## Also by Mary Wine

# Between a
# HIGHLANDER
## and a
# HARD PLACE

# MARY WINE

sourcebooks
casablanca

Published by Sourcebooks Casablanca, an imprint of Sourcebooks, Inc.
P.O. Box 4410, Naperville, Illinois 60567-4410
(630) 961-3900
Fax: (630) 961-2168
sourcebooks.com

Printed and bound in Canada.
MBP 10 9 8 7 6 5 4 3 2 1

# *One*

Grant Tower, 1579

"Hiding in me chambers again?" Brenda Grant was a beauty and had a lyrical voice to match. Symon didn't take any pleasure in it, ripping his bonnet off and throwing it onto a table before he landed in one of the huge chairs she had placed in her receiving chamber just for his visits.

The man had cracked two chairs before she'd ordered new ones made.

"How fortunate that we are first cousins," Brenda continued as she poured some whisky into a glass and offered it to him. "Otherwise, the gossips would say we are lovers." Her lips twitched as she tilted her head to the side. "No' that I am saying no one says such a thing, mind ye."

Symon glared at her and then at the delicate glass in his hand before tossing the whisky into his mouth and setting the glass on the table.

"I take the look on yer face to mean the bride hunting is not going well?"

Symon drummed his fingers on the table. "I've a fine, sharp memory, Brenda. The day is going to come when ye are the one being—"

Brenda humphed at him. In private, she didn't much care for how inappropriate interrupting the laird might be. He'd come to her chambers, after all. "I have been wed. Done my duty, and now I will have no more of it."

"I wed as well." Symon reached over and refilled his glass. But his taste for the liquor was gone, and he left it sitting on the table as he started to brood, the specter of his wife dragging him down.

More than one member of the clan had claimed they'd seen her ghost in the passageways.

"Do not." Brenda moved closer to Symon, reaching out to grasp his hand. "Ye must begin living again."

Symon tilted his head and eyed her. "I am no' the only one who needs to listen to that advice."

Brenda didn't care for the reprimand; however, she acknowledged it as her due. "There is a difference between us. Yer wife was taken by cruel fate."

"And yer husband was just cruel," Symon finished for her.

"Ye do nae become the property of yer spouse when ye take marriage vows," Brenda answered bitterly.

"This castle will always have open doors for you. If the man ye wed is in fact a bastard once he's won yer hand, there will be sanctuary for ye here." Symon spoke clear and firmly, a promise in his tone.

A promise she held dearer than all the gold in the world.

Silence hung between them for a long moment. Time enough for them both to feel the chill in the air. They were the last of their line, and the clan looked to them to maintain order by leaving a clear heir. No one wanted fighting over who would be Symon's successor.

It was more than just securing the bloodline. The castle needed life breathed back into it. Hope needed to be kindled before there was nothing left but crumbling stone. Their line was dying; both of them had wed and had no children. And now both of them were widowed as well. Perhaps if Symon's wife had not died in childbirth, Brenda might allow herself to be free of the burden of making sure their blood continued.

"I will join ye below," she said softly.

Symon slowly nodded. "So now ye will shame me if I do nae go as well."

"It is no' a matter of shame, for we have both faced our duty in the past." Brenda took a moment to check her appearance in a mirror. Behind her, Symon stood, the pleats of his kilt falling down to just above his knees. "Now 'tis more an act of desperation, for the truth is we are both entombed alive in this chamber. For all that I have no desire to wed again, sitting here is no' much better."

Symon grunted as he pulled his cap on. "Wait until you get a look at the men sitting at our high table, sweet cousin. Ye will understand true desperation once ye sit and listen to them trying to auction their kin to one of us."

"I have no doubt." Brenda took a deep breath and went through the door Symon held open. "Just as I do nae doubt ye came up here because ye have it in the back of yer head to see me wed first and save yerself from the same fate."

He made a low noise in the back of his throat.

Brenda shrugged.

They were a fine pair and the only kin either had left, so better to be united.

ᴄᴪᴖ

"I adore you, Athena."

She believed him. Galwell's eyes were full of appreciation as he reached out and delicately fingered one of her curls. A tiny one had escaped her caul and was hanging in front of her earring.

A love lock…

"You are simply perfect," he murmured as he trailed his fingertip across her jaw to her chin. He lifted her face, leaning down to press a kiss against her lips.

Her uncle cleared his throat.

Athena released a little sigh as she opened her eyes. Her uncle was working at his bench, carefully crafting wax into what would one day become a tiny flower made of gold for one of his clients.

"I cannot wait for our wedding day," she muttered softly to Galwell.

Galwell was dressed smartly in the latest fashion. His slops were paned and worked with lace. The doublet was made of silk and edged with pearls. He had the top two buttons open at his throat, exposing the blackworked collar of the shirt she'd gifted him when he'd asked her uncle to allow them to wed.

Her cheeks warmed as she saw the linen collar settle into position on him. She'd spent hours with it in her own hands, making it an intimate thing to see it against Galwell's skin.

He offered her an elaborate reverence, stretching out his leg in front of her to show off his trim calf encased in a knitted stocking.

"I must away to court," he announced as he retrieved his hat from where it rested on a table nearby. "Elizabeth Tudor enjoys having her courtiers dance attendance upon her."

Galwell settled the hat on his head, moving toward the door. Beyond it, his personal servants shifted as they noted their master's imminent arrival.

Galwell was a blue blood. As such, he had obligations to his family's name and reputation. As his wife, she would be expected to support him in gaining the Queen's favor.

"I will continue to practice my dancing diligently," Athena promised. "The coin you pay the dance master is not being squandered, I assure you."

Galwell turned and sent her a small smile. "Yes, practice, my dear. I shall have you dance for me next time we dine together. You shall wear the cream-and-green dress."

Athena lowered herself in obedience as the manservant waiting outside the shop opened the door for his master, and Galwell was gone with a flip of his velvet cape.

She felt her heart might burst. But her elation was cut short by her uncle's stern look. "He will attend to the contracts, Uncle," she assured her guardian. "Why else would he come to visit me if he was not sincere?"

Her uncle was a strict man. But she had learned to respect his sternness in all things because he did so in order to ensure his family did not want. He had taken her in when her own parents had failed to think what might befall their tiny daughter when they both defied their families to wed in secret. Her noble father had been promptly cut off without a silver penny to his name, and her mother had died in child bed. Once her mother was dead and she only a daughter, her father had returned home to beg forgiveness for his disobedience, leaving her to fate and the mercy of her uncle.

Her uncle, Henry, let out a little grumble. "You are dear to me, Athena. Do not begrudge me seeing to the duty of being a proper guardian."

She smiled warmly at him and lowered herself in truest sincerity. "I am fortunate beyond all riches to have you. You are always in my prayers."

He made another grumbling noise before sitting back down to work. "A good thing," he said as he looked up and bestowed one of his rare smiles on her. "For I have spent my life making things of gold that feed naught but vanity. The Lord will have something to say about my lack of Christian dedication."

Athena bit her lip to stop from arguing.

If they were in private, she might be allowed to speak her mind, for her uncle had always allowed her the freedom to do so. However, there were three apprentices in the workshop. Their eyes were on their work, but she'd be a fool to disrespect her uncle within their hearing.

Her uncle sent her a wink. "Off to your studies. Soon you will be a wife and have to prove I have provided you with an education worthy of Galwell

Scrope. He will need an accomplished wife. Make certain your French is flawless."

"Yes, Uncle."

She loathed French.

Henry knew it quite well. However, her uncle was correct. Galwell required a wife who could run his estate and make a good showing in front of the Queen.

So she would persevere and learn French.

And soon, oh so very soon, she would be Galwell's wife.

∽

Brenda and Symon sat together in the evening as the sun faded and the castle became quiet.

Deathly still…

"Ye do nae have to tell me I must decide on one of them," Symon muttered as he lifted a mug and downed the cider. "It is me duty."

"Ye have time."

Symon was making ready to take another drink when she spoke. He stopped, mug halfway to his lips, to look at her with a raised eyebrow. "Have no' ye been the one advising me no' to tempt fate by putting the matter off for another season?"

Brenda nodded. "The spring has not yet broken."

Beyond the walls, snow still lay on the ground. But the rivers had thawed, and frothy water flowing down from the melting snow could be heard through the open shutters.

"Hmm," Symon replied as he took the drink. "Are ye suggesting there may be other offers once the roads clear a bit?"

"Aye. For ye made it clear last year that ye would be wedding this year."

"I did." There was an unmistakable look of relief in his topaz eyes.

"So." Brenda reached for her mug and took a delicate sip. "It would be rash and perhaps even rude not to allow all the offers to arrive before making a choice."

"I've a feeling Bothan Gunn may be intent on a visit."

Brenda sent him a hard look. Symon merely raised his mug in a silent toast to her in response. "I'll no' have him," she declared.

Symon contemplated her. "Did ye no' just advise me to no' be hasty?"

"It's a very different matter, and ye know it well. Bothan Gunn has simply decided I shall be his. I know little of the man, and I shall no' be claimed like a prize." Brenda put her mug down and got up, her mind set.

"Sneaking up on ye is no' a simple matter. Admit the man earned some bit of respect for being able to do it too. Ye're running away like a startled mare, and the man is no' even here. Has he even kissed ye? If he did and it left ye cold, well, that is one matter. Yet if ye are to choose yer next husband for naught but passion, best ye consider how Bothan has managed to stir yers with only a single meeting."

His words stopped Brenda in her flight. She turned around so fast her skirts flared out before settling back down.

"Think on that matter for a good long bit, Brenda."

"I do no' need to contemplate Bothan Gunn at all," she announced. Her voice was carrying, and she didn't care if the other members of the clan heard her. Let them judge her as unbridled—she'd already done her duty and wed a horrible man for the sake of alliance.

"He unsettled ye."

Three little words were all it took to undermine her determination. Of course it was because Symon had sworn to honor his father's word that she was her own woman. He'd not force her to wed, but he would insist she stop hiding in her chamber.

It was an agreement between them: to keep the other from drifting away from life.

So Symon's words were ones she could not dismiss because he cared only about her happiness. Symon raised his mug to her.

"Good night to ye, Cousin. I thank ye for yer counsel today."

Brenda lowered herself, earning a few nods from the men sitting at the tables in the hall. Supper had been cleared away, but most of the men would sleep in the hall. As the weather warmed, more of them would find their way outdoors to huts near the fields. There would be weddings, and the fields wouldn't be the only things ripening by the end of the summer.

There would be babies in the fall.

He'd never seen the face of his child. His wife had died before giving birth. One week she had been glowing with happiness, her belly round and large and their child kicking so hard he'd been able to feel it.

A week later Tara was being laid to rest, her eyes sightless in death.

The babe had been turned wrong and too large, or so the midwife told him.

*And it's your duty to wed again…take another woman to
your bed…to face the same fate…*

Symon was no coward.

At least, not when it came to facing a battle, a
fight, or even the judgment of those men to whom
he answered.

But a woman…

It was his place to protect his family.

Everyone thought he still mourned because he'd
grown to love his bride. It was partially true. For all
that Tara's and his had been a negotiated union, he
had enjoyed her laughter and looked forward to joining her in their bedchamber.

Was that love? Perhaps. It had been affection at
least. And now, he was stuck facing fear. Perhaps fear
was too strong a word. He was a man who knew
when to be practical.

Reluctance, then.

And he truly was reluctant to bring another bride
into his bed where she'd accept her duty. For certain
he had the right to expect such devotion as the laird,
but he admitted he found it distasteful to have a docu-
ment written and sent off to a father who would pack
his daughter up and deliver her.

There was a coldness in the method that left him
with a bitter taste in his mouth.

Well, as Brenda had said, there was time yet before
he would have to conform to what was expected of
him. Duty was something he understood.

He'd shoulder his load.

❧

"Athena…"

Galwell was calling to her. In the last light of the day, with the bells of the evening service ringing out behind her, Athena turned to see her beloved leaning out the door of his carriage. It rolled up to where she was, the footman jumping down and rushing around to open the door for his master.

Galwell didn't come out.

"Join me for supper, Athena."

She wanted to.

Galwell noticed her hesitation. His lips thinned with annoyance before he schooled his expression. "You don't think I would try to lure you away without the permission of your uncle?"

"Of course not." A ripple of guilt went through her as she realized that was exactly what she'd been thinking.

Galwell smiled at her. "Come…supper awaits."

The footman stood with a hand out to steady her as she climbed into the carriage. The door was narrow and the ceiling low. But the seat across from Galwell was padded, even the back of it. The moment she was inside, the footman closed the door and ran for his seat on the back of the carriage.

Athena realized why he scurried so when Galwell thumped the top of the ceiling with his fist before the poor servant had even finished closing the door. The driver responded instantly, snapping the reins and letting the horses begin pulling them down the street.

She shouldn't dwell on the matter.

Galwell was the son of a baron. He paid his servants well because he needed to keep his attention for important matters.

Still…

*Hush,* she reprimanded herself. Everyone had bad habits. As Galwell's wife, she would endeavor to make certain his staff knew how appreciated they were.

Galwell's family had a townhome along the Thames. It was accessible by barge from the palace. However, soon the Queen would likely take to the country, leaving the city behind as the warm summer months made the stench of London grow. It was known as progress: a huge caravan of nobles and their households that took days to pass on the road as they ventured to country estates where the Queen would be entertained by her nobles and then move on, with her court following to another estate. It was rumored that one visit from the royal Tudor queen could destroy entire herds of stock animals as lavish feasting went on for days.

Athena felt jittery as her excitement grew. She hadn't dared to voice how very much she hoped Galwell would want to celebrate their union before spring fully arrived.

She might go with him on progress if he did.

She longed for the moment they might do more than court.

"Here we are, my dear," Galwell said as the carriage stopped. "Welcome to my home." He alighted and turned to offer her his gloved hand. "The city one, of course. We shall enjoy the country estate in summer when the grass is high and the berries in bloom." He pulled her close. "And I shall enjoy tumbling you on the riverbanks."

Her cheeks warmed as she pulled away. "When shall we take our vows?"

He waved his hand in the air and preceded her into the house. His servants were quick to greet him, rushing around as they took his cape and hat, cleaned his boots, and offered them both refreshment.

French wine.

It was strong. Athena found it warming her stomach and making her cheeks flush after only a few sips.

"Drink up, my sweet," Galwell encouraged her as he finished off his goblet. "We have merriment to be about this night."

Truly, he must have reached agreement with her uncle, for a feast was laid out. In the air, the scent of expensive spices floated, teasing her with their exotic smells.

Cinnamon.

Nutmeg.

Cloves.

"Oranges?" she exclaimed as she saw the table up close. "So early in the season?"

"The first ships have arrived from Spain." Galwell sat down and extended his open hand toward a chair across from him. "Her Majesty's lord chancellor is often generous and allows others to peruse the wares after she has had first pick."

Athena lifted an orange up to her nose, inhaling deeply. The last piece of fresh fruit she'd held was back in autumn, when the apples had been harvested. She wished she had worn a finer dress, but she had always attended service in basic wool.

The meal began with washing of hands. One servant brought in a bowl and held it beneath Galwell's hands while another servant poured water from a pitcher over them. Then a length of linen was offered so he might dry his hands. They came to her next and then disappeared, only to return with salt and stale bread. They sprinkled salt on the plates and used the bread to clean it away to remove any possible contamination. Rumor had it Queen Elizabeth always watched her plate being salted before she ate off it because she was so afraid of being poisoned, as she was still unmarried and James Stuart was now fourteen.

Musicians began to play somewhere out of sight. Their notes blended perfectly with the presentation of the supper. The oranges were not the only lavish fare on the table. There was meat, during the season of Lent when a special license was needed to allow them to enjoy it, and a tart made with sugar from the Caribbean islands.

Galwell was every bit the nobleman. He sat at the table, expertly commanding his staff. Athena finally sat back, unable to eat another morsel.

"Perhaps your stays need loosening, my sweet?"

It was a wicked thing to jest about and yet, because they were in negotiations to wed, not too scarlet a topic. Athena allowed herself to smile suggestively at him. "Soon, my lord."

His eyes flashed with something she'd only glimpsed hints of before. Now, she was treated to a full look at the desire he aimed at her. "Dare I hope this splendid feast was meant as a celebration of the announcement that our union will soon be brought to bear?" she asked.

He chuckled and finished off his goblet of expensive French wine as though it was no more than water. "Indeed, my dear."

Galwell was suddenly on his feet, working open the buttons of his doublet before shrugging off the garment and tossing it over the back of his chair.

Athena was frozen in place, staring at his shirt while she frantically tried to think of a reasonable explanation for his lack of propriety. Nothing came to mind though, leaving her facing a reality that was harsh with unacceptable familiarity.

"I believe the time has come for me to depart." She rose, pushing her own chair back because the servants seemed to have vanished.

Another ripple of unease went through her.

"Indeed it has," Galwell announced as he grabbed a handful of her skirt. He used it to tug her into his embrace. The French wine that had been so very delectable was now abhorrent on his breath. "Let us retire to the bedchamber."

"Galwell," she scolded him. "Your wits are pickled in too much wine. We are not yet wed."

"We shall never be wed," he muttered. "My father is arranging a better match for me."

Athena stood frozen in his embrace as he boldly confessed his thinking.

"But you, my sweet." He cupped her bottom through her skirts as he backed her into the table. "You I shall enjoy as a mistress, and you will be content with the arrangement, for no one will believe I have not had you tonight."

"Galwell! For shame… I would never have come away with you if I'd thought you intent on playing the scoundrel."

He snickered at her reprimand, pulling one of her

thighs up so he could press between them. "Enough games, Athena! Your mother was a tart. She lured your father away from his family, and now I will enjoy the same hot-bloodedness you inherited from her. It is the best arrangement you can expect."

"You claimed you desired marriage from me!" Her thoughts were spinning out of control. He looked like the man she'd trusted with her heart, but there was a cruel twist to his lips and a bright glow of anticipation in his eyes she did not recognize. "You fiend!"

Athena reached behind her and grabbed the first thing she might. It was a plate, and she swung it at his head. Galwell recoiled, releasing her as he jumped back and indulged in a long laugh at her expense.

"That's the spirit!" he encouraged her. "Enough with the virginal blushes and so forth. I crave a spirited ride, and I've gone to a great deal of effort to tempt you away from your chaperones."

"Is this some wager then?" she demanded as she made her way around the table. "Am I a prize merely for the sake of your pride?"

Galwell sent her another one of those smiles she'd never seen before. This one was sly and tore another chunk from her heart with its callousness.

She was naught but a conquest to him.

The truth sent a bitter taste into her mouth as the fine meal tried to erupt from her stomach.

"You truly thought to marry so well?" he scoffed at her. "Foolish. Your mother wasn't blue-blooded. My heirs must be pure noble."

It wasn't the first time she'd heard such a thing.

More than one well-meaning matron had taken the time to warn her of her circumstances.

*But I trusted him.*

Tears stung her eyes.

"I see you understand," he remarked. "Now, let us get to the matter of the arrangement between us."

"There will be no arrangement," she hissed.

He leveled a look at her, the same he gave his servants. She stiffened, forbidding herself to cry.

He was not worthy of her tears.

Or her heart.

"Oh, you may be quite certain there will be an arrangement that pleases me, if you know what is good for you and your family."

There was a large measure of arrogance in his tone, his eyes narrowing as he let his gaze lower to her cleavage and stay there.

"You shall please me," he continued. "In every way I crave."

"I am no whore."

His lips curved up in response to her rejection. "You have no choice. Your reputation is quite ruined now that you have been here so long," he remarked. "Your uncle will have raised the alarm, and I assure you, I have told my servants to speak freely as to where you have been tonight.

"Your lessons will continue, but with a different goal in mind," he continued. "You shall become an accomplished courtesan." His eyes glittered with excitement. "I have made all the arrangements for your tutelage. And I shall keep you very well, Athena. Now, come and allow me to introduce you to your duties—"

"Never," she growled.

He chuckled at her denial. "If you leave here without my blessing, I will have it said you were put out for thieving. Your uncle will be ruined."

It was so horrible an idea that the breath felt frozen in her chest while she struggled to force her mind to function.

"Why are you doing such a foul thing?"

Galwell raised an eyebrow. "Because it is the only way to have you. And I will ride you—"

"There are dozens of women competing for your attention because of your blood—"

"And yet none are as fair as you." He smiled brightly at her, sickening her even more. "The moment I saw you I knew you were to be mine. I am very good at getting what I crave."

The oranges...

The cinnamon...

The cloves...

The meat...

It was all as repugnant as the thirty pieces of silver used to pay Judas for his betrayal of Christ.

"Go abovestairs now and disrobe, or, I assure you, I will turn a deaf ear to your pleas when you return and beg for my attention because your uncle cannot put bread on the table." He sent her a confident look. She had the feeling she was far from alone in seeing it; there was far too much confidence in his expression for her to think she was unique in encountering this side of his nature.

Games.

A nobleman's pastime.

Clearly Galwell expected her to accept her lot.

"It takes a long time to starve to death," he continued as she hesitated. "The children die first. You shall watch as your uncle's daughter buries her family. A goldsmith out of favor with the court is a man with no means of income."

She felt as though a noose was tightening around her neck.

He knew it too, rolling his lips in with enjoyment.

"Abovestairs, if you please," he remarked casually. "I have been waiting a long while to see your tits."

Many would call her foolish. But none would label her a coward. She pushed one of the candles over onto the table covering. Galwell gasped, barking out for his servants. Athena fled as they rushed into the room.

❧

The difficulty with escaping was a person needed a place to go. Athena discovered the truth of her dilemma once she spied her uncle's home. The moon was rising, but the night was still bitter. The sturdy wool dress she had lamented wasn't pretty enough was now her dearest friend, for it kept her from shivering.

At least as far as the chill in the night went.

Inside her heart, there was ice forming.

*What a fool I was.*

And now, her lack of judgment was going to destroy everything. Galwell would do as he promised, she had little doubt. It felt as though his shell had cracked, allowing her to see what manner of foul creature he truly was. Well, she would not allow him to claim a victory over her. But how? Nobles controlled the world. His blue blood would be seen as more honest than her word. The sin of her parents would be taken as a stain against her account of what had happened.

He could accuse her of thievery. Have her flogged or any other manner of horrible fates. Yet there was nowhere else to go.

"Athena?" The door suddenly opened wide, the light from within illuminating her. "Thank Christ! I have been near to death with worry." Henry was pulling her inside, even as she tried to fend him off. She didn't really want to. No, he was her family, the man who called her his own when others had advised him to abandon her to an orphan's lot.

"Tell me true," he demanded once the door was shut and the warm glow of the candles on the table surrounded her.

Sweet Christ, she had not given enough thanks for how wonderful her home was. The world beyond the door was crueler than she might ever have imagined.

"Athena." There was a subtle reprimand in her uncle's voice.

Her memory rushed in with vivid recollection of Galwell's threats. "I must leave."

Henry's forehead furrowed.

"I must," she insisted. "Oh, Uncle, I have made a grave misjudgment of character."

Henry held up a hand. His fingertips were marked with scars from years of toil at his trade. She fought back nausea as she recalled how Galwell had promised to destroy it all in his quest to have her submission.

"Tell me everything. We shall find a solution."

"I must leave," she muttered, suddenly losing the

strength to stand. She lowered herself onto one of
the benches at the table. A place she had so often
enjoyed the company of her family. Now it was
empty, and she faced the knowledge that she could
not be there at dawn when they came down to break
their fast.

"Galwell…came upon me as I was leaving service…
in his carriage…"

Henry had always been a man able to keep his
thoughts hidden. Tonight she witnessed him fighting
for control of his temper. It flashed in his eyes as he
tapped the tabletop with his fist.

"I shall have to leave…" And yet she had no idea
where to go. "Galwell will ruin you."

"Aye, he's a black-hearted man and no mistake."

Her uncle stood, pacing about the kitchen. He
stopped as he came to some sort of decision. Athena
stood, ready to face whatever he might say as her due
for loving unwisely.

"We need time," Henry said. "I am not a man
without friends, but it will require planning to ensure
Galwell cannot destroy us. As a noble, his word will be
listened to first and with more weight. I will have to
make inquiries discreetly, for not many will go against
Galwell's blood. At least publicly. Behind closed doors
is another matter entirely."

There was a commotion on the street, the sound
of boots stamping against the cobblestones as men
approached.

"The priest hole," Henry whispered.

He didn't wait but grabbed her wrist and pulled her
toward a side of the hearth. There he ran his fingers

along a stone until he found the small indentation where he could open a hidden door. She had to turn sideways to fit into the hollowed-out section of the wall. Her uncle closed it, locking her behind the wall of the common room.

It was dark, but she'd often played in the space as a child. She drew in a deep breath and slid down farther, to where she could see into the kitchen through tiny places where the plaster had been removed so a hidden priest might see out.

Someone pounded on the door.

"What's all this?" her uncle asked gruffly. "Is that my niece at last? I'm sick with worry."

"We are here for Athena Trappes."

Through the peepholes, Athena saw the constables with their white staffs. All along the street, doors opened as the neighbors came to investigate why the sheriff had sent the constables out into the night.

Every honest man was expected to show he was not harboring a criminal by opening his door wide.

"And you come to me?" Henry demanded. "Why?"

It wasn't a lie. Athena realized Henry was a man who was bound by his honor. She bit her lip as her insides churned. Tonight her fate would be decided.

"Baron Scrope's son has accused her of setting fire to his London home."

There was a shifting among those watching in the streets. Fire was a grave crime because it might spread so easily in the tight confines of the city.

"You say my niece was with Galwell?" Henry demanded again. "Before he finished the contracts with me? He has offered for my niece and then takes her to his home? I will have satisfaction!"

"So will the sheriff," the captain of the constables said. "You shall—"

Henry interrupted the man. "You will return to the sheriff and demand to know why Galwell Scrope took my niece to his home when he had sworn to finish negotiating contracts with me, as he pledged his word of honor to do. What manner of a man is noble by birth and yet not honest in his dealing with a common man such as myself? He stood in my home and vowed to wed Athena! It is well known on this street! If my niece set a fire, she was likely attempting to escape from a man who is dishonorable at his core. Did he attempt to make her his whore?"

Now there was a mumbling among those watching, good men who had indeed heard Galwell say he would wed her. The constable captain was uncertain. He looked between Henry and the crowd moving closer.

"I will put the question to the sheriff."

The constables turned and marched away. Henry nodded to a few of his neighbors before firmly shutting the door.

She wanted to be relieved. But her worry only grew as she recognized just how much power Galwell wielded.

"Stay in there, Athena. I shall return."

Her uncle was gone a moment later, slipping out of the back door.

It left her alone with her thoughts.

Love hurt.

Her heart was torn. Oh, she understood she owed

not a single tear to Galwell, not after what he had done and threatened to do.

And yet her dreams were a pile of rubble at her feet, her world upside down, and even hope seemed beyond her grasp as she felt as though she was turning as hard and cold as the stones she was pressed against.

Perhaps that was for the best.

Yes.

It truly was.

She would never love again, for men were vile creatures. They declared themselves so many things, and beneath it all was naught but the craving to use women to satisfy their lust.

She allowed her memory to offer up an image of Galwell's gleeful face. It was an ugly sight, and she wanted it burned into her mind so she never forgot!

Never.

❧

"Athena, come now." Her uncle had opened the door to the priest hole. He reached inside and drew her out. "We've things to accomplish before dawn."

"Did you see the sheriff?"

Henry shook his head. "There is little point. The man is in Galwell's pay. I will need time to contact men who can keep him from blackening my name. Until I can, you must be hidden away."

Her uncle took her through the room and into the kitchen. He pressed her into the corner where the bathing tub was tipped up against the wall and the window shutters closed. There was light from the coals in the hearth.

"I have made arrangement for you to travel with Myles Basset. He's a young man trying to make his mark in the world by traveling to markets in Scotland."

"Scotland?" she gasped.

Her uncle nodded, taking up a bag that was sitting on the kitchen table. He dumped the contents out.

"I must send you beyond the Scrope family's reach until I can arrange a meeting with the lord of London. It will take several weeks. Galwell will have you broken and installed as his mistress long before that if you remain here." Henry looked at her, his face solemn. "He is the worst sort of man. One with family ties that will make others turn a blind eye to his dealings."

"I am sorry, Uncle," she murmured, feeling as though there was no escape. "Perhaps I…should…" She couldn't force the words past the rising bile in her throat.

"You shall not bend to his whim."

Henry was a mild man. Yet she heard the heat in his tone. He pointed a finger at her. "You shall never suffer the fate my sister did. I swore it before God on the night she died beneath this roof. Your father deserted her when you were born female and begged his way back into the good graces of his noble family. I took you as my own, and thank God your worthless father died before siring any of the sons he longed for. Sons he would have raised up to be exactly like Galwell. Black-hearted."

"You never told me…"

Henry shook his head. "It was not your sin. My sister was as beautiful as you and just as much of a phoenix. You are as powerful as you are fair. It was her curse, and fate seems to have made it yours as well. Know this: I will keep my word, and I will enjoy knowing Galwell shall not have you. Now." He held up a pair of breeches. "You will travel as a boy."

&

"Boy? Are you deaf?"

Athena jerked awake. It was barely first light, the morning gray and still dark.

"Still sleeping?" Will Tinker demanded as he reached over the edge of the wagon to grab a hank of her hair and yank on it.

"Sorry, Master." Still groggy, Athena forgot to mask her voice.

"You squeak like a girl," Will Tinker complained. "Get your arse moving. We'll never make it to the crossroads before May Day at this rate."

Myles Basset was a decent enough master, but he was also wise enough to know that dealing in Scotland meant he'd be best to employ Scottish men.

Will Tinker was given full authority over her and the others. He was vulgar and short-tempered.

It was raining again. Within moments of emerging from the wagon, she found her wool doublet soaked. At least she had a dry place to sleep, for their wares were fine cloth and had to be kept safe beneath heavily oiled canvas wagon covers. At night she crawled in and slept beside the bundles, making very sure she closed up the canvas when she left.

Will cursed at the two burly men who handled the horses, complaining about how slow the animals were moving. She hurried to bring the reins to them, earning a roll of eyes from the man named Tanner. She kept a smile from emerging on her lips because Will wasn't one to let mockery go without a good thrashing.

Still, she preferred him to Galwell.

In fact, it was remarkable how many things she found in Scotland that were to her liking. The weeks had passed and with them her heartache.

Love truly was the folly it was preached to be.

Or at least it was flimsy enough not to be anything she should ever trust.

No, better to plan a future with good, solid sense leading the way. As soon as she returned to England, she would happily allow her uncle to settle her future in a match of his choosing.

The plan was a logical one.

So why did it leave her so cold?

The reason was Galwell, of course. She was loath to trust any man with even friendship now, much less act as wife. She shuddered with revulsion as she remembered the way Galwell had stroked her.

*Ah, yes, like a fine possession…*

The rain was suddenly not so cold. She helped break camp and looked forward to the long day of travel because it meant doing something besides submitting to Galwell. Truly her uncle was the best thing in her life, for he had saved her from that fate, and she would not forget his parting words to her.

There would be no submitting.

Ever.

❦

*May Day*

Athena didn't have to be woken. No, she felt the excitement in the air before first light. It was the first time since leaving England that she'd felt too grubby to endure the male clothing she hid inside.

She left the wagon and moved away from camp, and she wasn't the only one doing so either.

"Hurry up, Rosslyn...ye do nae need yer shoes..."

Girls were moving away from the camp that had arisen in preparation for the market fair. It was the only day they were allowed the liberty of going unescorted. Of course, their male relatives weren't really duped. No, they were rolled in their plaids, pretending to sleep because it was tradition that the girls were allowed to sneak away to wash their faces in the morning dew.

A pagan tradition, but one the Church realized would never truly be forgotten.

Or at least no one was quite willing to defy fate by failing to raise a maypole and dance around it as Old Man Winter was banished so a good harvest might be ensured.

The ritual was older than anyone recalled. Better safe than sorry. They all placed their faith in God and yet took the time to perform the acts of good luck their ancestors had.

Athena's memory was filled with years past, when she and her cousins had whispered to one another as they hurried to walk barefooted across the new grass.

She didn't dare...

And yet she longed to so very much. Traveling as a boy had kept her from any attention along the road.

She was truly grateful and should keep her hat on and the dirt on her face.

But first light was beginning to break.

The birds called out to one another.

The breeze carried the scent of early spring flowers and flowing water.

And she simply couldn't resist.

With a quick look behind her, she moved off before dawn broke. Off toward the woods where the other girls were going. Athena stopped to strip off her breeches and doublet. Doing so left her in a shirt that fell to her knees, and she swore to herself she would only stay long enough to wash her face in dew and let her toes get wet before returning to her role as a boy.

Wasn't it right to ensure Galwell not be allowed to steal everything from her?

She'd have a bit of May Day happiness in spite of his black-heartedness.

The thought bolstered her confidence enough to have her stripping off her boots and stockings. The grass delighted her with its chill as the sun began to turn the horizon pink.

Now, she could see the other girls smiling shyly at one another as they moved off into the woods. Someone started to untie the braids that had kept Athena's hair tightly bound to her scalp, combing it with her fingers until it rose up in a fluffy cloud of gold.

Athena smiled, unwilling to use her voice lest her English accent be detected. But giggles seemed to be universal, and she happily indulged in a few as the sun began to warm her skin.

❧

Symon poked Brenda through the wagon cover.

He heard a soft grunt from his cousin. Tamhas and Lyall both looked up from where they were still "sleeping" to send him raised eyebrows. The wagon swayed as Brenda climbed down.

"I am no' a maiden," she groused.

"And I am no' in the spring spirit," he whispered. "But we both agreed we'd play along and no' sour the day for others."

She fluttered her eyelids before making her way toward the woods, her dark hair flipping back and forth across her back. Symon jumped when Tamhas grabbed a handful of his leg hair and yanked.

"We're"—his retainer gestured toward the rest of the clansmen—"supposed to be sleeping."

Symon returned to the ground, wide awake and more aware than ever of how bleak he seemed to find life. The truth was he was sick unto death of the hold the events in his past seemed to have on him.

He needed to move on.

Too bloody bad he was laird and no one seemed willing to kick his arse.

He needed it rather badly.

If he ran across Niul McTavish today, he needed to thank the man for knocking him across the jaw the season before. At least the fight had woken Symon up enough to shave off his mourning beard and try to live again.

The thought was bloody frustrating. May Day was something every man near him was looking forward to. Now that dawn had broken, they were creeping off to peek at the girls. Symon sat up, but his member wasn't stirring at the idea.

And it damned well should have been.

Which meant he was going toward the woods because he was damned tired of the way his blood felt like it was frozen in his veins.

It was May Day. The girls washed their faces with morning dew with their hair flowing free and naught on but chemises. The only men not stirred by the idea of it all were the ones wearing sackcloth in the monastery.

At last he grinned.

He'd done too many things to be considered for a life of piety.

Too many stolen kisses on summer days.

Ah, but Tara's had been the sweetest of them all. Shy little kisses that their wedding vows dictated she owed him, and yet he'd enjoyed coaxing them from her.

He moved through the woods, using skills he'd learned to stay alive during raids. Today was an anomaly. A day when McPherson, McTavish, Grants, Robertson, and others dispensed with their feuds in order to indulge in spring festival.

Today, he kept low to the ground and moved carefully in order not to be heard by the women. The game would last only until full light, when skirts and dresses would go back on, but the hair would be left down until sunset.

Of course the fun was catching glimpses of the girls in their chemises.

At last Symon felt his enthusiasm growing. He

wasn't sure if it was the promise of seeing a few well-turned calves or maybe just the idea of being able to sneak closer without being heard.

Not that it mattered. He crouched low, staying in the shadows close to the trees and making sure he was near enough to the river to allow the sound of the water to mask his motions. He pulled his plaid up to cover his head, the muted color of the wool allowing him to blend better with the surroundings.

Other men passed by, drawn by the soft sound of whispers farther away from the river. Symon decided to wait, leaning in so he was pressed against a thick tree trunk.

At first, he thought he imagined her.

While the other women moved deeper into the woods, this one hung back, content by herself.

Her hair was a golden cloud. Like a crown, and she wore it proudly. She was graceful but tall. It drew his attention because he was accustomed to dwarfing the women around him. She reached up, finding new spring leaves that the other girls hadn't been able to touch, and tipped them so that the dew dripped down on her face. The wind carried her husky laughter to his ears as he felt his lips being split by a grin wider than any he'd felt in a long time.

She was magnificent.

The first rays of the sun showed him the outline of the mounds of her breasts.

Handfuls.

Ones that would fit his hands.

His member stirred. She lowered her head, and their gazes met. Her eyes widened as her lips rounded in surprise. It might have been an hour that they stood there, staring at one another; Symon honestly couldn't have said. Her eyelids lowered, fluttering against her smooth cheeks.

He reached up and tugged on the corner of his bonnet.

Something flickered in her eyes as he performed the common courtesy gesture. A hint of trust perhaps. He fought the urge to move closer to her, caught between the need to close the distance between them and the fear that she'd take flight if he moved.

*Fear...*

He hadn't worried about a woman's opinion of him in a very long time.

Something rustled behind them, gaining her attention, and then she took flight. Her long legs carried her swiftly, right out of his sight, as he cursed.

The lad who had startled her stood gap-jawed while she disappeared.

"Was she real?" he asked as he stopped beside Symon.

"I'd no' be surprised to discover her a forest sprite." He patted the younger lad on the shoulder. "But ye can be sure I'll do me best to prove her a mortal woman before the day ends."

And that was a promise he was going to enjoy making good on

⤝⤞

Her heart was pounding.

It made stopping and fighting to get back into her clothing a chore and extremely frustrating. The strip of cloth she used to bind her breasts tangled as she fought with it. And her stockings felt twisted when she did finally succeed in drawing them up her legs. Why had she taken such a risk? It had been foolish.

*You wanted to spit in Galwell's eye.*

Well, that was the truth now, wasn't it? And so was the fact that she would see that pair of topaz eyes in her memory forever. Galwell was being burned away by the Scot. She might have been grateful if she could form logical thoughts. She'd never been so close to such a man.

Yes, she'd expected to see Scotsmen, for she was in Scotland, but he had been something so very different from what she'd expected. So very suited to his environment.

As she succeeded in getting her hair braided and pinned tightly to her scalp, her alarm faded, allowing satisfaction to fill the void. Her lips curved into a very satisfied smile as she shrugged into her doublet and buttoned it. The last thing was a skull cap that tied securely beneath her chin and then her flat cap.

He'd been the most savage thing she'd ever encountered, and yet there had been something about him that inspired trust in her. Such a strange combination, and with it came the oddest intensity. She recalled a multitude of details about him, all as clear as if he were standing right in front of her now.

Dark hair. He had it trimmed so it didn't quite brush his shoulders, and he wore a beard like so many men did, only his was trimmed short and he hadn't allowed it to cover his neck either.

She liked that.

Athena felt a blush sting her cheeks.

Really, she shouldn't like anything about the man. However, she decided ruefully, where exactly was the harm?

He had topaz eyes.

Almost golden and yet darker. Just like the rest of him. Dark was a word that fit him, for there was a hardness to him. He'd had his shirtsleeves tied up to expose his forearms, showing her how honed his flesh was. Galwell had often practiced his swordplay while she watched in order to impress her with his skills.

This man put Galwell to shame.

He'd also have towered over him.

There were more people awake now. Athena jerked away from her thoughts as men sent her smirks.

All in all, she passed for a boy well enough because of her height. There had been a few years when she despaired over the fact that she was taller than all the other girls, but her face had always captivated men.

*Such as Galwell?*

Indeed, and the fact left such a bitter taste on her tongue. Still, she enjoyed knowing she was somewhere she had never thought to go. Trudging back to camp, with morning fully broken, she found herself enjoying a sense of adventure. One so very unexpected too.

After all, the Church would have her in the stocks or worse if she were caught in breeches.

"What are ye about?" a girl demanded. "Have ye no shame?"

Athena ducked her chin as her ear was cuffed. Girls were enjoying the right to reprimand the men for a change. Plenty of them had their hair down still, proclaiming them maidens and unspoken for. It was a topsy-turvy day. The rules reversed for the sake of celebration.

"There ye are at last!" Will exclaimed as she made it back to the wagons. "Ye are no' being paid to dally on the green!"

Her cheeks heated as she considered just how many girls were coming back from the woods less pure than when they went out that morning. Even though the Church frowned on it, a spring pregnancy was considered an omen of good luck for the harvest. If the girl chosen as the May Queen failed to ripen, there would be worry about the harvest to come. There would also be a rush of summer weddings when girls declared themselves fruitful after a tryst on May Day morning and named the fathers of their babes.

All around her, she heard babies crying and being put to breast. They were three months old, the crop from the year before.

Immoral?

She didn't have the heart to judge them harshly. Not when there was such joy surrounding her. Such life. Couples came from the woods, hand in hand, offering each other longing looks before the men broke away to return to their duties or clans and the girls hurried to the side of their kinfolk. In a place where clans didn't mingle with other clans, she could see the advantage of May Day. For many of the girls, it was the only way to meet someone new.

*As you did?* The man in the woods had been tempting indeed. Part of her lamented the fact that she'd fled.

She blushed scarlet and kept her chin tucked to hide it. At least there was work to do. Plenty of things to carry to the booth Myles was preparing to open for the day. The lengths of fabric were carefully displayed, a canopy set up to shade them and oiled canvas kept beneath the table in case of afternoon rain.

"Well now, lads," Myles said in an attempt to speak Scottish. "Let us see if our efforts are rewarded in profit for this venture."

Athena took a moment to sit in the back of the booth, out of sight and alone with her thoughts.

She'd already reaped her rewards. Galwell hadn't forced her submission, and she'd even found the means of driving him from her thoughts.

At last fate was turning kind toward her.

May Day, it would seem, was still a day full of wonder for her.

❧

"It's time ye told me what ye are looking for."

Brenda turned around, facing him down with a look he knew well. It promised him Brenda wasn't planning on being denied what she wanted, which happened to be something Symon wasn't entirely sure he was in the mood to share.

"Is no' shopping about looking for things?" he asked her.

Brenda's lips twitched. "Ye"—she pointed at him—"never accompany me when I go shopping. Tamhas and Lyall are both looking for an excuse to check yer forehead for fever because ye are sticking to me skirts."

Symon turned and caught both his captains looking slightly guilty. They covered it quickly enough, hiding their emotions behind stern expressions.

"Now tell me." Brenda stepped closer. "Who are ye looking for?"

Symon tilted his head and looked down at her, but she shook her head.

"Ye spied someone this morning," she accused him in a hushed tone. "Do nae deny it."

"Well, if I did," he answered, "and I am no' saying I did…"

Brenda snorted softly.

Symon grunted at her. "There would be no reason for ye to take issue with me, since we have both agreed I need to find a wife this season."

"Why do ye think I am asking ye to share the details with me? I cannae help ye find her if I do nae know what to look for." Brenda turned and leaned in close as she looked at the booths they had yet to visit. "What color hair?"

Symon thought about not telling her.

Brenda poked him beneath his ribs. He was quick to grab her hand and spare himself the pain she seemed to know exactly how to inflict.

"Ye are a beast, Cousin," she muttered. "Hulking and huge. I will have a much better chance of finding her if ye hang back just a wee bit. Elsewise, ye will meet only her brothers as they stand in yer way to shield her from the wild highlander ye appear."

"So certain she's a foreigner?"

Brenda fluttered her eyelashes once again. "We know all the eligible girls from the clans represented.

Perhaps a cousin is visiting, hoping to meet someone. It's the time of year for that sort of thing."

"Gold hair," Symon supplied.

Brenda was pleased with herself. She made a little motion with her hand. "And what else do ye recall about her?"

*Everything.*

Brenda's eyes narrowed as she sensed he was holding something back. Symon tightened his expression. There were some things he wasn't going to share with his cousin.

"Lightest gold, like the first rays of the morning sun, and blue eyes like a mountain lake…tall…" He looked up at the crowd, feeling like he could hear the sand running through the hourglass. The thought of not finding her should not have been so important, and yet he'd be a liar if he denied it. He recalled every detail about the girl.

Well, woman.

Young and yet tall enough for him not to worry about taking her to his bed. She was passionate too, or at least bold, for she'd gone out in only a smock.

He suddenly realized it had actually been a shirt.

"Ye're taken with her," his cousin whispered. Brenda stared at him.

"I have nae even spoken to her," he defended himself. "I cannae be taken from a simple moment."

"And yet…" Brenda's voice trailed off. His cousin was normally so poised, it was rare to see her hold her tongue because she was uncertain.

"Do nae make more of it than…well, than it is. I would like to see her again is all," Symon said.

Brenda slowly smiled. Determination flickered in her eyes. "How tall?"

Symon used his hand to show her. She let out a little "hmm" before turning and contemplating the merchants waiting to try their hand at selling to her. "That will make it a bit easier. No' many women measure up like that."

It was the truth that at times, his cousin's brazen nature had tested his patience. Today Symon decided it was worth every moment of frustration he'd ever suffered, for Brenda Grant was many things, and good at getting what she went after was on the top of the list.

With the information he'd confessed, she was off and hunting with purpose, and he didn't even mind that part of her motivation was so she would no longer need to find a mate herself.

For the moment, he was content to let her believe he'd drop the matter.

In fact, he just might even think about doing it if Brenda found the girl for him.

Because the truth was he was taken with her.

❧

She was breathless.

Not out of breath, no. Athena had felt that way more than once while working under Will Tinker's direction.

This…this was something entirely different.

Her breath felt lodged in her throat, while her blood seemed to be racing along in her veins, making her light-headed, and all the while she fought the urge to giggle because she enjoyed it so very much.

He was there.

She had no name to apply to the man she'd encountered that morning, yet her memory didn't do him justice. Somehow, she'd failed to realize how large he was. Because she was taller than most women, men didn't seem overly large to her. In fact, there were several she looked straight in the eye. Her uncle had found it amusing, while her aunt had despaired of ever making a match for her.

Well, in Scotland, there were men who dwarfed her, it would seem.

His strength was measured in more than just height, though.

He was large through his shoulders and limbs, all the way to his hands.

He was also the most savage-looking man she had ever seen.

And there was a presence about him. Behind him, two other men seemed to be keeping guard, although she doubted he'd allow them to protect him. No, he was a hands-on sort of man. One who led and therefore deserved the respect of his followers.

She wanted to see his eyes once more...

*He'll know you for who you are if you look into his eyes...*

Athena looked down at a length of cloth, letting the plain color calm her thoughts. "Savage" wasn't really correct. No, he was hard, his arms thick with muscle that spoke of hard work. Clearly the sword he carried was something he knew how to wield.

Galwell had carried a rapier, and just like the thin Italian blade, his arms had lacked the muscle this Scotsman's limbs had.

*You prefer him…*

She chided herself. She preferred no man. None at all. She was simply fascinated by how very different he was from any man she had ever met. He wore a kilt, pleated up around his trim waist and belted to his body. His shirtsleeves were rolled up and tied to allow her to see past his elbows, proving that he was quite comfortable in his climate.

And then there were the topaz eyes. Not brown, but topaz. She didn't dare take another glance for fear he'd recognize her in spite of her male attire, but she wanted to look at him again.

Longed to, really.

"Alex?" Will snapped his fingers at her. "Bring the linen for this lady to see."

Athena responded to her male name, carrying the fabric forward.

"Soft and fine," Will said, expounding on the quality of the fabric. "Fit for a lady of your quality."

The woman offered him a soft chuckle. She reached out and stroked the cloth, her fingers slim and graceful.

"Have ye no women among ye to give testimony on the way yer cloth suits a woman's skin?" she asked.

Will stiffened. "It…it would not be proper to have a woman along the road with us."

The lady let out a little sigh. "However, it would be helpful. Men and women are very, very different."

"An excellent suggestion," Will offered in an attempt to soothe his would-be customer.

"Stop toying with the man, Brenda," the man with the topaz eyes chided her gently, and then turned to

Will. "Forgive me cousin. The winter was too long, and she has had only me to sharpen her tongue on."

So gentle a voice for a man of his size. He came forward with a purse in hand to settle the price. Athena melted back as they haggled. At last the deal was struck, coins exchanged hands, and the fabric was picked up by one of the men at arms attending the couple.

Cousin. Athena didn't care to admit how much she liked knowing the woman was not his wife.

*Well, he surely has a wife.*

There were six men set to walking with him. All of them faced partially away while he shopped to keep his back safe. And there was that purse. It jingled with silver and gold. The man's knitted bonnet was different from his men's as well; there were three feathers sticking up, while only one of his men had a feather.

An important man, which meant he had a wife.

She turned and busied herself making sure the stacks of cloth were perfectly neat. It was best not to look at him again.

Not that avoiding looking kept his visage from rising in her memory.

Would she never learn? Why was she drawn to yet another one instead of noticing how far she was from home because of her folly in dealing with men?

She needed to gain wisdom.

Needed to learn to ignore them.

"I see ribbons, Symon," Brenda declared. "Let us see if I can find some to complement me hair."

Symon.

His name sank into her mind in defiance of her determination not to think about him.

Clearly she was a poor student as well as being foolish.

As clear as the blush staining her cheeks.

# *Two*

SYMON FELT SOMETHING DEEP INSIDE HIM AT SUNSET. A lament rippling through his heart over the fact that he had not found her.

And it was the honest truth he was relieved to know he could feel such a thing.

"Is that Symon Grant?" Diocail Gordon slapped him on the back before peering at his face. "Truth is ye look like Symon, but ye've been shopping like a woman all afternoon." There was a round of chuckles from the retainers ringing them.

Symon took the reprimand jovially.

"I do wonder what yer new bride thinks of yer harsh judgment concerning spending time with female relations," Brenda offered softly.

Diocail tilted his head to one side and crossed his hands over his chest. "Well now, Mistress Brenda, it is no' the first time ye have found me lacking. Is it, now?"

"Ah yes, Harvest Festival," she muttered. "How is yer new wife?"

"Round with child."

Symon reached out to offer Diocail his hand. They

clasped wrists before Symon took a mug of cider Diocail offered. He toasted the setting sun, feeling a sense of loss that once more struck him as a good thing because he was feeling something at last.

Still, he'd wanted to find her. Now, at the end of the day, with no way to see her again, he might admit he had been taken with her.

Perhaps it was better he hadn't found her after all. Affection in a union was fine, but obsession led to distraction. What he needed was a female he found pleasing in company, one who would see to his home and be sturdy and strong.

She'd been tall and sturdy...

And captivating too.

Aye, well, she was lost as well. Better to focus on the good that came of the encounter. Fires were being lit now, the mood turning pagan as the moon began to rise. Children were hustled off to bed before the more wicked nature of the festival was unleashed.

The flames licked at the wood stacked in the center of the green. Behind it, the maypole turned scarlet as women with unbound hair began to dance around the fire. They spun their skirts high, baring their legs as they thrust out their hips in carnal display. Drummers accompanied them, playing ancient tunes.

"Go on," Diocail muttered gruffly. "Ye're a single man..."

There were many reasons why festivals were held at the crossroads. Clans could mingle more freely, and the Church was far away when it mattered.

Symon moved closer, the heat from the fire warming his face. But he was content to watch as women danced and men tried to lure them away into the woods for a tryst.

Some believed it good luck.

He smiled wryly. Some were simply good at finding acceptable ways to talk about lust, for that was what the night was full of: heart-pounding, blood-heating, carnal lust.

Symon peered intently at the dancers, seeking the woman he'd hunted for all day. If she danced by, she'd be his.

And God could chastise as He would for it.

~~~

"Stay away from the fire, Alex," Myles warned. "These are the highlands. Pagan practices abound. Guard your soul against them."

Myles muttered the Lord's Prayer as he walked away toward the wagon he slept in. Will Tinker waited until he was gone before snickering.

"Bloody English think themselves so pious." He flashed a grin at Alex. "Yet yer women still swell with babes. Christ did nae put them in those bellies, men did!"

It was a vulgar comment. Athena had become used to them, for anytime Myles was out of earshot, Will unleashed a volley of scarlet speech. Time had dulled her sensitivity to it, and Will pursed his lips together, clearly disappointed by her lack of shock.

"Maybe ye should get out and lose yer virginity, lad," Will offered. "Ye're sure to get a warmer welcome from a good Highland wench than those English chits back home." He rubbed the front of his kilt. "I

know I'll no' be declining should some wench make
me an offer."

Will wandered away.

Athena stared at the fire. There was a hypnotic pull
coming from the flames.

It would be wicked of her to go.

Yes. However, she realized she had done everything Galwell deemed proper. Conducted herself with
piety and submissiveness.

And what had it gotten her?

A position of being his pet. For all that a wife's duty
lay in obedience, it was a respectable position. One
earned through self-discipline and perseverance.

She had been such a trusting fool.

A timid little mouse.

Temptation was licking at her insides as surely
as the flames climbing up the dry wood. The night
seemed alive with a beat she'd spent the past few years
stopping her ears against. A wild tempo that sent her
blood rushing through her body with excitement and
made her feet itch to dance.

Not one of the Italian dances favored by court. No,
she wanted to spin around the fire and let her body
move freely.

*Well, you shall never have another chance…*

The voice inside her was too hard to ignore. And
why should she? Driven into hiding by a man who
was breaking a commandment by bringing false accusations against her.

Shouldn't she take advantage of the moment to
taste adventure?

Athena looked around, but everyone else had found

the time to sneak away. Myles was behind a flap on one of the other wagons.

Just a dance…

She wasn't going to give up her virtue, but by Christ, she was going to taste what it was like to be unbridled.

At least for a moment.

So she fought with her clothing, her breasts aching to be free. Once they were, she combed her fingers through her hair before looking around once more and leaving the wagon behind. She'd left her boots on to protect her feet as she moved closer to the fire. There was more light, and the heat drove away the chill of the night.

The drums were louder too.

Wilder.

The tempo caught her, seeming to pull her in with the girls dancing around the flames. Her flesh seemed to know the way to move, sweeping, turning, dipping, thrusting. Control vanished, leaving her feeling more free than she had ever been in her life.

And more aware of being a woman.

Yet it wasn't the sort of consciousness she was accustomed to. No, there was a sense of enjoyment now. A rush of delight connected to her gender that she had never experienced before. She was not the weaker sex, not the lesser in any way. In fact, she was the cradle of life, and it was a more precious thing than she had ever taken the time to realize.

The music came to a crescendo before stopping, leaving her with her hands raised toward the sky and the tail of her shirt fluttering about her knees while she arched her head back and looked at the stars.

Pagan.

Oh yes, it really was.

But she laughed in a husky tone before telling herself she must return to the wagon. So she lowered her hands and head and left the firelight before temptation became too great. The drummers were starting up again as she forced herself to leave them behind in favor of the cold night.

"So ye are no' timid."

Athena jerked her head around, finding Symon leaning against a tree. Once more he blended so perfectly with his surroundings that she was only a foot from him when he spoke.

"I wondered if ye were," he continued smoothly. "This morning when we met."

He moved, straightening. A strange little awareness of him went twisting though her insides. He made her feel small, which was something she had not experienced with many men.

"But the way that ye dance, well…that tells me ye are no' lacking in spirit."

There was strength in his tone and in the way he moved.

"Symon Grant."

She bit her lip, shifting away from him as she contemplated what to do. His attention was on her, and the truth was it excited her in some very odd way.

"Athena," she answered.

His lips twitched. "I wondered if ye were a woodland spirit this morning. It seems yer parents named ye well."

Despite the dozens of people still dancing and men

playing drums and couples making use of the darkness to enjoy each other's embrace, Athena felt alone with him. But she could hear a couple kissing passionately nearby, the rustling of clothing making her blush as she realized what they were intent on doing.

What the night seemed perfect for...

What he seemed perfect for...

"I should go." A taste of adventure was one thing; discarding common sense was quite another. Uncle Henry deserved better than her returning home soiled by some need to rebel against the unkind way Galwell had treated her. "Truly, I should."

His lips twitched into a grin. One that told her he understood her reasoning and had been raised to be obedient to morality. And then there was the way he tilted his head, like a child intent on snatching a tart before supper. He moved and captured her hand. "Have some cider with me."

She was frozen once more, his touch sending a ripple of awareness through her. She had never been so conscious of someone's flesh against her own. Never been so tempted to allow him to touch her more intimately.

"I couldn't." Her voice betrayed how unsettled she was. "I simply wanted to try dancing, naught more."

At least the last two words came out in a firm tone. Symon stroked the delicate skin on the inside of her wrist.

"Couldn't or shouldn't?" he asked intently. "Are ye promised, lass?"

Athena shook her head before she thought how much wiser it might have been to let him believe honor demanded he find another to share cider with. She would have had to lie though, and she didn't care for the bitter taste that filled her mouth at the idea. She would far rather maintain her honor. Galwell wasn't going to rob her of her morality. "Yet I am not loose with my favors." She tried to tug her wrist from his grasp, but he held tight. "A dance was all I wanted."

"Perhaps I might tempt ye to want more…"

*Oh could he…*

Something shifted between them. An awareness, an understanding of some sort. The truth was she didn't really think all that long on it because she was too busy responding. Impulses were bubbling up inside her as if she hadn't recently learned the price of following such things.

No, nothing seemed to matter except the way his touch delighted her. He smoothed his fingers along her inner wrist, sending ripples of enjoyment through her body.

And he knew she liked it.

His touch.

She watched the way his eyes narrowed as he read her reactions through their locked gazes. She'd never been so aware of Galwell. No, now she was face-to-face with the difference. It felt as though time had slowed down just to allow her the opportunity to notice how very handsome he was.

His attractiveness wasn't in the classical sense. No, it was in the way his jaw was tight and sporting a couple of faded scars. He hadn't applied any powder to cover them because he was comfortable in his world, a place where strength, not fashion, was the true attractive trait.

He drew in a deep breath, pulling her closer while stepping to the side to turn her around and put her back to the tree he'd been leaning against. The action made her gasp because he'd very neatly pinned her, his larger body between her and freedom as he leaned down and sealed her mouth beneath his.

She'd never been kissed before.

Sweet mercy, had she been naive!

Symon's mouth moved across hers, awakening a thousand more points of sensation than she'd ever imagined her lips might be capable of. He moved slowly but firmly, taking command of the kiss as he slid his hand into her hair.

He tasted good.

She heard a little sound escape from her as she succumbed to the moment, intoxicated beyond reason by the way his mouth moved against hers. Reaching for him was a necessity, one she couldn't have quelled if it had meant her very life to defy it.

Touching him was something she craved.

She smoothed her hands along his upper arms, finding more hard muscle beneath the thin fabric of his shirt. Everything inside her was heating, warming, as she opened her mouth and kissed him back.

His chest rumbled with a male sound of appreciation. It was a strange compliment and yet one she felt her confidence blooming in response to.

"Tell me yer family name, lass." His tone was husky.

Athena blinked, trying to remember exactly why she needed to keep such information from him. He leaned down and inhaled against her hair.

"Tell me the name of yer father."

There was command in his voice. Authority she realized he'd likely earned.

"I can't," she muttered, trying to move away from him.

"Ye would rather I kiss ye and make ye no honorable offer?" he demanded as he stepped into her path of escape.

She froze, looking up into his face, so very pleased with the sense of honor coming from him. "You're a good man."

His jaw tightened. "That's another name I want from ye, Athena. The name of the man who makes ye doubt me."

He didn't sound like he was going to take no for an answer either. She enjoyed the intensity for a moment, loath to leave him, even though she realized she must.

"Ye're English," he muttered.

A shiver went down her back. Disguised as a boy, she'd heard plenty of slurs against the English since she'd crossed into Scotland. They were in the Highlands now, where the English were hated.

"Yes, so you see why I can't have cider with you," she said, more disappointed by the barrier between them than she should have been. "I must go now."

He caught her hand and stroked it. "Tell me…yer family name." There was a flicker of determination in his eyes.

"Boldness won't help you change my thinking."

One of his dark eyebrows rose. "Are ye sure about that?"

She heard the promise in his tone a moment before he was kissing her again. He just turned her around, surrounding her as he claimed her mouth. This time, there was more passion in the kiss. She shivered beneath it, realizing he was introducing her to the boldness she'd warned him wouldn't help his cause.

It did…

She responded to his determination with a surge of need, wanting to give as good as she got. She reached up and threaded her fingers through his hair, enjoying the way he pulled in a hard breath and the fact that she was close enough to hear it. He pressed her lips open, teasing her with the tip of his tongue before he thrust it inside her mouth.

"Ye bastard, Grant!"

Symon grunted, lifting his head and turning it to look toward the fire where the curse had been flung.

"Ye get yer filthy hands off me sister!"

There was the hard sound of flesh connecting with flesh as women screamed and a fight broke out.

"Stay here," Symon ordered before he was gone, his kilt flapping up as he ran toward the fray.

She felt like he'd been ripped from her, the night air harsh with its chill, reprimanding her for her rash behavior. Athena pushed away from the tree and scurried through the darkness toward the wagon.

She'd dared too much.

And yet, once she was secure beneath the oiled canvas, she found herself stroking her own hair.

It had been good to enjoy being a woman. Life was full of so many who told her she was less for being born into her gender. Tonight she'd felt so very happy to just be who she was.

She couldn't lament it.

Not really.

But she would end it. The strip of linen she used to flatten her breasts was nearby, and she sat up, slowly winding it about her body and tucking the end in.

Yes, all things must come to an end.

At least the memory would always be hers to treasure.

❧

Will Tinker slowly lowered a mug. He was grinning, and it gave way to snickering now that he'd swallowed.

Alex was a girl.

And not just a girl, a woman of rare beauty.

His master was too devoted to his faith to realize what was right beneath their noses. Will never took things for what they seemed. He was a man who made his living by his wits alone. His clan wouldn't welcome him back, so the life of a tinker was his lot. More than one of his countrymen had sneered at him during the day for working for an English merchant.

Ah, but there was profit to be had in Myles Basset's employ.

He grinned again as he faded into the darkness to see what other secrets he might learn.

❧

She was gone.

Symon swept the darkness again, but there was no way to know which wagon she'd disappeared into, and he wasn't going to be very popular if he started rousing the occupants in a search.

That didn't mean he didn't want to.

Symon quelled the urge. It wasn't easy with her taste clinging to his lips. Christ, he could still feel her hair between his fingers.

Perhaps he shouldn't have kissed her.

The only reason he lamented his action was that it had frightened her off.

He should have courted her more.

But Christ! He'd felt like discovering what she tasted like was a need instead of a desire. The only time he'd ever felt so desperate for a woman had been back when he'd been a beardless lad, still at the mercy of his cock because he hadn't yet developed the control a man learned over his lust.

Tamhas shifted, making Symon aware he wasn't alone this time. His men didn't care for the times when he went off by himself. It was foolish, but tonight Symon wasn't thinking about who might have slipped a dirk between his ribs while he was distracted.

No, he was stuck on the thought that if he'd allowed Lyall or Tamhas to do their duty, then maybe one of them would have seen which way his woodland sprite had headed.

He'd gone and gotten the fever.

There was no other explanation for how agitated he was.

And there were too many tracks for him to be able to deduce which ones belonged to Athena.

But he'd find her.

On that, she could be assured.

Will was smirking at her.

Athena tried to ignore it, but by evening the next day, there was no way to convince herself that the tinker wasn't taking more notice of her than he had before.

She must have done something to make him question her.

So she kept her chin tucked and her attention on her work. Still, the tinker was the one who brought her a plate of supper.

"We're going north," he explained jovially. "Toward Sutherland, to sell our wares. I've a few friends who have promised us safe travel through the Highlands."

Athena put a chunk of bread into her mouth to keep from having to answer. Will's "friends" were clustered about the fire: a rough-looking bunch of men who had swords strapped to their backs and filthy clothing. Their faces were smudged with dirt and grease, and she didn't care to be downwind of them, for it was clear none of them bathed.

Symon had smelled nice…

The memory heated her cheeks. At last Will wandered back toward the fire and the company of his cohorts.

"You are a good lad." Myles surprised her by speaking directly to her. "Making no complaint. We'll have a larger profit to split once we head home. Your dedication to duty will yield reward."

She nodded and kept her attention on her bowl of stew. Myles wasn't quite finished though.

"I rather applaud you for keeping distance from the men at the fire. They are a disreputable sort for certain.

Best for you to keep your thoughts to yourself. Can you read?"

Athena nodded.

Myles bestowed an approving smile on her as he handed a book of common prayer to her. "Keep your eyes on the scriptures and away from Will Tinker's associates. Their ways will leave a stain on your virtue."

Deceiving the man was a sin.

Athena felt regret over it, but at least she had earned his approval. It was a small thing, and she found herself longing for home as she battled against the regret of knowing she was lying to him.

Damn Galwell for making her do it.

And yet there was a part of her that wouldn't have missed meeting Symon Grant. He was burly and hard, like the men at the fire, and yet so vastly different. His chin had been scraped free of stubble and his hands were clean. There had been honor in him as well.

*"Are ye promised, lass?"*

He'd been a rogue, kissing her so boldly. Yet not before he'd made certain it wouldn't leave a stain on her virtue.

*You must stop building him up in your imagination…*

Perhaps if she were home, Athena might have listened to her voice of reason. But here? On a lonely road in the Highlands? She had only her thoughts, so better to keep company with herself. Besides, she would never see Symon Grant again.

And she didn't care for how sad that made her.

Not at all.

❧

Spring and summer offered merchants the chance to take their wares into the Highlands. May Day might have been the traditional day for festivals, but in the north there was still snow, so there would be market fairs throughout the season.

Athena was English, so she was traveling with a merchant.

Symon took to the road. If she'd been Scottish and promised, he'd have had to accept she was beyond his reach. But English, well, that was another matter.

He might claim her as a prize.

That thought sobered him. He'd never been one to raid—well, not for women anyway. Athena seemed to have awakened a very odd determination in him.

Perhaps he was just trying to find something to do other than return home and look at the offers for him.

Now there was something he wasn't ashamed to admit to. The letters sitting in his study were a penitence he wasn't looking forward to facing. In other clans, there were plenty of kinsmen who would enjoy being laird. Symon grunted as he thought about how they'd find the position less grand than they'd dreamed.

There was duty aplenty. His was sitting in his study, and he turned his horse toward the road leading to the next market day fair. He would find her and bring her home. Discovering if they suited one another would be better than looking at ink on parchment.

At the least it would help him understand why he was so determined to see her again. His men thought he'd gone mad. They rolled their eyes when they though he wasn't looking. Tamhas wasn't fast enough though, and Symon had caught him.

"I thought ye wanted me interested in a woman enough to go and claim her."

Tamhas rubbed his beard. "But…English?"

"A woman is a woman. And this one is…well…I suppose we could cut east…no doubt there is plenty to do with it being planting time."

"No." Tamhas was quick to interrupt him. "Ye said it yerself, a woman is a woman, and now that ye mention it, I'm enjoying running her down."

His men were suddenly eager to keep going. Guilt nipped at him a bit, but Symon didn't really let it get the better of him. They'd all done their share of work. But it had been a few years since he'd ridden out just to enjoy stirring up a bit of mischief.

Was it even about Athena?

Perhaps. And then again, maybe he was just feeling more alive than he had in a long time. For that reason alone, he would track her down like a fox.

They rode until the sun was gone and stopped at a tavern to see what news might be gathered from those enjoying a warm meal inside.

Lyall joined him at a long table as serving wenches began to set bread and stew out for them. "Glad to see ye taking interest in a lass. Some of the lads, well, they were beginning to wonder if ye had unnatural tastes."

Symon shot his captain a hard look. "Ye know better, and I've bought ye plenty of cider to keep yer mouth shut about just how ye came into that knowledge."

Lyall slowly grinned. "Well now…back then, we were both lacking wits aplenty. But those Campbell sisters, now there were the finest pairs of tits."

Symon shook his head. A whistle came from ahead of them. He looked up as Craig turned around.

"Looks like Marcus McPherson coming in just to see what we're about."

Marcus McPherson was the war chief for the McPhersons. He was bastard born and well suited to his position. His retainers swept the room before they entered. Symon stood and offered the man his hand. They clasped wrists, and both their men returned to their conversations as Marcus settled down across the table from Symon.

"What has ye so far from home?" Marcus inquired.

Symon found himself somewhat hesitant to admit his purpose.

"He's looking for a lass," Lyall answered when his laird didn't.

Symon sent him a warning look that only earned him a chuckle from his captain.

"Someone I know?" Marcus asked.

"Truth is he knows only her first name," Lyall was happy to reveal.

"Enough." Symon gave Lyall a shove. "I've a bad enough reputation as it is."

Marcus accepted a mug of ale but declined to indulge in a peek down the serving girl's bodice.

"Still in love with yer wife, I see," Symon said.

Marcus lifted his mug in a toast before sampling it. "If ye're chasing a female up this way, ye must understand me feelings for Helen."

Symon shrugged. "It's folly. Lyall has reason to rib me about it."

"Yet ye are still here."

It wasn't a question, but Symon nodded anyway. "Met her at the May Day festival."

"Hence the reason ye have only her first name," Marcus replied. "That is going to make finding her a chore."

"She was English," Symon added. "And tall for a woman."

Marcus chewed bread, but the serving wench behind him looked startled. She masked it quickly when she realized her guest had noticed she was listening in.

"Mistress." He was half off the bench as she started to scurry back to the kitchen before her master took her to task. "What do ye know of the English lass?"

Lyall had joined a table behind Marcus. He turned around, swinging his leg over the bench and standing up along with a few other retainers so the girl couldn't escape.

"I didn't see any English lass," the serving girl insisted.

"Ye saw something," Symon insisted. "Yer eyes went wide when I spoke."

"We had an English merchant here yesterday," she admitted.

"And?" Marcus asked. "What else?"

"One of his men, well, he was asking to buy a dress, one for a tall woman, but no' just a common dress, mind ye. He wanted something pretty and cut…low…"

Something shifted inside him.

Symon dug a coin out of his purse. "Where were they heading?"

"North."

"Did they get a dress?"

The girl looked at the floor, her cheeks brightening. "I heard...heard Will went down to...the place at the edge of town for one."

"Will who?" Marcus demanded in a gruff voice.

"Will Tinker. He's a McGregor by blood but does nae wear the colors. Works for an English cloth merchant."

A memory flashed through Symon's mind. Brenda had bought the cloth, and there had been a boy. Now that he thought on it, the lad had possessed some very delicate fingers.

He had seen her and not even realized.

Symon placed the coin on the table. The girl was quick to take it and push it into her bodice for safekeeping. She made a show of wiping down the tabletop before she hurried away.

"Careful, Symon," Marcus advised. "It's possible there is nothing amiss." He caught Symon's look as he whistled to his men to make ready to ride. There were a few groans, but they were already stuffing the last of their supper into their mouths and mopping up their bowls with bread. "She might be willing to wear the dress."

"If that was the case," Symon replied, "she'd have brought her own along. My guess is she has no idea one of her own is making ready to sell her."

"Pretty, was she?"

Symon nodded. "And dressed as a lad."

Marcus grunted and let out another whistle. "In that case, we'll ride with ye, for if I catch them on McPherson land, ye'll be needing me to hold ye back, by the look on yer face."

Symon knew he was too intense about the entire matter.

There was no denying it. Truth was he wasn't going to waste time debating the issue with himself. Athena had been an innocent. She'd trembled when he'd kissed her, shaming him with how quickly he'd pressed her for the intimate touch.

She wasn't a whore, and he was going to enjoy choking the life out of the man who thought to sell her as such.

Will Tinker had best sleep lightly.

❧

She was tired of her own company.

In spite of that fact, Athena wasn't pleased to see Will Tinker walking her way. There was a flash of something in his eyes that made her skin crawl.

She knew it wasn't a very Christian thought; still, there was no hiding from the way she felt. His comrades had turned to watch him, the smirks on their lips making her shift uncomfortably.

They'd made it far north. Myles was ecstatic with the way people came out of their homes to see his cloth. He'd bought larger portions of supper for them all as he smiled, content with the profit from the day. With the sun starting to set, the village church bell began to toll. Myles smiled brightly.

"I'm off to give proper thanks. You must stay and mind the wares and horses."

Athena had nodded, gaining another pleased look from her employer before he dusted off his hat and started toward the church.

The moment he was through the doors, Will started toward her.

Apprehension gripped her as she realized she recognized the look in Will's eyes.

It was the same one Galwell had aimed toward her.

She turned to flee but found herself facing one of his cohorts. The man smiled at her, showing off his rotten teeth before he brought the pommel of his short sword down on her skull. Blackness grabbed her and dragged her away from the moment, giving her only enough time to realize how very helpless she was.

Damn all men to hell.

❧

Someone threw a bucket of water in her face.

Athena woke up, sputtering. She used her hands to sweep the water from her eyes and heard snickering.

"There she is," Will remarked. "Our little dove."

Her skull cap and hat lay on the floor. Will's friends looked at her hair, greed shining in their eyes.

"Just as I promised." Will opened his hand and gestured toward her. "She'll fetch a fine price tonight. Far more than Myles is paying us."

Athena sat up, looking around the room they were in. It was a kitchen with a large hearth, and the door was behind Will and shut tight.

The sounds of revelry could be heard through the door. She caught some music mixed with bawdy laughter. A solid knock sounded before the door was pushed in by a woman in a silk dress that rustled when she moved. She stopped in front of Athena, the front of the dress shockingly low.

"Well, get her cleaned up and into that dress," the woman exclaimed. "I can't hold the men back from the other girls for much longer. They came for bed sport and are eager to get to it."

"I am no whore," Athena exclaimed. "No matter what you have been told."

The woman's eyes narrowed. "Ye're English and in the Highlands. Better learn to keep yer mouth closed and me pleased with yer actions. I can make yer life hell."

She picked up the front of her skirt and shot a warning look toward Will. "Get her ready."

The moment the door shut, Will grabbed Athena by the hair. She cried out as he hauled her up by the grip, not caring how much pain he caused.

"Ye'll do everything I tell ye and do so with a smile on yer lips," he rasped. His breath was foul, but she turned away out of revulsion over what he'd suggested. Will released her, and she landed back in a chair.

"I do nae know who ye are or why ye have been traveling as a lad," Will began. "And neither do the men behind that door. But they will be happy to help ye accept yer lot as a woman." He rubbed his crotch. "If I tell them"—he gestured toward the door—"what ye have been about, they will throw ye on the table and rut on ye like a pack of dogs. There are no constables here to stop them, and even if there were, no clansman would worry about the fate of an English witch who needs to be reminded of her gender. Mind ye, most of them would know well enough that ye are no witch. Not that it would stop them from having a turn on ye. They came to fornicate, and a free ride is a free ride."

Nausea threatened to bring her supper up. She pressed the back of her hand against her lips as Will's companions nodded, their eyes bright with lust and the desire to join in the described fray. She looked around, desperation making her heart beat at a frantic pace. Will grabbed her hair again.

"So ye will agree that one man will be preferable to a dozen of them?" he demanded. "Better to be auctioned off to only one man."

"That is no agreement," she hissed. "Only a matter of survival."

He offered her a bright smile of victory. "As to that, I agree, for I am a man who has to work hard to earn enough to survive. Here in the Highlands, it's no' easy to earn enough when ye have no clan."

He made a gesture with his hands. "Get yerself bathed. Emilia runs one of the finest brothels in the Highlands. Men come here from all over to see their tastes satisfied. Ye"—he pointed at her—"are a novelty. One they will pay handsomely for."

The way his eyes flashed with anticipation was sickening, but she bit her lip because she needed time. Time to think of a way to escape. And she needed Will and his companions gone. He thought her beaten, beaming at her with victory glowing in his eyes.

"I'll send the lads in with water for a bath. Ye'll fetch such a fine price once ye're cleaned up," Will informed her before he licked his lips and turned to his men. "Let's get some whisky, lads, and toast to a job well done."

They left her at last. Quelling her panic, Athena forced herself to look around the room. However, short of climbing up the chimney, there was no escape. There was only the one door.

She refused to accept defeat. There had to be a way; she just needed to think of it.

Money might help. After all, that seemed to be the thing everyone was willing to sell their souls for. Sitting down, she tugged her boot off and found the coins Henry had given her in case she found herself in need. The candlelight shone off them. One was a full-gold angel. It was a small fortune.

Athena tucked it back into her stocking, selecting one of the silver coins to keep in her palm. She finished just as a girl opened the door and came in.

"The mistress sent me in to help ye with yer hair."

The girl was timid, scurrying to do what she'd been told to do before she earned any more bruises like the one she had on her left cheek.

"I can pay you," Athena whispered, "if you will help me escape."

The girl shifted. "Mistress Emilia would have me whipped. She's promised the men a treat."

Athena fought to mask how revolting she found that idea. She lifted the silver coin.

"This," she said, "is enough to pay for you to travel far from here and even have some for yourself."

The girl's eyes brightened. "I could buy me own sheep, and by next year, the fleece would be worth a considerable amount." The girl rolled her lower lip in and set her teeth against it. "I do nae know how…we might do it…"

"Is there a boy serving in the kitchens?" Athena asked.

The maid nodded.

Athena thought fast. She avoided admitting to herself how very desperate she was because she needed her wits.

"Call for him…and send him out…for something…make him go back and forth, you as well. The guards will lose track of who is inside and who has left. Tell them my hair needs washing and it will take time to dry."

The girl considered the plan. For a long moment, Athena found herself waiting to see if she'd agree. The girl looked at the coin at last, hope flickering in her eyes. She was off to the door in the next moment, slipping through while Athena breathed a sigh of relief.

Will Tinker could choke on his victory.

She fully intended to claim her own.

And she refused to think about how easy it might be to fail.

⤜✦⤛

She paid the kitchen boy to bring her a grubby bonnet and piece of wool for a kilt. He showed off missing teeth as he watched her try to dress, finally coming to her aid and finishing the task. She pulled the bonnet on and took a deep breath.

"Ye are too clean," the girl said as she stooped down and rubbed her hands in the soot near the edge of the hearth. Her hands were black when she lifted them and rubbed them over Athena's face. The soot made her want to sneeze as her eyes watered from the harsh scent.

"Better."

Athena passed the silver to her and another coin to the boy. With a deep breath, she gathered up the soap and linen the boy had brought and carried them through the door. Will looked up but dismissed her and went back to his drinking.

Somehow, a room had never struck her as so very large before.

Each step seemed to take a small eternity, and every footfall sounded far too loud. Around her, there were women laughing as they attempted to captivate their male customers. There was the swish of ale and whisky being poured and music coming from a corner.

She mustn't run.

But quelling the urge to take flight took every last bit of determination she had.

Fate decided to be kind, or maybe the word was merciful. Athena made it to the door and slipped through it without anyone raising the alarm. Normally the dark street would have been something she avoided; tonight she walked eagerly into the night, seeking relief from the world of greed and men's lust.

"So now it's a Scottish lad…"

She jumped, but the man emerged out of the night, clasping her arm and stopping her.

"Ye play a very dangerous game, Athena."

Symon Grant wasn't pleased with her. But he looked up to where she'd come from, and she watched the way his jaw tightened.

"Maybe ye've been introduced to yer folly, lass." He pulled her around, his grip tight but lacking the pain Will had inflicted on her. "That bastard tried to sell ye…did nae he?"

"How did you know?" she asked.

He locked gazes with her. It was unsettling the way something inside her shifted. There was determination in his eyes, but not the bright glow of lust. For a moment, she almost believed he was an honorable man.

Except that she no longer believed such nonsense. Men were beasts. She really needed to learn that lesson for good.

"I followed ye," Symon answered while pulling her down the street. "And ye're fortunate I did. I would like to know what ye think ye are doing, but for the moment, I cannae take the time to listen to yer story. We needs be away from here before someone sees ye dressed like this."

She heard the soft sounds of horses. Symon took her toward them with a stride that had her hurrying to keep pace. She felt the tension in him, and it kept her silent as he lifted her up and onto the back of a horse.

She needed to escape, so she'd not quibble over the means.

Symon Grant was certainly better than Will Tinker.

⁂

Symon didn't call a halt to their riding until the next day. Athena dropped off the back of her mare with a sigh of relief.

The feeling was short-lived. Symon was suddenly there, clasping her arm and taking her into an inn. She didn't really have time to look around as he hurried her toward the stairs.

But once they were abovestairs, he spun her loose

and stood between her and the door, looking like he was trying to decide just how to take her to task.

"I owe you my thanks," she said.

He tilted his head to one side. "Aye, ye do."

"And I have thanked you." She drew herself up straight. "But I did not ask you for assistance."

"Because ye are a bloody fool for traveling dressed as a lad."

He was furious with her. His tone chafed her pride.

"You think I am not aware of the risks I have been forced to undertake?" she asked. "Well, I assure you, Laird Grant, I am painfully aware of my circumstances."

Something she'd said caught him off guard. He started to say something but shook his head before voicing whatever his thought was.

"We'll discuss this after we both eat," he informed her tightly.

She didn't think for a moment that he was making the suggestion for his sake. He was far too imposing for something like an empty belly to keep him from speaking his mind when he felt it was rightful to do so.

"Do not pity me."

She should have kept her lips sealed. He wasn't anyone she should be reaching out to for solace or even approval.

He grunted. "Now ye're the one being right unkind toward me, lass." He crossed his arms over his chest and swept his gaze over her from head to toe. "Ye're a mess, and I know Will Tinker bought a dress to auction ye off in. The look on yer face tells me he told ye exactly what he'd planned for ye."

"I escaped."

Symon's lips twitched. "Aye, ye did, but no' so much as ye think ye did either. Truly escaping from anything means ye need somewhere to go. Ye're in the middle of the Highlands. Ye'd no' have made it out of that village without someone else helping ye, for ye could no' return to the cloth merchant."

He was correct.

So very horribly correct.

Despair tried to claim her, making her fight to maintain her composure while he watched her with his keen eyes.

"I can't believe all…Scotsmen are dishonorable…"

He grunted. "We're not."

She nodded. "I would have found someone to take me south."

"Ye found me."

She contemplated him for a long moment. Somehow, she'd forgotten how large he was. Now that she was taking a moment to consider her circumstances, she realized there was no way she'd make him do anything he didn't want to.

"A meal," he said gruffly. "And some proper clothing. It's no' decent to gawk at ye."

He was gone a moment later, turning and affording her a look at his wide back before he disappeared through the door.

*"No' decent to gawk at ye…"*

It wasn't the first time he'd seen her in only a shirt. The knowledge gave her hope that he'd left her in order to afford her privacy. He was honorable. A decent man. One she'd hoped, prayed to find.

*You are grasping at straws...*

She was; however, beggars simply couldn't be choosers. So she'd cultivate her hope and refuse to accept anything less than victory over the dire fate Will Tinker had planned for her.

&

It wasn't the first time Symon had battled the urge to do what he wanted over what he knew very well he should.

Right versus wrong, a dilemma as old as time.

He stood for a long moment just outside the door separating him from what he craved.

*Well, if ye want her to see ye as more than the men who would have sold her, ye'll leave her.*

Was that what he wanted?

He snorted as he went down the steps. More the fool than ever, it would seem, for he knew precious little about her and there he was, placing her on a pedestal. He had no idea if she was worthy of such thinking, and yet he would have challenged any man who questioned the matter.

"Symon Grant."

Symon froze. Cormac Sutherland was taking full advantage of how distracted Symon had been by Athena. Heir to the earldom of Sutherland as well as being in line for the lairdship, Cormac wasn't a man easily overlooked.

He sat with his back to the wall, his men enjoying supper at the long tables. The innkeeper's wife scurried to serve them.

"Traveling light?" Symon masked his surprise by looking at the six men wearing Sutherland colors.

"Truth is my sister heard of a cloth merchant up from England." Cormac shrugged. "It was an excuse to stretch me legs."

And Cormac wasn't fool enough to announce who he was by riding out with a large number of men or to allow anyone to see just how many men he had. Symon didn't need to look for them; he knew they were somewhere nearby.

"Have a drink with me," Cormac said. "And reassure me ye have no' resorted to buggery."

Symon grunted and watched as one of the innkeeper's daughters escorted Athena down the stairs and toward the kitchen where she might bathe. He shared a look with Tamhas. The retainer reached up and tugged on his bonnet before turning with Craig in tow to follow.

"'Tis a lass." Symon lifted his leg and straddled a bench.

"Which only brings more questions to me mind," Cormac muttered thoughtfully.

Symon accepted a bowl of stew from the mistress of the house and broke a round of bread open. "Truth is I followed her here."

Cormac's eyebrow rose. "I see the rumor is true: Ye're finished with mourning at long last."

"I said I followed her, not that I'm ready to declare meself."

Cormac shifted his attention back down the way Athena had gone. "I enjoy a lass with enough spirit to defy everything around her. Perhaps I'll get a look at—"

"She's mine," Symon declared.

"By what right?"

Cormac was toying with him. Symon knew it,

honestly expected it from the man. He pointed his dagger at the heir of the Earl of Sutherland. "Do nae be casting yer eye on the lass. Yer father is busy contracting ye an heiress, from what I hear."

"And ye're rumored to be home, sifting through the offers for ye," Cormac countered. "We both know what we should be doing. What I'm more interested in is what we *are* doing."

Symon shrugged as he used his dagger to spear a piece of cheese and lift it toward his lips. "I met her on May morning, followed her."

"In a shift? With her hair unbound?" Cormac said. "Ye have an unfair advantage." The bench he was sitting on started to slide back as he made to get up. "I'll remedy it and see if she's worth fighting ye over—"

"Have ye ever loved a woman?"

Cormac chuckled. He sat back, tipping his head up and laughing. "Me father would be quick to enlighten ye as to just how much of a rogue he considers me to be. But I rather think ye mean affection of a more… emotional sort."

"I came to have affection for Tara. Call me what ye will for it, but I preferred it to a cold marriage."

Cormac's lips split in a grin. "I've managed to enjoy plenty of heat in me liaisons, I assure ye."

Symon swallowed and sent Cormac a hard look. "That heat dwindles, and ye know it well. That is the true reason ye seek new entertainment and earn yer sire's reprimands. Because it matters very little who is warming yer bed. It's as fickle as yer appetite when looking at a feast table."

Cormac went silent for a moment, contemplating

what Symon had said. "So ye have followed this female here…to what end? Ye claim affection for her?"

Symon offered his friend a shrug. "I confess I stole a kiss from her on May Day, and the craving for more has kept me awake more than I should admit."

"Allow a female to know ye crave her, and ye will discover yerself dancing to her tune," Cormac muttered.

It was a jaded idea, but Symon knew more than one man held the opinion to be true.

"Truth is," Symon continued, "I heard her escort had bought a dress for her without her knowledge. Her being an English girl, I followed farther to make sure there was no trouble."

Cormac's eyes narrowed. "Did ye find it? Trouble?"

Symon chuckled. "I came away with the prize, so that is all that matters."

Cormac smiled slowly. "Morning will be interesting, more so than I first thought. I cannae wait to gain a glimpse of this creature who has enchanted ye."

Enchanted?

Symon didn't care for the word.

But he couldn't deny how hard it was to sit at the table through the evening when all he wanted to do was go up the stairs and confront Athena.

Better to let her think she didn't have that sort of a draw.

Besides, she would be leaving with him no matter her circumstances.

⁂

She'd meant to go down and talk to Symon.

Athena made a firm decision to do so, right after she

ate the stew and bread waiting in her room. Her hair was drying and her head was much clearer with a full belly.

She'd thank him once more.

And use her money to secure passage home. With any luck, Henry would have found a resolution to her situation, and she might settle back into her life with a very hard lesson learned.

But her eyelids were simply too heavy. With her belly full, braiding her hair seemed an impossible task. She'd sat on the bed because the only other thing in the loft was a stool in front of the fire.

The bed was so soft.

Weeks and weeks of sleeping in a wagon had made her conscious of just how wonderful a true bed was. She lay back, just for a moment, to indulge herself.

And didn't wake until first light.

A knock on the door roused her. She brushed at the tangle her hair had become during the night, staring at the unbound strands in confusion as the door opened.

"Morning, miss." One of the innkeeper's daughters lowered herself before shutting the door firmly. "I've come to help ye dress. The laird is already making ready to depart. Ye should be preparing as well."

She should, but not because she was not leaving with Symon.

*Do not be peevish.*

Athena recalled her resolution to thank the man again. The girl brought her boots and helped Athena to lace them tight over the stockings she'd slept in. Standing up, Athena reached for her hip roll and tied it tightly. It was strange the way the garment felt after so long in breeches.

The underdress was next, which earned a little sigh from her because lacing the front of it did not smash her breasts but supported them instead.

The overgown cut the chill of the morning air. Athena happily turned so the girl might attach each sleeve with a lace through eyelets worked beneath the shoulder epaulet.

"Ye are so fair." The girl marveled as she gathered up Athena's hair.

"It has brought me more grief than pleasure."

The girl froze for a moment. "Still, Laird Grant is a handsome man. I heard last night that Laird Sutherland believes Laird Grant is enchanted by ye." She let out a dreamy little sigh.

Athena discovered herself loath to shatter her illusions.

The truth was she wished she might return to a day when she was still enamored of Galwell.

*Then you would never have experienced Symon's kiss…*

Athena felt her cheeks heat. The girl backed away, smiling at the picture Athena made.

"Thank you."

"No trouble at all," the girl replied. "When the lairds are here, I have the chance to catch the eye of one of their captains. It would be a fine match, so much better than what me father is thinking to settle me in."

She opened the door and held it wide for Athena.

Indeed, it was time to go.

She didn't care for knowing her time with Symon was at an end.

No, and she wasn't going to dwell on it either.

She'd made her decisions, using logic and good sense to guide her. Staying because she enjoyed his kiss would be folly indeed, and she'd learned how easily allowing affection to influence her thinking might burn her.

So, it was time to go.

❧

"Now that is a fair sight, to be sure," Cormac muttered next to Symon. "I like a woman who is nae too delicate to tussle with meself."

"Ye will nae be tussling with her."

Cormac smirked, but Symon didn't really give the man too much of his attention. He was staring at Athena.

Named for a goddess, and she fit the image.

The dress complemented her fair skin and gold hair. She looked at him with eyes as blue as a summer day, and her lips were rosy pink. Now that she was dressed as a woman, he gained a glimpse of her breasts, plump and inviting, just as he'd suspected they were when he'd kissed her.

Christ, he needed to gain control of his thoughts before he made a fool of himself.

Or tossed her over his shoulder.

The truth was both were likely options. He should have felt a nip of guilt for thinking about the fact that she was English and at his mercy.

She deserved better from him.

Or perhaps it was more correct to say that he wanted to be better for her so she'd not see him as a savage.

❧

He was more handsome than she recalled.

*Well, it had been dark...*

Now she could see his dark hair clearly, and the topaz eyes were there, just as she'd remembered, not a figment of her imagination.

He was also just as imposing. When he stood, she felt small by comparison, lifting her chin so they might maintain eye contact.

She was already halfway into the room before she recalled any sort of manners. She lowered herself, a bit clumsily for how long she had been performing such courtesies.

"Good morning, Laird Grant. I apologize for not answering your questions last evening," she began softly. She looked at the other man, noting the silver brooch pinned to the corner of his bonnet. The crest proclaimed him a man of noble heritage.

"Cormac Sutherland," he offered as he held his hand out for hers.

She hesitated before placing her hand in his.

"She's no' so easily charmed, Cormac," Symon informed his friend.

"She's comparing me to ye," Cormac replied. "Likely thinks I'm as much of a savage as ye to sneak out on May morning…"

"Ye don't go out on May morning because ye never sleep alone."

Symon's men chuckled. Athena felt her cheeks heat. She glanced at them as they cleared their throats, nodding and tugging on the corners of their caps before escaping. The girl who had helped her dress brought a bowl of porridge and placed it on the table, then sent a shy smile at one of the remaining men.

Symon gestured toward the bench. She realized

she'd been tense. She was relieved to discover him waiting patiently for her to consume her breakfast. However, she found it nearly impossible to eat while under his scrutiny. He didn't grant her any mercy but waited until she'd finished the bowl.

"Now tell me, lass," he asked at last. "What has ye fleeing into Scotland?"

"It was my uncle's plan, one formed out of necessity."

Cormac was listening intently; however, it was Symon Athena couldn't look away from. The intensity in his stare held her spellbound as she relayed the details of Galwell and his plans to accuse her of thievery.

"And so," she ended her tale, "my uncle sent me north with Myles Basset to afford himself time to gather support against Galwell and his accusations."

There was silence for a long moment, both men contemplating her story. Cormac softly chuckled. "Me sister would do something like that, dress as a boy instead of allowing anyone to put her in a thieves' hold."

"Do nae encourage her." Symon sent her a reprimand with those topaz eyes she found so fascinating. "Ye are more than fortunate I found ye."

"I have expressed my gratitude." She stood up.

"Aye, but no' admitted to yer foolishness." Symon towered over her as he stepped into her path.

"I will certainly not apologize for not staying where Galwell might have me thrown into prison simply because he is a noble," she informed him sternly.

Symon offered her a tilt of his head. "It's true there are men who allow their lineage to inflate their egos."

Cormac made a scoffing sound. Symon locked stares with him. "The Earl of Morton comes to mind."

Cormac came around the table. "Well, fair enough when ye mention that man's name. He is a fine example of just what ambition can do to a man who sells his soul for his position."

"It's a relief to hear you agree with me," she said. "If you would be kind enough to direct me to where I might secure passage back to England, I will not take up any more of your time."

Both men didn't care for what she asked. She watched the way Symon gripped the sleeve of his shirt.

His hands were just as large as the rest of him.

She really wished she didn't notice such details about him so very often.

"Ye'll come with me," he informed her with a tone thick with authority.

She wasn't having any of it. In fact, something flickered to life inside her that made it an absolute necessity to refuse.

"I couldn't impose," she said smoothly.

Frustration drew Symon's features tight. "Ye're in the Highlands, lass."

"I am aware of that." She tried to go around him. Cormac stepped up and blocked her path. "I realize the situation is poor at best. However, I will not allow Galwell's plans to succeed. Uncle Henry has likely had enough time to gather support now. I will return and place my faith in justice prevailing."

"As to that," Symon replied, "I'll send a message south and see what the man has to say. Ye will be me guest until I know ye can return without fear."

Athena felt a warning prickling across her skin. Some sort of awareness of the fact that while Symon might have come to her aid outside the brothel, now he presented an obstacle she truly had no way to dislodge if he chose to be stubborn.

And Scotsmen were known the world over for their stubborn natures.

"I couldn't."

Symon tilted his head to the side. "Ye must."

Her own frustration was growing. "For all that I am in your debt and properly grateful, you are not a member of my family. I owe you no obedience."

"Go back out there, and ye are only going to end up the property of another man," Symon informed her without a shred of mercy for her pride.

"So I should just agree to be your property?" she inquired.

His jaw clenched. "Are ye saying ye prefer Will Tinker's plans for ye?"

"That is not what I am saying," she said in her own defense. "You are twisting my words to suit your own ends."

"Maybe so," he informed her gruffly. "But at least I'm intent on seeing ye safe."

Which meant she'd be alone with him.

The memory of his kisses rose in her mind.

Athena shook her head. It wasn't that she was refusing his offer; it was more of a case of knowing that she lacked the self-discipline to be too close to him. "I simply cannot accept such an arrangement."

His fingers clutched into fists. She watched his knuckles turn white before he uncrossed his arms. "In that case," he murmured, "I will have to insist."

There was a warning in his tone, one she heard

loud and clear. She stepped back, reacting out of instinct. The single step was inadequate. Symon moved, lowering his body as he twisted and captured her wrist. He gave a quick jerk on her limb, and she tumbled forward, falling over his shoulder before he straightened and turned toward the door.

"Put me down!" She didn't care for how ridiculous she sounded, rather like a kitten hissing at a full-grown man who had plucked it up by the scruff of the neck.

Symon seemed as unimpressed with her demand, carrying her out the door to the delight of his men. They laughed good and long over her plight, as their laird deposited her on the ground.

"Now ye can get up on this horse and ride, or I promise ye, I will bind ye and toss ye across the saddle like a bundle of fleece," he informed her.

She wanted to refuse.

By Christ she wanted to tell him no, but he sent her a look that dared her to defy him.

Somehow, she'd managed to miss just how power-ful he was. It was more than the strength of his body. It was also the fact that he was laird. His men stood around them, completely obedient to his will.

He cupped his hands and offered them to her. Resistance made it hard to lift her foot off the ground and place it in his interlaced fingers.

His men enjoyed her submission, chuckling as they mounted, while Cormac Sutherland observed with his men. He caught her eye and reached up to tug on his bonnet.

She was sick unto death of men and their plans for her.

Yet that seemed to matter not at all. Symon mounted,

his stallion sidestepping with its eagerness to get going. He raised his fist, and his men moved into formation behind him, her mare knowing its place already.

At least they headed south.

Small comfort, but all that was going to be afforded her.

So she concentrated on it, hoping to cultivate a positive outlook on her circumstances. The problem was all that thinking did was return her to the way she'd enjoyed Symon's kisses.

There would be no more kisses, and that was final.

Of course, she had no true way of ensuring that any of her choices would be respected. She'd battled long and hard to keep helplessness from creeping into her thoughts since she'd left her uncle's house, for if she gave in to it, despair would follow.

# Three

"WE'RE STOPPING TO REST THE HORSES."

The man called Tamhas took a moment to tell her what they were doing while he collected the reins of her mare and took the animal down to the water's edge.

"Ye can…go up a bit…there…for some privacy…"

Athena moved off before he'd finished. She really did not need to hear him complete his sentence. She had a feeling he'd be very blunt if she lingered.

At least she was farther away than she had been from any of Symon's men all day. She ached from the pace they set, enjoying the walk because it soothed some of her muscles.

All around them, the land was lush and green. She climbed to the top of a hill and witnessed the sight of snow hanging on the mountains in the distance.

"That's Sutherland."

She jumped, finding Symon off to her right. He pointed to the mountains. "Cormac calls it home."

"You live south?"

He nodded. "No' much farther now. Ye'll find it welcoming, Grant Tower."

"I will not be staying." She sounded less than grateful, but there was no help for it. "You simply must understand that."

He crossed his arms over his chest. "Ye'd return home before knowing ye are not returning to a sentence of prison?"

"I can't very well stay with you." She tried to sound reasonable. "It would be…well…"

"Better than prison, I assure ye."

Authority was back in his voice as well as a look in his eyes that made it clear he expected her to submit to his will.

"I have had quite enough of this, sir." Her temper was bright, too bright for her sense to hold her tongue. "My uncle will have the matter resolved. Henry has always been a good provider for me, even sent me north because he knew he needed time to set Galwell on his ear. I will not submit to this…abduction."

His lips parted, flashing his teeth at her. "I do nae care for submission either, lass, but ye kissed me back, and that is what has me thinking a little time together will be interesting at the least."

"Interesting?" she demanded. "So I am an amusement to you? Is that it?"

"At the moment," he replied, his voice dipping low with warning, "ye are me guest. I suggest ye do nae test the limits of that word."

"I told you, I will not submit to you."

He reached out and caught a handful of her skirt. She'd misjudged his reach, and he pulled her toward him as she gasped in surprise.

But he didn't kiss her.

She expected him to.

Her cheeks heated as she realized her disappointment.

"As I said, lass, I do nae care for submission." His breath teased the delicate surface of her lips, bringing up a perfect recollection of how his kiss had felt. "Test me, and, I promise ye, I will rise to the occasion."

She'd flattened her hands on his chest—to keep him back, of course—but now her palms were against his shirt, soaking up what he felt like.

Hard.

And yet she was drawn to him. As though she was fashioned to melt against him.

"Kiss me."

"What?" she demanded.

His lips twitched again. "Kiss me. I see the desire in yer eyes."

"That doesn't mean I should…" She stopped when she realized she'd admitted he was correct. He softly chuckled at her horror.

"I want ye to," he said. "Kiss me."

Her cheeks caught fire. "People do not…they do not discuss such topics."

She pushed against him, but the waistband of her skirt held her in place, and he had a big enough handful of the pleats of her skirt to keep the stitches from tearing.

"They should," he answered her. "What better way for a couple to be the best of lovers than to discuss what they enjoy?"

He released her. She stumbled back but caught herself as he grinned at her.

"I wanted ye to kiss me," he continued on as

though the topic wasn't scarlet. "Now, ye might have thought I would like ye to do it, but then, if I had no' told ye, ye might be beset by guilt for thinking I wanted a kiss...when I did nae..."

"So...it was for my benefit?" She was losing track of just exactly what they had been discussing. "Wait... we are not going to become lovers." She propped her hands on her hips and glared at him. "Put that thought right out of your mind, Symon Grant."

His face transformed into an expression that left no doubt he was thinking exactly that.

"I am not staying with you."

And she was also certain she'd never meant anything more in her life. Symon absorbed her words, enjoyment flashing across his eyes before his expression settled into one of solid determination.

"As ye like, lass," he muttered softly. "Ye come as me prize."

∼

Clearly she'd been seduced.

Just as Athena had always heard in church, she'd been taken in by the pagan ceremony on May Day.

Because somehow, she'd been taken in by the moment and completely overlooked how very dangerous Symon Grant might be.

In the dark, his kiss had intoxicated her, dulling her senses and leaving her with the opinion that he'd somehow be reasonable when it came to listening to her.

The rope binding her hands was a harsh reminder of just how foolish she'd been.

"I know well ye do nae care for yer circumstances,

lass." He crouched low next to her, watching the way she tested the strength of the knots he'd used. "And I doubt ye'd believe me when I say I've no liking for it either."

She battled against the gag he'd pushed between her teeth, but all that emerged was an unintelligible mumbling. Symon locked gazes with her, giving her a glimpse of the unrelenting determination in his eyes.

"We'll get to hearing yer thoughts on the matter later. For now, best sleep while ye can. We're only stopping to rest the horses."

He reached out and tugged a length of wool up and over her shoulder. All around them, his men had unbuckled their wide belts and let their kilts down so they might roll themselves in the length of fabric. They wasted no time settling in and closing their eyes, giving weight to what Symon promised about not resting for long.

He stood, giving her a glimpse of his back as he walked away to join two men who were on watch. He didn't settle down but joined them.

Was his behavior weighing heavily on his mind? Athena wondered but couldn't find any true revulsion in her. Which left her contemplating Symon Grant.

At least, that was what she intended. Her body had other ideas. All day in the saddle had left her spent. She felt fatigue nipping at her.

Well, better to sleep then. For she would be rested and he would not. It was a sound enough plan. Until she recalled what he'd said.

"*Truly escaping from anything means ye need somewhere to go.*"

Perhaps she should recall that wisdom was the greater part of valor. Of course that meant admitting Symon Grant could physically do as he pleased. But that didn't mean she needed to accept defeat.

Will Tinker had certainly learned that lesson.

And they were going south.

She held tight to that thought as she drifted into sleep.

Yes, Symon Grant was taking her where she wanted to be.

And that was all that mattered.

❧

"I do nae often question ye," Lyall began.

"Today is no' the best day to begin," Symon warned his captain.

Lyall wasn't intimidated. Of course, he wouldn't be one of Symon's captains if his knees weakened when Symon sent him a hard look. Lyall's place was to ask the questions that needed to be asked.

Especially when Symon didn't want anyone broaching a subject.

Symon adjusted his mood and looked toward Lyall. "I could no' leave her to the hand of fate."

Lyall reached up and stroked his beard for a moment. "Ye could have, but I agree it would no' have been very Christian of ye. Still, life is no' the fairest of things. Her plight is none of yer doing. A man cannae feed every orphan he crosses paths with." Lyall was still fingering his whiskers. "She could have uses. Ransom, perhaps. Did she no' say her uncle was a goldsmith?"

"Aye." Symon limited his reply to the single word. The truth was it bothered him to contemplate seeing Athena as goods to be bartered. In fact, he felt something building in his gut that felt a lot like a defense of her.

At the moment, she'd not thank him for it.

Which only made him want to grin.

Christ, maybe his men were right to worry he'd contracted some sort of fever. His thinking wasn't right, and that was a fact. A few stolen kisses should have set him to thinking about which offer to select when he returned home, because the heat in his loins proved he was ready to get on with living.

Instead he was hauling a captive Englishwoman home.

"I cannae see yer cousin being very pleased by the arrival of a female in bonds," Lyall remarked.

Symon stiffened. "Brenda will likely have nothing good to say, and that's for sure."

Lyall shrugged. "Still, perhaps yer cousin will spend a wee bit more time out of her chambers if she feels the need to watch ye."

Symon lowered his brows as he tried to follow Lyall's thinking.

His captain cleared his throat. "Ye might… happen…to have guests at the high table, some of those who have been trying to court yer cousin."

Symon slowly nodded. "And Brenda may not be so quick to take herself off to her private chambers."

Lyall grinned. "Exactly."

"Or Brenda just might decide to murder me and call it justice," Symon said.

"I would no' say it couldn't happen that way also, but ye are the one who carried that English lass out of the tavern."

"Maybe I just wanted to deny Cormac Sutherland the prize."

"Tell yer cousin that one," Lyall advised. "And she'll slit yer throat for certain."

Symon gripped his belt, looking back to where Athena was lying. Her chest rose and fell in a slow rhythm, telling him she'd fallen asleep.

He wouldn't bother to deny how satisfied it made him feel to know she was there, under his protection.

Was he a beast for feeling that way?

Possibly.

He might dwell on the very real fact that she'd not have fared well if he'd left her. Cormac wouldn't have hurt her, but he'd certainly have realized someone would take advantage of her if he allowed her to walk away.

Many might call her foolish.

He preferred naive.

Unjaded.

He didn't care to be the one to disillusion her.

*Galwell.*

The man's name rose from his memory of the tale she'd told them. His temper heated, and the truth was he would have enjoyed getting his hands on the man. Athena was far from the first person to discover a noble bloodline that had led position and money to blind her to what truly mattered in a man.

His word.

A man was naught without integrity or honor. An

honest beggar was worth more than an earl if the earl was a liar and cheat.

He wouldn't stand idle while Athena returned to a place where such a man held power over her.

She would just have to come to terms with his decision.

Although he did admit to the fact that he was rather looking forward to her distemper over it.

Aye, beast it was then.

⁓

He untied her at first light. Athena flexed her hands and sent him a scathing look as she rolled over and gained her feet. There were a few things she'd enjoyed calling him during the night, but now, privacy was all she longed for.

"Do nae make me run ye down."

He would.

She grumbled on her way toward a bit of privacy, more annoyed with the fact that she wasn't willing to risk spending the day bound. Her mouth was dry as dust from the gag. At least that was something she could remedy. Moving down to the river's edge, she scooped up a handful of water and found relief from at least one of her complaints.

"Say what is on yer mind, lass."

Symon hovered over her.

"There appears to be little point," she answered. "You seem to have your mind set."

He crossed his arms over his chest. "I am no' the only one."

She shouldn't argue with him. No, she should

find the dignity to ignore him and give him only silence.

But her temper was completely unwilling to cooperate.

"You hardly have a complaint," she began. "I am not telling you I consider you some manner of prize."

He slowly grinned. "A man can dream."

She shook her head. "That was not meant to please you."

He shrugged and offered her a piece of bread as he crouched down near her. She took it and ate some of it while he continued to watch her.

"It's really not amusing to label someone a prize," she added. "You are just trying to frighten me because you know what is said about Highlanders in England."

"Ye'd prefer me to act like yer nobleman?" he asked with a serious note in his voice.

Athena froze and locked gazes with him. There was a challenge in his eyes, one that dared her to answer him honestly. "No."

He nodded once before pushing back to his full height. "Something for ye to think on while we travel today."

She did indeed discover their conversation keeping her company. No, she didn't want him to be like Galwell, but how did she reconcile herself to agreeing to her own abduction?

God, it was ridiculous to discover she was truly being abducted.

And that it was the better of her options.

When exactly had the world gone mad?

Tamhas was a captain.

By the time they stopped for the night, Athena had learned who was in charge of the men traveling with Symon. There were Tamhas and Lyall. Both of them had a feather sticking up on the side of their bonnets. When Symon called a halt to their day, the two captains made quick work of making sure the horses were seen to and fires started to roast the rabbits the men had caught along the trail.

Symon didn't shirk from the duties.

She found herself watching the way he pulled the saddle from the back of his stallion, just like the rest of his men. No one served him, and he didn't stand about expecting anyone to either.

All the activity made her feel rather lazy because she didn't know her place. She settled for collecting wood, searching beneath the tree limbs for dry sticks. When her arms were full, she moved toward what was going to be the center of camp.

Tamhas nodded approvingly at her. He reached into his saddlebag and pulled out a comb. "Thought ye might like to work some of the tangles from yer hair."

She took it with a smile, withdrawing to sit on a large rock. Lyall reached out and shoved Tamhas.

"Ye do nae tell a lady her hair is needing attention," Lyall exclaimed.

"How else is she going to know?" Tamhas demanded. "She does nae have a maid with her."

"Do ye think she knows how to comb her hair?" One of the other men asked from behind the horse he was rubbing down. "English ladies do nae do things for themselves."

They all turned to look at her together. Athena pulled a few more pins from her hair, earning a couple of nods from them.

"Seems the English are no' the only ones telling stories about their neighbors."

She jerked her head around to find Symon watching her from the trees. He'd pulled up the part of his plaid that hung down his back to cover his head. The result was a very effective camouflage. She realized a few of his men had done the same, doing a very good job of hiding how many of them there were.

"I did nae think ye actually did no' know how to comb yer own hair though," Symon confided in her.

"I should hope not."

He was grinning at her again, in that way that warned her he was making ready to say something she probably wasn't going to like.

"After all, ye had it all down and flowing on May Day, so ye must know a bit about putting it all back up."

Heat teased her cheeks. His gaze lowered to the stain.

"It proved ye are spirited, Athena."

"Foolish is a better word," she answered. "I should have stayed disguised."

"Normally I'd agree," he muttered. "But I would no' have met ye, and I'd be a liar if I lamented our introduction."

She choked. "It was hardly an introduction."

His lips were parted in a grin once again. "A more honest sort than most introductions. I knew yer nature from yer actions."

And he'd been frank in what he wanted from her.

Her fingers went still on her hair. She didn't have to

guess with him. There was something to be said for it, even if she was struggling to deal with how very direct he was being about what he wanted from her.

Honest. Blunt. However, she could not label him secretive.

Someone whistled behind them. Symon looked past her, his body stiffening. There was an alertness to him that she admitted to admiring. He was extremely well suited to the wildness that was the Highlands.

He came out of his hiding place, moving down as another group of men came through the forest. They wore a different plaid than Symon's men, but Symon greeted their leader with a firm clasping of wrists before they settled down to converse.

The newcomer was Symon's opposite, with blond hair and blue eyes. He looked at her for a moment before giving his full attention to Symon.

◦❧◦

"Bruce Robertson," Symon greeted his friend. "I've no' seen ye for a fair bit."

Bruce offered him a shrug. "Ye were too busy shopping with yer cousin on May Day. But that was more than a week ago. What has ye returning just now?"

"The same thing that had me distracted on May Day," Symon replied. "Her."

Symon watched the way Bruce looked at Athena.

"That is a fine thing to be distracted by," Bruce murmured thoughtfully.

"Ye can forget ye've seen her," Symon insisted. "She's mine."

Athena heard them and gasped, turning to shoot them both a glare. "I am not yours, Lord Grant."

Bruce's lips split into a huge grin. "English?" He raised his voice and rolled right over his back and onto his feet so he could make it closer to her before Symon cut him off. "Where did ye find a beauty like this to steal?"

Athena's eyes widened as she stood up and backed away. "It is not amusing," she scolded him.

"She sounds a bit tart, Symon," Bruce remarked.

"She was dancing by the May Day fire in a smock sure enough," Tamhas added. "Wild as a fae forest creature…"

Symon snapped his head around toward his captain as Athena gasped. Tamhas shrugged. "I was about me duty, watching yer back, Laird."

Athena felt her cheeks burning with a blush. The men sitting with Tamhas were all grinning at her, making it plain that her meeting with Symon had been far from private.

"She kissed him quite well," Lyall added. "They'll have a wee one in no time at all."

"We shall not!" Athena declared as the comb slipped from her fingers.

Bruce was clean-shaven, but he was fingering his chin as though he had a beard there to stroke. "It sounds as though ye have no liking for Laird Grant's plans for ye, mistress. Perhaps I should be of assistance to ye and take ye home with me."

"Over my dead body…" Symon growled.

Bruce winked at her before he faced off with Symon. "My plan exactly."

The men let out cheers as Symon and Bruce started circling one another. Athena shook her head, backing up as they charged at one another like bears. The connection between them was hard, like a thunderclap. Symon threw Bruce to the ground first, but Bruce rolled over, flashing his bare backside at her before he was on his feet again and his kilt fell back down to cover him.

Symon went down next, courtesy of a hard hit on the side of his jaw.

"There's a Robertson kiss for ye, boy!" Bruce exclaimed.

Symon charged into him, closing his arms around his midsection and hoisting him up and off his feet as he rammed him into a tree. He left him there, backing away as Bruce slid down to his feet.

"I prefer lasses," Symon explained.

They were both breathing hard, but it didn't stop them from going at each other again. Their men yelled encouragement. She turned around but found herself facing Lyall. He reached up and tugged on the corner of his bonnet before looking back at the fight.

She retrieved the comb and moved off to another rock, putting her back to the display going on behind her.

She wouldn't encourage them.

But she did smile, since no one was there to see her. Symon did know how to embrace life. Part of her was envious of his freedom.

*That's why you went and danced on May Day...*

Yes.

*And why you kissed him...*

True.

*And why you aren't as outraged about him calling you his prize...*

She drew the comb through her hair and frowned at her own thoughts. It was terribly wrong of her to be pleased by the way Symon was taking her to his home. Protesting was a matter of pride.

*You do want to kiss him again...*

She drew in a deep breath, trying to get her thoughts to clear.

Because she truly needed to stop thinking about Symon Grant.

❧

"It was just good fun."

Darkness had descended by the time Symon came near her again. He brought her some of the roasted meat that had been teasing her nose for the past hour.

"Do ye have any brothers?" he asked.

Athena shook her head and offered him the comb to return. He plucked it from her fingers. "Truth is I'm surprised Tamhas owns a comb."

"Your men are not so unkempt."

Symon nodded. "Aye, now that ye bring it to mind, Will Tinker looked as though he was fit for the barn floor."

"He smelled like one, sure enough."

Symon lowered himself into a crouch next to her. "Can ye no' agree then that me company is no' so terrible?"

Guilt nipped at her. He might be different from the men she'd known in her life, but he was not black-hearted as Will Tinker had been.

"It is not a matter of opinion but of principle," she explained. "I cannot agree to be your prize."

"Well, as to that matter," he muttered, "I'm rather looking forward to changing yer mind, lass."

"You should not speak like that," she admonished him.

He tilted his head as one side of his mouth twitched up. "Like what, precisely?"

"So…boldly." She fought to keep her voice steady. "It's not modest."

He chuckled softly, the sound threatening to elicit a smile from her.

He was such a rogue.

"I strike ye as such a timid man, then?"

She lost her battle against her amusement. He watched her fight to control her laughter.

"As I said, fair Athena, conversation between lovers is a fine thing."

"You've had so many…lovers, that is…to know?" she asked before she realized how jealous she sounded.

His expression became serious. "Me wife was everything a woman is supposed to be. Demure, obedient, and I realized I did nae care for knowing she was in me bed because she'd been told to be there."

It was a shocking revelation. One she had never expected to hear. The wife was submissive to the husband. She'd been raised to understand it was how good women behaved.

"You are the most unconventional man I have ever met, Lord Grant," she said thoughtfully.

"And ye, Mistress Athena, are the most surprising Englishwoman I have ever encountered." He stood.

"You don't know many Englishwomen."

He touched the corner of his bonnet with two fingers. "That does nae make me words untrue."

He rejoined the men around the fire, but she didn't think for a moment that she was alone.

No, Symon was far too aware of his surroundings. She realized that was another strength. He knew how to survive in his world.

Just as she'd done what was needed to survive. She wouldn't look back on any of it as a shame. At least, not her shame.

Galwell, he was another matter altogether.

One she had no intentions of wasting her time thinking about.

❧

Symon Grant lived in a true fortress.

Athena looked at the towers as the mare she rode picked up its pace. The stone was dark from the growth of moss in the moist Highlands. Three towers rose up against the green mountains behind them. Each one was taller than the first, and there were walls running between them.

She heard someone start to ring a bell. It tolled a few times before a second joined it and then a third until bells were ringing along the entire length of the walls. By the time they rode through the gate, the yard was full of people who had come out to greet their returning laird.

One of the retainers offered her a hand down from the horse. There were squeals as wives threw themselves into the arms of their husbands. Children wore

bright smiles as they waited to be picked up and have
their hair tousled.

The sight sent a shaft of loneliness through her. All
of the time with Myles and alone hadn't been as bad
as seeing people who had family. It was almost more
than she could bear, bringing to mind Henry, his wife,
and the children who were always underfoot. And then
there was Henry's sister, who lived two blocks over
and always managed to time her visits with suppertime.

The lady she had seen with Symon at the market
fair was there as well. Brenda stood on the top of the
steps leading into the largest tower. She was beautiful,
with a fine-boned face and delicate limbs. She found
Athena, surprise flickering in her eyes a moment
before her lips curved into a very pleased smiled.

"Ye found her." Brenda glided up to Symon's side.
"And have come to an agreement as well. I am happy
for ye, Cousin."

Brenda wrapped her arms around Symon's neck,
cutting off his chance to reply, and then she turned
toward Athena.

"I am Brenda, Symon's cousin. Welcome to Grant
Tower." Brenda's eyes sparkled with happiness and
excitement. She looked back at Symon. "Have ye
wed already? Did ye deny me the chance to celebrate
it with ye?"

There were a few sputters from the men around
them. Most of them suddenly became extremely interested in helping to move the horses down to the stalls.

"We have not wed," Athena answered sweetly.

"I would no' have blamed Symon for no' waiting,"
Brenda explained. "It has been time for him to select a

new bride for a long while." Brenda clapped her hands together. "Come! I will show ye yer new home, and ye may clean the dirt of the road off ye. After ye settle in, we many discuss the details of yer nuptials."

Brenda wasn't taking no for an answer. She reached out and clasped Athena's wrist, intent on pulling her along.

"Your cousin"—Athena aimed her comment toward Symon—"is very much like you."

Brenda laughed, missing the look Athena sent toward Symon. She intended it to be stern, but he only grinned at her before flashing his teeth when his lips parted in a full smile. He reached up and tugged on the corner of his cap as Brenda pulled Athena right up the stairs and into the tower.

Beast.

For certain, her friends would have used the word "Highlander" to convey the same idea, but "beast" stuck in Athena's mind.

*Remember, be docile. Men are prideful creatures. Allow him to think you broken, and he will never notice when you leave.*

❧

Grant Tower looked fierce on the outside, but it didn't lack amenities inside.

The stone was dark, which sent a shiver down Athena's back as she followed Brenda up the steps and into the first tower. It was round and rose several stories up into the air.

Symon's cousin was at ease though, guiding Athena toward the kitchens.

They were huge, with three large hearths; two had

meat being turned by shirtless boys whose skin glistened from how hot they were so close to the flames. The third hearth had large shelves built into it so bread might be baked. There were long tables filling the center of the space in front of the hearth. Preparations for the evening meal were in progress, and the maids who had come out to welcome the men home were now returning to the tables to take up whatever they had been doing when the bells rang.

They looked at her without shame, sweeping her from head to toe as Brenda guided her toward a door at the back of the kitchens.

"Ye can bathe abovestairs if ye prefer," Brenda explained. "But it's warmer here."

The room was built next to the last hearth with doors to provide privacy. Two maids scurried in to take one of the tubs that was leaning against the far wall and place it on the floor.

"No, get Symon's tub," Brenda instructed. "Yer new mistress will not use one of the common tubs."

"It is quite well," Athena said. "You shouldn't go to any great effort. I will be delighted to be clean."

Brenda was a strikingly handsome woman with red hair and blue eyes. "I cannae wait to hear how me cousin managed to win ye."

Her eyes sparkled with joy. Athena bit her lip and focused on unlacing her boots. She just couldn't bear to kill the other woman's happiness.

No, Symon could have that chore all to himself.

*He's hoping to wear you down…*

Well, for the moment, she was content to go along with Brenda's plan to bathe her. All the weeks on the road had left her with a new appreciation of being allowed a true bath.

A hot one as well.

Athena didn't hesitate but hurried out of her clothing as the maids returned with steaming kettles. They poured the hot water into the tubs.

Brenda had disappeared, granting Athena the opportunity to stash her coins inside her boot. She climbed into the tub before Symon's cousin returned with a lump of soap.

"Rosemary soap," Brenda declared with a little smile of victory. "The last of it until spring brings us more rosemary."

Athena wanted to refuse, but Brenda handed it off before fixing her with a firm look. "Give me that smock," Symon's cousin insisted. "It's only women here, and if ye've been on the road, ye need a fresh one."

Brenda reached right over and caught the back of the garment, pulling it over Athena's head before she had much of a chance to argue.

And then Brenda was off, muttering instructions to the maids.

Her absence gave Athena the chance to bathe. Which she did with all haste because Brenda was as much a force of nature as her cousin. Athena didn't doubt for one moment that Brenda would return and scrub her from head to toe if Athena didn't manage the chore herself.

She ducked down to rinse her hair, enjoying the scent of rosemary replacing the smell of dust. She was up and out of the tub by the time Brenda returned.

"Well then, I suppose I should show ye abovestairs."

Brenda was still giddy, snapping her fingers at a maid who had a dressing robe in her arms. Once Athena was in it, the maid hurried toward the opposite side of the room where another door was. She opened it and peeked out.

Satisfied that no one was in the passageway, the maid waved Athena toward her. Narrow stairs went up the side of the tower. It was a different tower from the front one. This one was wider, and Brenda kept climbing until they were on the third floor.

"These are nice chambers," Brenda said as she pushed the doors wide.

Someone had lit beeswax candles, the scent welcoming Athena as Brenda swept her inside. A maid was just carrying away a stack of folded covers, which must have been over the furniture. Even with the sun setting, the window shutters were open wide to air out the rooms.

The entry chamber gave way to a receiving chamber where comfortable chairs and a table for food were set off to one side. A small decanter was there already, two goblets waiting should Athena decide she wanted some wine.

Brenda was welcoming her in high style, sparing no expense.

"I can dress myself," Athena said. "You have already been so very gracious."

Brenda dismissed her statement with a wave of her hand. "Ye'll be needing help dressing, for I've brought ye some dresses that have back lacing."

There was a swish of fabric as Brenda and two maids carried the bundles into the chambers.

Brenda stopped and considered her. "I think the blue will complement yer hair best."

The maids sprang into action, bringing forward undergarments and helping to get Athena into the stockings, hip roll, and corset, and then she sat down so one of the girls might work to braid her hair.

It had been so long since her hair had been dressed.

Athena enjoyed the sight as the maid held up a small handheld mirror behind her so she might see the creation on the back of her head. The girl had woven ribbon into the braids and crafted a masterpiece out of Athena's hair.

"Thank you," she said in all sincerity. How long had it been since she'd felt pretty? Yes, it was good to discard vanity, and after the way Galwell had torn her trust and heart in two, she'd been content to hide in plainness because he'd wanted to make a possession of her.

A pretty pet…

Symon had never seen her at her best. Something shifted inside her as she contemplated that fact.

He liked her the way she was, and she would be a liar if she denied enjoying knowing it.

Brenda was still overseeing everything. Athena felt a twinge of guilt but couldn't decide if telling the woman there would be no wedding wasn't worse, for Athena would be speaking ill of her family.

"Alba will put yer boots in yer wardrobe. For tonight, wear the shoes," Brenda decided.

The maid was already taking the boots away. Athena lowered her eyes as she let the shoes be put on her feet.

No one would know her money was tucked into

the boot. At least not if she didn't appear distressed by having them taken away.

The blue dress was made of wool. Athena decided it suited the chill the stone tower seemed to have inside it. Darkness had descended, leaving her fighting shivers, but the wool was very comfortable. The maids began to close the shutters and turn down the bed that lay beyond the receiving chamber.

"There," Brenda declared with a smile and a clap of her hands. "Ye look quite pretty. However did my cousin manage to contract ye? Yer father must have had dozens of offers for ye."

One of the maids was just finishing buttoning the bottom of the sleeves as Brenda spoke, the girl's gasp drawing Brenda's attention to where the rope had left bruises on Athena's wrists.

"What in the name of Christ?" Brenda asked as she came closer.

Athena pulled her hands back, but Brenda's expression turned thunderous. "He…stole ye?"

Brenda wasn't waiting for an answer. She turned in a swirl of her skirts and stormed through the doorway. Athena was left facing two very startled maids, who slowly began to grin as though it was a fine amusement.

"Well now, if ye are going to be stolen…all the better to have it be done by a laird," one said.

The other let out a dreamy sigh that sent Athena out of the chamber and down the stairs to see what Brenda was going to do.

Clearly Scotland was an insane place.

Or her mind had finally snapped.

Honestly, she wasn't sure which one it was, only that she was caught in the center of a crazy dream.

❧

Symon was in the great hall.

As far as halls went, it really was to be admired. There were long tables running up and down it with space for three hundred men, perhaps more. Bread was already sitting on the tables for the evening supper. Brenda marched past them to where her cousin was talking to an older man.

"Ye are a horrible excuse for a cousin!" Brenda informed Symon.

He held up his hand, but Brenda wasn't going to be quieted.

"How dare ye bring a captive home?" Brenda demanded. "How could ye allow me to think she is yer bride and content!"

Athena was fascinated by the way Brenda went after Symon. She'd stalked toward him, uncaring of the fact that Symon was twice her size.

Symon stood still, allowing his cousin to have her say. But he looked past Brenda to where Athena stood near the doorway that opened into the passageways of the tower. "I suppose it was too much to think ye'd not tell her all the details."

Athena caught the hint of disappointment in his topaz eyes. He really didn't have any cause to appear wounded.

And yet it needled her to see he was so.

*You mean you feel guilty…*

Athena refused to acknowledge her inner thoughts. Really, she needed to stay well away from the idea of caring for Symon Grant's personal feelings. Such an admission would mean she cared about him.

And she couldn't do that…

"She said nothing," Brenda was quick to inform him. "I saw the bruises on her wrists. Have ye taken to frightening innocents as well as deceiving yer own kin?"

Brenda wasn't any sort of meek or obedient female. She faced down Symon, her eyes blazing as his men tried to hide their smirks behind their hands by pretending to stroke their beards.

Athena was fascinated by the display, but it was also an opportunity to leave while Symon was distracted.

Part of her truly loathed the idea of getting back on a horse.

*You are clean.*

Yet her belly was empty.

She lowered herself and left the hall while Brenda demanded to know whether Symon had any shame at all. The passageway was quiet as everyone was in the hall for supper. She made quick work of the stairs and found her way to the chamber. Her boots were sitting just inside the door. She checked inside the right one, a little sigh of relief escaping her lips when she found the coins wrapped in a scrap of leather.

The chamber was inviting and welcoming after so long on the road. The bed with its fresh linens and curtains would be divine after so many days sleeping in the wagon.

*Maybe you should see if you grow to like him…*

She forced herself to turn around and reach for the door, pulling it open, but instead of an avenue of escape, she stood facing Symon Grant.

"No' so fast, lass," he informed her slowly as he backed her into the room.

Her insides twisted, and she realized it was with excitement.

*You must not!*

And yet she felt the surface of her cheeks heating as he faced off with her, uncaring of the fact that the door was closed and they were very much alone.

"You should not be in here with me." She drew in a little gasp when she realized how raspy her voice was. "It is indecent."

"And ye." He pointed at her, his eyes lit with determination. "Ye are no' so meek, miss. To be running to hide simply because me cousin was arguing with me. Ye hoped to…sneak away while I was distracted."

She shifted back, her eyelashes fluttering. She felt like he could read her thoughts right through their joined gazes.

"You barely know me," she tried to argue.

He made a soft, male sound in the back of his throat. "I know ye have a streak of passion in ye, Athena. One that sent ye up to dance in the light of the May Day fire in naught but a shirt like a wild creature."

"I shouldn't have…" Oh, but it would be a lie to say she regretted it. She couldn't resist looking at him, and their gazes locked.

A shiver went down her spine.

But it pleased her greatly.

"Do nae lament it," he rasped out, stalking her. Closing the distance until she was certain he could feel the heat of her body. "For I would never wish to forget that moment when I saw ye dancing so freely, so very comfortable with yer nature."

He was weaving a spell with his recollection. It was like the memory was reaching out and around them both like a flame of a candle on a pitch-black night.

"I couldn't have resisted kissing ye…" He reached up and fingered the curl of hair that had escaped her braids near her ear. "And ye kissed me back."

His face hardened. It was a shocking transformation, one that shook her to her core with how dramatic it was. The memory vanished, leaving behind the hunger their first encounter had kindled. She witnessed it flickering in his eyes and realized the same fire licked at her insides.

He bit back a word but leaned toward her.

He was going to kiss her.

But what made her gasp was the fact that she wanted him to do it so very much. There was an insane twist of anticipation going through her belly. The intensity of it delighted her because she had never realized she might feel in such a way. It was like discovering her body had capacities that she had never dreamed of.

But the kiss was no recollection from her mind while she slept.

No, he captured her, closing his arms around her body as he stepped forward and then to the side to make her turn. She was off-balance, but his arm was there around her waist to steady her while his mouth claimed hers.

She twisted, reaching out to grasp the front of his doublet as she struggled to find something solid to cling to while her world spun off-kilter.

He was the only fixed point in her universe. He was a flame, and she went toward him as happily as a moth, her fascination leading the way.

And yet, as she began to move her lips in unison with his, Athena realized she was no beguiled creature. No, she was a counterpart. The orange flame to his scarlet one. No fire was ever a uniform color, not if you looked closely. Together, they formed the blaze, twisting around each other. His hand was in her hair, threading through the braids as he cradled the back of her skull and held her steady for a kiss that shocked her. He swept his tongue across her lower lip before pressing her jaw open so he might thrust inside her mouth.

It was intimate.

Carnal.

And she stroked his tongue with her own. The fabric of his clothing suddenly frustrated her. She stroked his chest, seeking a way beneath the outer garment. The top few buttons were open, allowing her to push her hand inside and connect with his skin.

The contact felt like lightning had struck them. She heard him groan, felt his body tighten. Inside her belly, there was an answering twisting of some need that she'd thought she'd felt before, but the truth was now was the first time she'd truly felt the full intensity of the cravings.

And only he was going to satisfy them.

She suddenly jerked from his hold, stunned by her own reactions.

The room was chilly, and yet she was fevered, her breath coming in pants.

She was wanton.

And Symon was aroused.

She felt like she was learning the true meaning of those words for the first time, in spite of having heard them in lectures and sermons. The look on his face made it clear what passion was about.

It truly was the thing of spells. She felt intoxicated, just because he was close.

"Ye're correct, lass," he rasped out. "I should no' be in here with ye. At least no' while there is no' an agreement between us."

"What do you mean by that?" she questioned him, still breathless.

One of his dark eyebrows rose. "I mean…" He stepped toward her, and she felt her heart quicken its pace. "Ye…kissed me back."

"Why shouldn't I? I thought you wanted me to kiss you." Oh, it wasn't a wise thing to have said at all. Athena was shocked by her own daring, but something flickered in Symon's topaz eyes a moment before his lips curled up and he flashed a very pleased grin at her.

"By all means, lass." She'd misjudged how large he was. What she thought was a pace from his grip proved to be nothing of the sort. Symon reached out, grabbed a handful of her skirts, and pulled her back against him. "Kiss me some more," he growled.

It was a challenge. One issued in a half growl a moment before he claimed her mouth. This time, there was raw hunger in the kiss, and God help her, she found she had the appetite to match his.

"Take yer hands off her, Cousin."

Athena opened her eyes in time to catch a flash of

temper crossing Symon's face. It was fierce and hot, but he turned and faced Brenda with his jaw clamped tight.

"Aye, ye know ye should no' be in here, Symon," Brenda informed him in a tight voice. "Now take yerself off to the hall before I have the priest deal with yer lack of morals."

He moved past her, turning and reaching up to tug on his bonnet before he disappeared out the door.

"Some time in the stocks might just do him good," Brenda exclaimed. "However, he is correct, ye were kissing him back…" Athena found herself caught in Brenda's keen gaze. "We're going to have to make certain ye have a chaperone, or yer name will be in tatters by the week's end."

It was the wisest course of action.

So why did Athena detest the idea so very much?

❧

Myles Basset was beside himself with regret. He delayed leaving the village for three days, hoping Athena would return.

Will Tinker watched the merchant, an idea forming in his mind.

"Ye're fretting about the lad."

Myles nodded. "I would be a poor excuse of a Christian not to worry about his fate. For all that Queen Elizabeth has no quarrel with Scotland, there are many here who recall that her father wasn't content with allowing Scots to be their own country."

"Well now, there's a solid truth," Will agreed. "Would ye like me to see if I can discover any news of the lad's fate?"

Myles's face brightened. "I would be in your debt."

"Well now, first off, I would need some coin for bribes."

Myles considered the request, nodding at last. "Of course. I must make certain the lad is not lingering in some thieves' hold. Such would be a blight on my eternal soul."

The merchant reached into his pouch and withdrew a small coin purse. Will enjoyed the way it jingled. Myles replaced the purse with a heavy sigh. "I will be praying for your success."

He turned and made his way toward the church at the end of the village. Will's companions moved up next to Will.

"That was a fine bit of business to watch ye manage," one of them remarked.

Will was counting the silver. He divided it among his comrades, earning chuckles from them. The silver disappeared quickly into doublets and boot tops as they looked around to make sure no one took notice of their business.

"Perhaps we might even earn more," Will suggested softly.

His comrades leaned in to hear his plan.

"What…" he began. "What if we discovered the location of that lad and convinced Myles we could retrieve him—for the right price?"

⁂

Symon summoned Athena the next day before the morning was even half gone.

The young maid lowered herself before helping Athena dress.

"This way, mistress."

The girl led her through what seemed like an endless maze of passageways. Sunlight was coming through the windows, the shutters open to allow the fresh air in, and yet a chill clung to the stones.

Her steps echoed between the stone walls, and it was all she could do to keep her thoughts from comparing the place to a tomb.

It was simply a castle.

She'd lived so much of her life in a city house; she needed to remember that castles were different.

And she would not be staying.

"Here, mistress."

A large wooden door was in front of her. The maid used a fist to pound on it before she hurried away.

Athena stared at the way the girl nearly ran.

"Enter."

Short of fleeing herself, Athena was left to open the door herself. She reached out and pulled it open. Inside, the space was far more welcoming than the passageway. Several of the walls were covered by tapestries, one of them depicting Saint George as he slew the dragon. Another was of Mary as the angel of the Lord appeared to her. The threads were vibrant, making the figures appear almost lifelike.

"Me mother made that one."

Athena realized she'd been staring at the tapestries and completely ignoring Symon. She lowered herself as she felt her cheeks heat.

"She'd often warn me to remember she might be

either Saint George or Mary and I'd be wise to behave or I would be the one being slain if I decided to act like a dragon."

Athena smiled. "I imagine you gave her more than one reason to take after you with lance in hand."

Symon was sitting behind a large desk. Off to his right was another man, sitting at a smaller desk with a quill in hand and a blank sheet of paper laid out in front of him.

She faced the laird.

Symon softly chuckled. "Surprised to discover me a man of learning?"

The heat in her cheeks increased. His eyes narrowed, his lips curling in a small, pleased expression.

"I need yer uncle's name," he explained.

"Henry?"

Symon had returned to business. He sent her a stern look across his desk, and she realized he was making an effort to stay behind the piece of furniture for the sake of propriety.

So unlike Galwell…

"I promised to send a letter to him, but I cannae do so without his name."

She set her teeth into her lower lip. Symon's eyes narrowed. He lost the battle to stay still, moving around the desk. While he'd been seated behind it, she'd only seen his doublet, making him look like any other lord. As he came around the desk, his kilt caught her eye, reminding her he was very much a man of the Highlands.

*You do not even know exactly what a Highlander is…*

No, but she was learning that Symon was not a man to allow words to intimidate him.

"Do nae be stubborn, Athena."

It was her turn to raise an eyebrow. "Aren't you the pot calling the kettle black."

He'd perched himself on the edge of the desk, looking almost as if he was using the contact with the furniture like a chain to restrain himself.

*You are being vain…*

"I'm correct," Symon informed her. "But by all means, explain to me why I should allow ye to go riding off on yer own. Are ye going to tell me yer uncle allowed ye to roam so freely? It would be a fine thing to hear ye tell me that we are more civilized here in the Highlands than down in England. More than one of me kin would enjoy laughing over it."

The secretary choked on his mirth.

"You are making sport of me."

"Nae." Symon was serious once more. "I am trying to open yer eyes."

"My eyes are open quite wide, thank you," she retorted. "Men are beasts who preach about honor but deviate from that course the moment they feel they might."

Symon slowly nodded. "A great many men fit that description. Which is why I insisted ye stay with me instead of going off and running into another one who would sell ye."

He'd stolen her.

She should have been more outraged about it too. She could almost feel the rope still biting into her wrists.

Symon's attention shifted, and she realized she was rubbing her wrist.

"I did no' mean for ye to be bruised." He'd risen and captured her wrist, turning it up so he could inspect her skin.

"It is naught," she stated and pulled away.

Or tried to.

Symon held her limb for a moment. She should have been angry over his daring. Instead she noted again the way he controlled his strength, while Will Tinker had used brutal force without any regard for how much pain he inflicted.

"I disagree."

He was being obstinate, and yet there was something about his insistence that endeared him to her. His knees that peeked at her and the rough stone of the passageway walls would have had anyone she'd grown up with declaring him a savage Highlander.

Yet he displayed more of the virtues of honor than many of the loudly proclaiming Englishmen who seemed not to understand that actions spoke louder than words.

She offered his secretary the details of her uncle Henry and his residence. The secretary dipped his quill in an inkwell and recorded the information. Symon nodded before moving back around his desk.

"Now, if ye will give me yer word that ye will wait for a reply from yer uncle, I can give ye free rein while ye are me guest."

Athena took a step back. Symon's lips thinned with disapproval. She witnessed the sparks in his eyes and felt something inside herself rising to battle.

Why? Well, the reason didn't appear to matter all that much, only that he was attempting to bind her to his will, and something inside her refused to be ruled. Even if conceding made good sense.

No, she was responding to something else about him, the instinct too powerful to resist.

He stood up, slowly, and she should have been wary; instead, she felt her chin rising.

The desk suddenly looked too small to keep him from her.

And part of her enjoyed that image a great deal.

But a bell started tolling and then another. The sound gained instant reaction.

Symon came around the desk and caught her wrist. He pulled her right through the door and into the passageway. There were others hurrying along the stone-lined walls, and a few disappeared up narrow stairwells while Symon took her into the great hall.

"Stay here, Athena, until I discover who has come to me gates."

Symon sent her a serious look before he strode out of the hall, leaving her with the rest of the women.

"Well, I don't intend to stand here and wait." Brenda was suddenly there, sending her a wink. "Let's go have a look for ourselves."

Athena followed Brenda through the kitchens. She barely had time to notice any details, only that Grant Tower obviously had many people living in it because a small army of women were working to produce the midday meal.

Brenda waved her forward as she ducked into a stairwell that was almost hidden behind the edge of one of the great hearths. It had been so long since

Athena had worn a dress that she forgot to yank up the front of her skirt and tripped on it.

She recovered quickly enough, climbing up to where the sunlight was bright and they could look over the wall through an archer opening.

"Looks like Diarmid and—" Brenda sucked in her breath.

"And who?" Athena inquired.

Brenda turned wide eyes toward Athena, but she was also rolling her lips in and trying not to laugh. "Becuma, the…"

Brenda was choking. A quick look back at Symon showed he was standing with his hands propped on his hips and his head cocked to one side while a woman who didn't even stand as tall as his chest pointed at him with a time-weathered finger.

And he was taking whatever she was giving him, too.

Lyall was at his laird's side, but he turned and caught Athena watching. He whistled and pointed at her. The Grant retainers who had taken positions along the wall when the bells began to ring suddenly looked Athena's way. Two of them started toward her as Brenda gasped.

"Who is that woman?" Athena demanded as the retainers tugged on their bonnets but sent Athena looks that made it clear they intended to take her to Lyall.

"She's the veteran midwife here about," Brenda answered before Athena was swept down the stairs and back through the kitchens.

"Oh, for Heaven's sake," she groused at her escort. "Show me the way. There is no reason to haul me about."

Her argument gained her little. The two men didn't release her but held tight to her biceps. Honestly, she wasn't even sure her feet touched the ground.

Lyall and Symon had come into the hall. Two more retainers were quick to carry a padded chair up to where Becuma stood leaning on a cane. The midwife shook her head.

"I'm no' here to waste the day," she informed them. "Where is the bride to be?"

Athena recoiled. The two men pulling her along suddenly had to invest more effort, and Symon turned at the sound of her shoes skidding against the stone floor of the hall.

"As I explained." Symon sounded like he was a breath from exploding with frustration. "There is no arrangement between us."

Becuma humphed in that way that only a matriarch could do and sound respectful. "All the more reason for me to have a look at her now before ye become attached to a woman who is not a good match in stature. Ye"—she poked Symon in the center of his chest—"are large and need a wife with ample hips."

The two men deposited Athena next to Symon. They took up position behind Athena as the midwife turned her wrinkled face toward her.

"Well now," Becuma murmured thoughtfully. She made a motion with her hand for Athena to turn around.

"We are not intending to wed," Athena said.

Becuma wasn't impressed with her outburst. The old woman clicked her tongue, and the Grant retainers watching sent Athena disapproving looks. She started turning, without really realizing she had decided to comply.

Clearly some things were the same in Scotland as in England—an elder was respected no matter what you thought about their requests.

When Athena finished and stood facing the midwife once more, there was a thoughtful look on the midwife's face.

"I see promise in her. I will inspect her," Becuma announced.

The Grants surrounding Athena suddenly smiled. There was even a ripple of pleased sounds going through the crowd as though Athena had passed some manner of test. The only thing that kept Athena silent was the look of frustration on Symon's face.

It was rather interesting to find the burly Highlander as bent into submission by expectations as she so often was.

Such a curious thing, to discover she had something in common with him.

"Becuma, with respect, I cannae force me guest to endure such—" Symon began to argue.

"There is no one forcing anyone to do aught!" Becuma interrupted her laird. "The pair of ye will both be inspected."

"But we are not negotiating to be wed." Athena tempered her tone, and she was fairly certain it took every last scrap of patience she had because the need to flee was becoming overwhelming.

Of course, with the crowd of Grants around her, all intent on making certain Becuma's word was honored, Athena would only find herself delivered to a chamber for the midwife to inspect her.

Becuma smiled slowly, in that manner only an elder, who had seen far more of life than others, could. Athena felt her shame rising and her chin lowering.

"A man does no' steal a woman he has no interest in. This house has had too much death. We will make certain ye are suited to each other before either of ye can form any attachment to each other. It is the reason I have come up to the tower this morning." Becuma's tone made it clear she wasn't going to listen to any arguments.

"There is no attachment being formed," Athena insisted.

Becuma slowly raised an eyebrow.

Athena felt her cheeks burn. Symon cleared his throat nervously. Lyall and Tamhas nodded when the midwife shot them both questioning looks.

The midwife drew in a deep breath and let it out. The hall was so silent that the sound of her breathing was clearly heard. "I've lived me entire life in the Highlands," she began.

Athena felt her eyes widening. There was something else that was very much the same in England and Scotland. When an elder was confronted with resistance, they fell back on softly spoken words that were as sharp as a needle. She felt her shame rising before Becuma even got to talking about just why Athena was wrong.

"So it's the truth I do nae know the ways of those living in England, although I cannae see as how the matter of how babes are brought into this world differs all so much just because of a border…"

Symon cocked his head to one side, his jaw tight as he waited for Becuma to strike.

"However…"

Athena felt it coming, and the look in Becuma's eyes proved she was anything but a mild-tempered old woman. No, her eyes snapped with her intentions.

"It would seem to me that it would be best"— she looked between Symon and Athena—"to put to rest any questions as to yer health and Christian nature."

Athena's mouth went dry.

Christian nature. What she meant was witch marks.

"It's a sad fact to say," the midwife continued smoothly, "that I've heard me fair share of gossip already about ye and yer arrival and the fact the laird went looking for ye after seeing ye dance by the pagan firelight on May Day."

"Enough," Symon declared.

Becuma turned on him. "Is it true?" She poked him in the middle of his chest with her cane.

"It was May Day," Symon exploded with frustration. "The way ye speak makes it sound like there were no' a hundred others doing the very same thing."

"Ah," Becuma said. "Those others are nae Englishwomen dressed in breeches, and ye are laird. If ye were taken in by foul means, well, that would bring a bad harvest on us all."

Athena gave in, turning around, but the retainers who had delivered her puffed up and blocked her path. "I believe the chamber I slept in last night is a better place for an inspection, or do you all intend to see me stripped bare here?"

One of them choked on a snicker. A moment later there was a hard connection of flesh on flesh as Symon launched himself at the man and landed a solid hit against his jaw.

"Ye'll mind yer thoughts when it comes to the lady," Symon warned his clansman.

The retainer stumbled but recovered quickly. Another man grasped her by the biceps and moved her out of the way as Symon and the man faced off.

"You shall not fight over me." Truly, she'd had no idea she intended to voice an objection. There was no reason at all to think anyone in the hall might listen to what she had to say, much less respect her wishes.

But a soft chuckle, crackling with age, came from behind her. It drew Symon's attention as he turned to look at the midwife.

"No' formed any attraction?" Becuma questioned, her mirth clear.

Symon snapped his jaw shut and sent Athena a frustrated look.

"And ye," Becuma punctuated her comment with a firm jab from her finger into Athena's shoulder. "Ye were ever so quick to defend our laird…"

There was a mutter of agreement. It rippled through those watching as heads nodded and a path cleared in front of her and Symon.

Athena wanted to snort with frustration. She settled for taking advantage of the cleared space in front of her. At least walking gave her a smidge of relief because she could no longer see so many pairs of eyes on her.

The relief didn't last very long, though.

The chamber that had previously been a delightful haven transformed into a place of unbearable torment as Becuma followed her, bringing five matrons and Brenda along with her.

*You'd have been expected to endure this if you'd wed Galwell…*

And now she was facing it due to the fact that she'd fled from the man.

At least Brenda was merciful.

"Best done quickly," Brenda said in a low tone as she came forward to begin unlacing Athena's dress. "I will no' let them linger."

There was a promise in Brenda's eyes. A flash of understanding that made it clear she'd endured the same. Athena managed a quick nod as the other matrons converged on her to strip away every last garment she had.

Gossips deserved to be damned, and that was a fact.

Becuma didn't neglect any part of her duties. She had taken her time, finishing with Athena before making a slow trek toward Symon's chamber. Symon had already stripped down, grumbling about taking his boots off when there was work to be done.

Becuma clicked her tongue at him before scrutinizing every last inch of his skin.

At last, the midwife made her way back into the hall. It took a long time for her to climb the stairs up to the high ground where the laird's table was set. Tamhas and Lyall tried to help her, but she shooed them away with a wave of her age-withered hand, insisting on leaning on her cane while struggling to ascend each step.

Symon stood in front of the laird's chair, waiting

for her. His people were nearly chewing their lips off with anticipation.

Athena stood on the lower corner of the high ground.

Becuma settled at last, a mug of cider in her hand that she took a sip from before flattening her hand on the table. Her palm made only a soft sound, but the hall grew deathly still in response. Christ, he was pretty sure half his men were even holding their breath as they waited for her to speak.

"The girl," Becuma began, pointing at Athena, "is fine and healthy."

There was a ripple of approval.

"And…" Becuma lifted a finger up to add authority to her next statement. "She bears no witch marks. I have heard her tale, and it is the right of any girl to choose virtue, even if such a path requires extreme measures. English nobles are nae known for their honor."

There was agreement in the hall. Becuma flattened her hand on the table again. "Yer laird is in fine health."

He might have been wrong, but Symon got the feeling Becuma was enjoying her duties a little too much for his comfort. He felt heat climbing up his neck as she nodded with a grin that lifted the corners of her mouth.

"They are well suited to each other." Becuma slapped the top of the table with her statement.

A cheer went up.

"We have no agreement to wed." Symon might as well have saved his breath. His people were busy celebrating. No one heard him over the chuckles and excited giggles.

He let out a snort as he sagged back in his high-backed chair. He rubbed at his forehead, trying to relieve the tension pounding there. All he managed was to open his eyes and discover Becuma scrutinizing him.

"I stole her because it was the right thing to do," Symon informed Becuma.

The midwife flashed another grin at him. "She's a fine, ample lass. It's the truth that I do nae have faith in matches made before inspections might be done. We do nae need another lady too slight to bear yer babes. Far better to have the inspections seen to first. Now, ye may proceed knowing there is no concern as to her ability to provide issue from the union."

His head started pounding again.

But his Head of House was busy bringing in pitchers of cider and ale to celebrate the moment.

Well, he felt in need of a drink rather badly at that!

❧

Once again she didn't really walk.

Athena found herself lifted right off her feet and seated next to Symon as the Grants began to toast to her and Symon. He sent her a frustrated look.

"They're your people," she insisted, trying to turn around when someone put a wreath of rosemary on her head.

"And they seem to have their own ideas about just what I'm doing," Symon replied.

It was a fair enough statement. The Grants were busy toasting and draining their mugs.

"I am going back to England," she informed him.

"No' until I hear back from yer uncle, ye are nae." Symon answered firmly.

"You will not tell me what to do." She pushed against the floor with her feet, moving the heavy chair enough to slip out of one side.

But Symon lunged after her, capturing her wrist. "Ye will listen to me, Athena."

"I won't—" She froze as she realized the hall had gone quiet and everyone, absolutely everyone, was staring at them.

The silence broke as laughter erupted throughout the celebrating masses. Symon was distracted, giving her the opportunity to break free and dash down the steps and onto the main floor of the hall.

People gave way, clearing a path for her as they looked to their laird.

"After her!"

"Run her down, Laird!"

"She's got spirit!"

Her chest was heaving by the time she made it to her chamber and closed the door.

*Ridiculous.*

That was the word for it all.

She was not going to marry Symon Grant. No matter what his people seemed to think.

No, she wasn't.

❧

*England*

"Sir Galwell, ye are my champion today, it seems."

Elizabeth Tudor was every inch her father's

daughter. She had the passion Henry the Eighth had brought to every aspect of his life. The candlelight lit her red hair as she watched Galwell perform an expert reverence, stretching out his leg so she might gain a long glimpse of his calf.

The Queen of England fluttered her lashes as her face transformed into a pleased expression.

"Yes, you must accompany us tomorrow on the hunt," Elizabeth announced. "You shall ride as my personal escort."

The court was in attendance. Galwell preened, sticking out his chest as he sent an adoring glance toward the Queen. She chuckled softly before turning and leaving, with her maids of honor filing in behind her.

In the shadows, Robert Leicester's eyes narrowed. He contemplated those who had been in attendance, settling on the dowager Countess North Hampton.

"My Lord Leicester." She lowered herself.

Robert acknowledged the gesture before slipping beside her so he might whisper in her ear. She was an older woman but still quite radiant.

"Galwell," Leicester began, the question clear in his tone.

"Yes, I understand he was to wed the goldsmith's daughter, but now there is some talk of his father attempting to contract him with one of Baron Barkley's daughters. I doubt it will happen. Their dowry is too great."

"Discover the details of the goldsmith's daughter. I would have him wed."

Robert sent her a hard look. She fluttered her eyelashes but inclined her head.

She must have fallen asleep.

Athena blinked and rubbed her eyes. She rolled over and sat up, trying to decide what had woken her. She smelled a hint of smoke and looked to where the lantern sat on the bedside table. The flame flickered, like a wind was blowing through the room.

But the air was still.

A strange prickle of sensation traveled across her skin.

The door moved, grabbing her attention. But it was just open, left ajar as though someone had been peeking in on her.

She should bar it.

Instead, Athena picked up the lantern near her door. There was still the chill lingering in the chamber that she'd noticed earlier in the day.

Obviously the days of travel and work had taken their toll on her, and she'd slept the entire day away.

But she'd fallen asleep in her dress, and now her hips ached from the padded hip roll she had on. She'd twisted and strained, but there was no way to reach the laces on the back of the bodice.

She stood for a moment, trying to decide what to do, and her belly rumbled long and low. At least now she understood why she'd woken.

The door was still partially open. She eyed it, certain it had been shut. Perhaps someone had looked in on her, a maid thinking to help her disrobe before seeking out her own bed for the night.

Athena went toward the door and opened it, going straight out into the passageway, seeking any sign of movement. The window shutters rattled, but there was a flash of motion ahead of her.

"Oh please...wait..." Athena was after whoever it was, hurrying around a corner and pausing when there was no one in sight.

Another flutter at the base of the stairs gained her attention.

So slight she might have imagined it, if she took the time to ponder it.

"Please wait," she called out, picking up the front of her dress as she began to climb the stairs. They went around the inside of the tower, round and round, rising higher as Athena felt her heart pumping hard to kept pace with how fast she was moving.

But there was no one in sight at the top of the stair-case. Just another stretch of passageway. The shadows were deep here, the walls above her narrowing into the roofline.

"Hello?" She stepped away from the stairs as she spotted the closed double doors ahead of her. "Brenda?"

There was nothing but silence.

She might knock.

But she had no way to know who the chambers beyond the doors belonged to. With a sigh, Athena turned and went back down the stairs. Perhaps she might remove her hip roll and be comfortable enough. It would do naught for her empty belly, but she didn't dare wander the passageways alone at night.

Not in a Scottish castle.

Well, not in any castle, really.

She started to turn toward her chamber, but she saw the girl this time. Up ahead of her, going around a corner.

"Please…" Athena ran after her, around the corner, but there was no one there.

But there was another corner. She went around it and down the length of passageway and up more stairs. She searched the shadows, seeking any sign of the woman. By the time she was out of breath and stopped, she realized she had no idea where she was. There were two sets of stairs now, but which ones had she come up?

*Don't panic…*

No, losing her wits wouldn't solve anything. Athena sucked in air, waiting for her heart rate to slow down so she might think clearly.

A shadow shifted at the edge of one of the flights of stairs, and she blinked, but this one didn't disappear like the girl had.

It grew.

She stepped back, feeling her eyes widen.

"I'm sorry, lass." Symon emerged from the shadows. "I suppose I am the last person ye wish to see."

"Considering I'm lost, I am in no position to argue against whoever comes to my rescue," Athena answered.

A hint of moonlight was coming through the center of the closed window shutters. It illuminated him, casting him in white light.

"What are ye doing up here?" he asked her.

"Well, I woke and thought I saw someone, a woman…" It seemed a foolish story. Like something a frightened child might babble on about. Athena ended up biting her lower lip as she felt her cheeks sting with a blush.

But her belly rumbled low and long again, and there was no way to hide the sound in the small space at the top of the stairs.

Symon chuckled. "Brenda said ye'd fallen asleep." He nodded. "Me cousin checked in on ye before she retired. It seems yer belly has roused ye. Come, I believe I still remember how to sneak into the kitchens, although it's been a few years since I did it."

"Seeking tarts before supper, no doubt."

He chuckled again as he gestured her to follow him down the stairs. Once they'd made it to the bottom floor, he turned with confidence down a passageway.

"Before me beard came in, there was naught I desired more than sweets."

The blush burning her cheeks deepened.

He was being frank, and she found it warmed her insides.

A flash of moonlight showed her the short beard still on his chin from their travels. It wasn't long or unkempt.

He reached up and ran his hand along his jaw. "Do ye no' care for beards on men?"

She was blushing scarlet now, grateful for the shadows. Such talk was that of lovers, or at least she imagined it was something like this when liaisons occurred.

"I really...don't know."

Perhaps she should have stayed quiet.

Except it felt much like being a coward, and she was so very tired of being meek.

Symon lifted a finger to his lips to warn her to be

quiet, making her recall just how much she'd enjoyed having him kiss her.

He peered around a corner and then gestured her forward. She caught the scent of roasted meat in the air and felt hunger gnaw at her insides. The hearth was still lit by coals, casting the kitchen in a ruby glow. The long tables used to prepare meals were clean now, large racks of herbs hanging above them.

Symon plucked a bowl from where it had been left to dry and began to fill it with food that had been left wrapped in cloths for the morning meal. Two boys snored in their bunks against one wall. Symon repeated his warning to be silent as he turned and retraced his steps toward the passageway they'd entered through.

She followed him, enjoying the strange sense of excitement pulsing through her blood. She felt more alive than ever and eager for something she really couldn't name.

Symon took her back through the passageways, the darkness never impeding his process.

Of course it didn't. He was in his home. The edges of his kilt flapped as he moved, giving her a glimpse at his thighs, but he didn't seem to feel the night's chill.

"Here we are, lass." He'd found his way back to her chamber, pushing the door open and placing the bowl on a table. She could smell the scent of the bread and cheese now and followed him in.

There was a spark as he struck a flint stone left next to a small bowl with tinder inside it. The sparks fell down in a shower and the dried grass ignited. He held a candle to the flame, placing it on the table when the wick caught.

The shadows were pressed back by a golden pool of light. It surrounded them just as magically as a fairy bubble. Nothing beyond the sphere mattered because it was so far removed.

"Supper for ye, lass." He opened his arms wide and offered her a courtesy.

"So very gallant of you to come to my aid, sir." She sank low in an answering reverence.

"Our parents would be impressed with our manners, to be certain." Symon straightened and grinned at her. "If no' a bit alarmed at the circumstances, for we have no chaperone."

"Well," she muttered, suddenly back in the grip of reality, "I have done my best to adhere to moral conduct and found obedience doesn't always bear the fruit promised."

"Is yer heart broken, then?" Symon surprised her by asking. "Is it still his?"

Athena shrugged. "No. It's the truth I wonder how I might have been so blind as to think myself in love."

She shifted away from him, wondering why she'd been so free with her feelings. Clearly the silence of the night made it seem permissible to be less guarded than she should.

Symon was contemplating her in that way that made her feel as if he could see straight into her soul. As though he knew her intimately, when there was no possible way such a thing might be true.

It was foolishness on her part, plain and simple.

"Thank you for helping me." There, that was better. Polished and impersonal and controlled, just as she had been raised to conduct herself.

Symon reached up and tugged on the corner of his bonnet. "I suppose I should leave ye."

"Yes, it would be correct."

And she didn't care to admit how hard it was to force those words through her teeth. She had a longing for his company.

"But not as much fun," he muttered.

She gasped, but the air came back out as a husky giggle. Athena raised her hand to cover her lips when she heard it, certain she'd never sounded so very brazen in her life.

She heard him chuckle in response. A very male sound of enjoyment that teased her with ideas of whispers and liaisons and stolen kisses.

If only she dared...

"I didn't tell your cousin anything...about how I got the bruises." Athena wasn't certain where the impulse came from to defend herself. Only that she still saw the hurt in his eyes.

He let out a long breath. "I believe ye. Brenda is no' one to miss details."

"I wager your mother might have been pleased with her taking you to task," Athena remarked as the two tapestries came to mind.

Symon offered her a smug grin. "But me sire would have praised me for no' allowing ye to meet with a foul end."

Her eyes narrowed, and his lips curved up farther. They were at an impasse, and yet she struggled to contain the impulse to argue with him.

*You want to keep him here...*

Well, the look in his eyes told her he wanted to stay.

*Maybe...*

Symon started to turn away but stopped. He looked back at her, clearly debating something. She watched the way he pressed his lips into a hard line before clearing his throat.

"Do ye need help...with yer laces?" His tone was gruff. "I do nae mean to alarm ye...but I remember Tara...me wife...needing help with hers."

His question sent a blush onto her cheeks.

Symon watched the way her color deepened, but what drew his attention more than the blush was the way her eyes glittered with anticipation.

Her eyelashes fluttered, but she returned his gaze without fear.

Christ, he liked the spirit in her.

It was a tangible thing, and he felt it warming him as he turned to face her all the way. Her cheeks were dark, and yet she felt the pull between them and didn't shy away from it.

"Turn around, Athena," he suggested softly, fearful his tone might spook her. "Ye need yer rest. Trust me to be a man of honor."

There was a long moment as she stared at him.

Deciding whether to trust him.

It tugged at something inside him, something he'd not felt stir since Tara had died. Only this time, he realized he was far more conscious of the fact that it was her choice.

She started to move, rotating until her back was toward him.

He noticed the way she trembled. The slight quaking of her limbs before she clasped her hands tightly in front of her to hide it.

Symon caught her scent before he touched her laces.

It gave him a moment of pause, and he realized his fingers shook as he reached for her laces.

*Trust...it is not something to betray...*

He caught the knot on the lace on the back of her bodice and pulled it into view from where it had been tucked into the top of the bodice. Once it was loosened, he heard her draw in a deep breath as the dress sagged. Pulling the loops of lace free one by one, he was certain he'd never been so conscious of time before.

It was creeping by, allowing him to notice every detail about the moment.

The way her hair shimmered in the candlelight.

Or how her breasts rose and fell in a rapid motion because of how aroused she was.

He could smell that too.

Her body was heating for him. Beneath his kilt, his cock was throbbing and hard. Symon set his jaw, determined to maintain his control.

*She'd trusted me...*

And he'd never wanted to be worthy so badly in his life. Beneath the gown was her corset. He dipped his fingers between it and her skin, watching the way gooseflesh rose along her nape.

He wanted to taste her...

No, he needed to press his lips against her skin and feed the craving driving him insane.

The knot in the corset lace was tighter, but he worked it loose, and her breasts sagged further. He heard the little sigh of relief come from her lips.

She crossed her arms over her chest, hugging her

clothing to her as he pulled the last of the lace from the corset eyelets.

"Thank you."

She shifted away, raising denial throughout every inch of his body. He caught her around her waist, never realizing when he had decided to do it, only that he couldn't seem to master his own impulses.

"Ye did nae answer me question." He looked down into her eyes. She was startled, and yet excitement shimmered there as well.

"About…what?" Her tone was raspy and edged with need.

A craving she didn't completely understand, he reminded himself sternly.

"About me beard," he clarified.

Her eyes widened.

"But I understand it's on account of ye never having been kissed by a man with one, so…" He leaned down and pressed his mouth to hers, controlling the way he handled her, easing his mouth onto hers and tasting her gently before taking the deeper kiss he craved.

Athena felt the tension in Symon's body. He pulled her close and cradled the back of her head with one of his large hands. She felt his strength, felt the way he held himself in check as his lips glided across her.

*He is waiting for you to kiss him back.*

She knew it.

Sensed it.

And felt something loosen inside her because of it.

As though she might be bold without fear of him taking advantage. She opened her mouth wider, rising onto her toes so she might press her lips against his.

She wanted more.

Something harder.

The craving flickered inside her, stunning her with its intensity. She felt his hand tighten on her head as he kissed her hard, the tip of his tongue extending inside her mouth to touch hers.

She gasped, but he didn't relinquish the ground she'd given. For a moment, she was his possession, the kiss hard and inescapable. She writhed beneath it, yearning to release her hold on her gown and just allow the layers of clothing to slip down her body and be forgotten.

The idea seemed to cut through her reservations like a knife.

She rose up onto her toes, reaching for him with her fingers. The gown started to slip, but Symon jerked back, releasing her and leaving her standing in a disheveled mess of fabric and rapid breathing.

"Good night to ye, Athena."

He didn't want to go. She witnessed the battle in his eyes before he turned and firmly shut the chamber door behind him.

It felt like he'd been torn from her.

She sank down onto her knees, biting her lip to keep from calling him back.

Good night?

It would be very far from that indeed.

Myles Basset was shocked.

Will Tinker rubbed his beard to keep his amusement from showing on his face.

"A woman?" Myles whispered, horrified by the idea.

"It would seem so." Will did his best to sound perplexed by the situation. "Got herself stolen away by Laird Grant."

Myles's expression turned disapproving. "It would seem I was deceived, and yet I cannot leave her to such a fate. Henry is a good friend of mine. Do you think there is any chance we might recover her from this Lord Grant?"

Will pulled on his beard some more. "Perhaps, but there would be a ransom to pay. Most likely why he took her. Likely thought an English lass would be worth something. Highlanders make their money whatever way they may."

"Where do we find him?" Myles asked. "Lord Grant?"

"Well now, that's the simple part. He's gone back to his land. All the better for demanding ransom, ye ken, for the lass will be there with chaperones and all."

Myles let out a sound of relief. "At least I shall be spared knowing I brought the girl to ruin." He nodded firmly. "Well then, we must proceed to this Grant land and retrieve Alex. Henry will simply have to compensate me for the money. He brought her to me, after all, and gave his word that she was honest."

Will let out a whistle that had the rest of the men making ready to go. He turned his back on Myles before letting his lips part in a bright smile. He'd have enough by the end of it all to buy a small farm.

His own land.

A dream that was suddenly within his reach. All he had to do was steal one English lass back from the Grants and pocket the ransom.

Since he'd been a thief his entire life, it would be no trouble at all.

# *Four*

"HOW DO WOMEN WISH TO BE COURTED?"

Brenda was still in her smock when Symon appeared in her dressing chamber the next morning. He shut the door when one of her attendants tried to enter and stormed across to sit next to her.

She put her hair brush down. "I am no' decent, even for close family."

He grunted and turned his back on her but didn't budge an inch beyond that.

Brenda snorted and then dissolved into a round of snickers.

"I've a fine memory, Brenda," he warned. She could see he was gripping his shirtsleeves with his fingers because his arms were crossed over his chest. "I've no' slept, except for dreams of her. Instruct me on how to woo her."

Brenda sobered. Truth be told, she was envious of the tone Symon used. She'd heard it only a few times in her life. Once was when Bhaic McPherson told her of his love for his wife Ailis. For all that the pair had been forced to wed at gunpoint, Bhaic had grown to love his enemy's daughter.

Aye, she was envious of the affection growing in Symon's voice.

"To hell with ye being indecent." Her cousin turned on her as she remained silent.

"I am thinking," she offered kindly. "For it is no' a simple matter, and I can hear that it is important to ye."

Symon drew himself up and grunted. It was a male form of apology.

"Ye need to spend time together," Brenda began. "And I do no' mean time spent doing things ye should have the priest's blessing on before ye do them."

Symon looked at the ceiling, his jaw clenched tight. When he lowered his head, there was a hard glint in his eye. "She'd no' be a maiden this morning if I had no' figured that bit out on me own."

Brenda's eyes narrowed. "What were ye doing in her chamber last night? Athena is virtuous. Otherwise she'd have taken the position of mistress for the gain it would have brought her family. Do ye ken how rare that is in a beauty such as her?"

"I know," Symon exclaimed. "She has no guile, plays no games, and it draws me to her. But I fear she'll no' wed me straight away today if I declare meself, so…" Symon sent her a hard look. "How do I woo her?"

Brenda was out of her seat. She stepped toward Symon, her finger out. "What did ye do with her last night…exactly?"

Symon cocked his head to one side and sent her a stony expression.

"If ye want me suggestions on what to do next,

I need to know what ye have and have no' done." Brenda pressed him.

"She was wandering the passageways with an empty belly. I took her to the kitchens and back to her chamber."

Brenda pursed her lips when he stopped talking.

"And I helped her unlace because she could no' sleep in that gown and corset," he admitted.

"She allowed it?" Brenda was astounded.

Symon was agitated and having trouble standing still. "I asked her to trust me, and…she did…so I couldn't very well do more than kiss her and keep me honor, now could I?"

Brenda smiled slowly. "No, Cousin, and I see it's a fine thing that ye came to me on this matter. If ye wish to woo her, show her what manner of lover ye'll be."

His eyes lowered. "Ye said no' to cross the boundary of intimacy before taking her to a priest."

Brenda crossed her arms over her chest and sent her cousin a frank look. "Do ye know how to please a woman with more than yer cock? Or with it, for that matter?"

Symon backed up a step. Brenda sent him a hard look. "Ye brought this to me, Symon. Leave if ye are too blinded by yer own vanity as to think only men should enjoy bedsport."

"I know how to please a woman in bed." He grunted. "But Tara was sent to me with the agreement already signed by her father. She had to get into me bed and allow me to touch her."

He started pacing. "Ye likely think I'm a fool to care if Athena feels as though I have no' given her a choice.

Last night, Athena trusted me, and I cannae explain how much I need her to choose me." He dropped into the chair she had for him. "I've lost me mind."

"Much like Bhaic McPherson."

Symon had dropped his head into his hands. He looked up as she spoke. The story of his best friend wooing his forced wife was often recounted in the Highlands.

"It seems to me," Brenda began, "that time is on yer side, for ye have sent the letter to her uncle."

"She can hide in her chamber until he replies," Symon groused. "That is one place I cannae force her from."

"If she is so timid, ye would do well to send her home," Brenda advised.

Symon's face betrayed a memory from the night before. Brenda watched the passion flare in his eyes and then suddenly held up her hand. She walked across the chamber to the window. "Ye may stop worrying that she is intent on hiding in her chamber, Cousin."

Symon was behind her in a moment. Below them, Athena ventured out into the castle yard. More than one Grant retainer stared at her, trying to decide what to make of their guest. She inclined her head in a very polite manner as she made her way.

"Christ, she's heading right for the gate." Symon started for the door.

Brenda indulged in another round of giggles before she turned around to see what would happen when he caught up with Athena. The Englishwoman had all of the spirit Symon said she did and then some. There was going to be no simple wooing; on that matter, Brenda would wager her last silver penny.

It was certain to be a spectacle.

❧

First light had given way to dawn.

Athena made it down the stairs and through the hall faster than she'd thought possible. She heard the maids in the kitchen as the Head of House called out instructions. She knew there would be a flurry of activity going on as the day's bread was being put out to rise and bake. At the front of the keep, she watched the butcher and his assistants walking toward the kitchens with a newly spitted hog.

She crossed the yard she'd ridden into the day before and received only a few nods as Symon's clan dealt with the morning chores. A maid passed by with her apron full of fresh eggs while the hens squawked at her in displeasure. Two more men were busy beginning the process of cleaning one of the coops in which the hens resided as the roosters battled one another.

Boys came up, their shoulders laden with yokes holding buckets of fresh milk from cows kept somewhere beyond the castle walls.

The gate itself was wide and high. The horses would be somewhere downwind from the castle.

"Where are ye thinking to go, Athena?"

Athena jumped and then chided herself for being so responsive to Symon.

Her damned belly quivered.

He reached right out and pulled her around to face him.

Somehow, the night had made her forget how tall he was.

"Am I to be imprisoned in that chamber?" she asked.

He'd crossed his arms over his chest and braced his feet wide. "There would be a man at yer door if I intended to keep ye under such conditions." His brows suddenly lowered. "Ye did nae give me yer word yesterday," he said softly. "Becuma's arrival interrupted us before ye agreed to stay and wait for yer uncle's reply."

She rolled her lower lip in and froze when his gaze went right to the little guilty motion.

His eyes narrowed. "Ye'll give it to me now. The Highlands are no place for an English lass to be on her own. A fair number of me countrymen harbor a great deal of hatred toward yer blood."

Some of those watching them nodded. It drew her attention to the number of men who had come closer to watch them. Chores were forgotten, and women leaned out of the windows to get a better view. The grins on their lips reminded her of the way they'd all insisted on her submitting to the midwife's will.

"You only want my promise so you can keep me here and marry me."

She was being tart and less than respectful.

Far less.

But she couldn't seem to stop herself. Her heart thumped against her breastbone, like a bird fighting for its life.

Symon's complexion darkened. "I've plenty of offers."

"Then why are your people shoving us together?"

she questioned. "You just told me they have no love for my English blood."

She opened her hands wide, but he didn't look at the crowd ringing them. No, his topaz eyes were directly on hers, a flicker of determination brightening them.

"I am no' yer damned Galwell," he grunted before he moved toward her and tossed her over his wide shoulder once more.

She let out a squeal of rage.

He smacked her bottom in response.

Her face turned red, leaving her sputtering as Symon carried her back inside the tower to the delight of his men.

"You...beast!" she snarled as he put her down and she spun away from him.

"Beast?" he demanded. "I could have had ye last night."

She gasped, horror choking her because it was a solid truth.

And she didn't want to think of him as that sort of man.

"Christ," he growled. "Ye have no cause to look at me so wounded."

"Does it bother you to have me disappointed in you?" she demanded, realizing he'd taken her back to his study.

"It does."

His response shamed her. Or at least it made her shut her mouth because she realized she was fighting just because there was something about him that made her want to hiss at him. For no other reason than to see what he'd do.

Like a mare snapping at a stallion.

"This is madness," she whispered, looking past him to where the door had closed behind them. "We must not be alone. Why did you bring me here?"

He snorted and pointed at a table behind the desk. "To show ye those. Plenty of offers for me."

He'd put her down and placed himself between her and the door. It made it simple to look at the open letters, proving his statement true.

"Do nae insult me by saying we can no' be alone. I would no' rape ye."

"You wouldn't have to." She really, truly should learn to hold her tongue. "You must forget I said that."

She needed to forget she'd thought it...

His expression softened. "How can I when the truth is I saw ye from me cousin's chamber because I was asking her how to woo ye?"

It was her turn to be stunned into silence. Which pleased him. She watched the pleasure glitter in his eyes before she managed to make her tongue work once more.

"I am English, hated by your countrymen, as you just told me."

He nodded. "Aye, I know it well."

She pointed at the letters on the table. "You should spend your day making a decision on which of those girls to marry. It will clear thoughts of me from your mind."

And she intended to leave the study so he might do just that.

Symon stepped into her path. Athena jerked to a halt two paces from him, her skirts swaying forward.

He contemplated her for a long moment, his topaz

eyes locking with hers as she felt he was seeing straight into her soul. "I prefer ye."

It made no sense.

And yet his words pleased her greatly.

*Stop reacting to him.*

"This is madness…" Her tone was husky once more. She barely recognized it. "You are Scottish, and I am English—"

"We are still a man and a woman. We would no' be the first union composed of different countries. Royals do it quite often."

"You cannot mean to offer me marriage," she exclaimed. "We know naught about one another."

He crossed his arms over his chest and leveled a hard look at her. "I offer it." His voice was stern and edged with hard promise. "For ye will no' compare me to yer Galwell, Athena. I will walk with ye this moment to the church, for it's the truth I want to bed ye something fierce, but I am a man of honor. Ye took the risk of traveling as a boy to preserve yer virtue, and I will no' disrespect ye with less than the offer of marriage. Ye are worthy of it."

She opened her mouth, but words failed her. All she seemed able to do was listen to his words ringing in her ears.

And how welcome those words were…

Did she dare?

"Think on that and go, for ye're correct to call this pull between us a madness. I would have ye consider me offer before I touch ye and we both forget all reason."

It was the logical thing to do.

So why did her feet feel rooted to the floor?

Symon stepped aside, his fingers digging into his shirtsleeves. She finally managed to force herself forward, but she stopped at the door, turning around and lowering herself in a courtesy that was among the most sincere she had ever bestowed on anyone.

Today she meant it more than the expected, well-mannered greeting; she sank low and stayed there a moment before straightening up and leaving.

He was an honorable man.

~~

They did not know each other.

*Ha! You thought you knew Galwell, and see what happened?*

Well, she was English and in Scotland.

*No one has treated you unkindly…*

Athena let out a snort of frustration. Logic was supposed to help her reason out exactly why she shouldn't marry Symon Grant.

It was the truth that she'd never felt so much passion for Galwell.

*There!* An excellent reason to insist on returning home where Henry would arrange a match for her based on solid reasoning.

Myles came to mind. The merchant was everything sound and decent, and the thought of kissing him made her shudder.

But not in a good way.

Someone was coming down the passageway. Their steps were hurried. Athena looked up as Brenda rounded the corner and drew to a stop as she saw her.

"Well…good then," Brenda muttered as she came

toward Athena. "I half feared I would walk in on something ye might prefer I did no' see between ye and me cousin."

Athena felt her cheeks sting with a guilty blush because she could not in all honesty deny something would have happened if she'd stayed inside Symon's study.

"Your cousin is an honorable man." Symon deserved her speaking up for him.

But Brenda's eyes narrowed with suspicion.

"I need something to do." Athena decided to direct her thoughts toward something less provoking than Symon Grant. "I slept yesterday away. Certainly there must be chores needing attention. I am ready to be useful."

Brenda tilted her head to one side. "Well then, I'll introduce ye to Feenet, the Head of House. It's certain she'll have plenty for a pair of willing hands to take on."

Athena felt relief flowing through her but only made it three steps before she recalled that Symon had said he'd been asking Brenda for advice on how to woo her.

Brenda was someone she couldn't trust, for the Scottish woman was in agreement with Symon wedding her.

*Would it be so terrible?*

*Wedding him?*

Honestly, she didn't know. But she did know that the man was unlike any other she'd ever met, so she wasn't going to wed him before learning his middle name.

*You'd discover that at a wedding ceremony…*

Christ! She needed work. Hard work and plenty of it.

"How do ye plan to get her out of Grant Tower?"

Will Tinker looked around before he looked back at one of his men. "I'm planning it all out."

He twisted the end of his beard. Several strands had broken off because of how much he had been fingering it in the past few days.

Myles was abovestairs in the tavern they'd stopped at in the village beyond Grant Tower. He'd advised the merchant to stay where no one would hear that he was English.

In the common room, men stopped in for a warm meal and some ale to keep their blood heated.

They were also interested in hearing all the latest news.

"I heard the laird brought home an English lass, tossed her right over his shoulder in the yard this morning."

Will turned, catching the attention of the man speaking. He flashed Will a bright smile, making it clear he enjoyed knowing Will was interested in listening to his tale.

"Aye, it's true," the man continued. "A true beauty as well. Still…English, and word is the laird thinks of wedding her."

There was a snort from one of the men sitting nearby. His beard was silver with age. "Damned English bring naught but misery to the Highlands."

He spat on the floor before placing his fingers around his mug and settling in to grumble about years long past.

Will grinned and waited. The common room grew quiet as the fire burned low and the innkeeper's wife sought her bed. Men lowered their heads to the tabletops to sleep beneath the roof instead of venturing out into the uncertain Scottish weather.

Will moved closer to the older man. "Men do foolish things when faced with beautiful women."

The older man cracked one eye and chuckled. "Are the gossips still talking about me, then? I'm old enough to admit to me sins now."

"I was thinking about the laird," Will clarified. "I've no love for the English."

The man grunted. "I'm too old to do more than grumble about them now."

"Maybe we should join together," Will suggested slyly. "Get her away from the laird before he does anything rash."

"I may have no love for the English, but I do nae spill the blood of women."

"If she's English, there's ransom to be gained," Will explained. "I say we lure her away from the towers and send a letter to her kin. Split the money between us."

The older man sent Will a suspicious look. "What do ye need me for?"

Will gestured to himself and his friends. "She'd no' trust us. But ye, well now, ye might convince her to follow ye."

"Where?"

Will was thinking. "The stables…a woman of quality would have learning in the healing arts… Tell her yer grandson took a fall or something."

The older man eyed him. "Ye will nae hurt the lass?"

Will spread his hands wide. "I'm a Highlander too. I do nae fight me battles through women, but I'll take a little gain when the opportunity presents itself. And if it keeps the laird from doing something foolish while he's beguiled by a pretty face…well, it will be for the best in the end."

Ransom was a game long played in the Highlands. A gleam entered the old man's eyes as he reminisced for a long moment. He reached out and offered his hand to seal the agreement.

※

"Are ye avoiding me?"

Athena stiffened, realizing she'd been trudging through the passageway without noticing where she was going.

Or the fact that she had nearly walked into Symon. Again…

"No," she muttered as she rubbed her sore hands. "Truthfully, I was half asleep. You may rest assured in knowing your Head of House does not squander a moment of time. Hers or anyone else's under her direction."

Symon's lips twitched. "Feenet put ye to work?"

"I offered my time," Athena replied, still trying to ease some of the stiffness from her hands. "Idleness leads to mischief." She eyed him. "I refuse to believe you spent the day accomplishing naught."

His grin widened enough to flash his teeth at her.

He stepped closer, fascinating her once more with the way he moved. She had never really been so aware of the way a man walked, but she seemed to notice the smallest details about him.

He still had the beard.

Yet his neck was clean, proving he was not one to ignore personal grooming.

"Still deciding if ye like it?" he asked.

She knew what he meant, and yet her tongue tied up in a knot as she attempted to answer him as calmly as he was speaking to her.

The topic was intimate.

He reached out and captured her hand. She felt the connection between their flesh like a jolt. Something hard and fierce that shook her down to the soles of her feet.

"It is not something we should discuss…"

He rubbed her hand, sending delightful relief through the sore muscles.

"Ye know well I disagree with ye on the matter of having discussions." Symon's tone told her he was enjoying himself.

And he eased closer, tilting his head so he might look down and lock gazes with her.

She caught a hint of his scent. Her heart accelerated, but there was a flicker in his eyes that betrayed just how aware he was of the effect he had on her.

"You only want to bring up the topic of kissing again, so…" She pulled back but didn't really gain any ground because she bumped into the wall behind her.

"I can kiss ye again?" he asked in a raspy voice as he closed the single pace she'd managed to put between them. "Aye, I did have that in mind." His gaze lowered to her lips. "I do want to kiss ye."

And he didn't waste any time making good on his intentions. He cupped the back of her head, tilting her face up as he slipped his other arm around her waist, so suddenly she was pressed against him, her skirts shifting as he embraced her and claimed her mouth.

He didn't rush. No, he didn't need to because she was his captive in that moment. His embrace was controlled, and yet she felt the strength in his arms, and the solid wall behind her proved he knew how to trap his prey.

He also knew how to kiss.

She'd never realized how much sensation might flow from a pair of joined lips. A soft sound escaped her as he moved his mouth against hers, enticing her to mimic his motions.

She knew kissing him back would lead to madness.

And yet she rose up on her toes even as the thought passed through her mind in an attempt to warn her.

Just as it had always been with Symon, her reason dissipated and rose like steam as he heated her blood.

Now, there was only the desire to touch him. His doublet was open, granting her the chance to slip her hands inside it. She heard him draw in a stiff breath, lifting his mouth from hers for a moment as his eyes glittered.

"Touch me, lass…"

Only the linen of his shirt was between her hands and his skin. The thought set fire to something inside her, kindling a blaze that stole her breath and made her tremble.

And Symon watched her.

His keen stare locked with hers, waiting to see if she was bold enough to answer his demand.

She was.

And honestly, Athena was certain no threat of reprisal would have kept her from slipping her hands along his chest, discovering the way he felt, learning where the hard ridges of muscles lay on him.

His eyes narrowed, pleasure thinning his lips.

She was captivated by the way his face showed her his truest emotions. Never once had she ever felt so very in tune with another soul. She moved her hands again, enthralled with the way he let out a soft, male sound of enjoyment.

It would seem she was not the only one driven to wantonness.

His eyes opened, freezing her in mid-thought as she caught the flicker of need there. A moment later, he claimed her mouth in a hard kiss that drove all reasoning from her mind as the cravings in her body rose up and burned everything else away.

There was only Symon and her need to get closer to him. Their clothing frustrated her with the barrier it presented, and yet she wanted to hold him as tightly against her as she might. Athena reached up and gripped his neck, kissing him back as her heart beat so hard she knew it would burst soon.

And she cared naught.

"Enough of that!"

Symon growled. "Be gone."

"I will no'," whoever was behind them informed them. "Mistress Brenda gave me stern instructions to see Mistress Athena to her chamber. Enough of that now."

Athena was mollified.

Her reason returned in a rush, like the bed-curtains being pulled aside so that the bright light of day shocked one with how lazy one had been to linger in slumber.

Feenet stood behind her laird without a care for how awkward the moment was.

"After all, Athena has no' agreed to wed ye, and I will nae have her casting doubt upon yer good name, Laird."

Symon grunted but turned and faced his Head of House. "So ye are protecting me good name, is it?"

Feenet fought to maintain a stern expression, but the corners of her lips twitched. "With half the families in the Highlands sending ye offers for their daughters, I would be a poor Head of House if I did no' ensure there is no gossip attached to yer good name. What sort of father would be willing to send his daughter here if yer name is tarnished?"

She reached past him and grabbed Athena's hand, tugging her away from the wall.

"I would no' care to have Athena telling one and all in England that we Highlanders have no Christian nature."

Symon crossed his arms over his chest and smiled menacingly. "I am in yer debt."

There was a double meaning in his statement that none of them missed. But the Head of House only lowered herself before turning and urging Athena down the passageway. When Feenet's back was to him, Symon sent Athena a look full of the unsatisfied passion still burning in them both.

But she turned and made her way to her chamber, offering courtesy to Feenet before the older woman took her leave. It left Athena alone with her thoughts, although there was really only one true item lingering on her mind.

More like stuck...

True, she had hoped to forget it before making it to

her chamber, but it was still there, tormenting her with just how impossible she was finding it to brush aside.

She didn't like hearing that she would be returning to England.

Not a bit.

Did she dare to follow passion? Wasn't that the very foolish action that had landed her in her present circumstances?

Athena lay down in her bed, still marveling at the comfort of having a true bed when she had spent so many weeks in a wagon.

So wasn't it ridiculous to even entertain the idea of embracing her whims when she'd so very recently had a taste of what consequences might be hers after such folly?

And yet Symon's kiss lingered on her lips, following her into slumber where her dreams were full of him and how much she longed for him.

❧

"Ye sent Feenet after me?"

Brenda was brushing out her hair. Symon was accustomed to seeing her, and yet he realized how very stunning she really was. Her hair was the color of an autumn sunset. There was red hair aplenty in Scotland, but Brenda's looked like fire had been caught up in the strands.

"Athena needs to be reminded of what a fine catch ye are," Brenda informed him as she put her brush aside and turned to move across her receiving chamber to where she kept a collection of fine spirits. She was graceful and poised as she poured him a measure of whisky.

Of course, she'd been raised to be the perfect wife, and her father had wed her to an excellent match of noble blood.

"Ye and Athena have a few things in common," Symon remarked as Brenda offered the goblet to him.

"By that do ye mean we are both free to make our own choices?" Brenda asked as she returned to her dressing table.

"I mean ye have both discovered noble blood does nae ensure nobility in a man."

Brenda offered him a little pursing of her lips. For a long moment, the only sound was the fire crackling. Symon realized Brenda's chamber didn't hold the appeal it had for the last year. He felt stifled within its walls, as though he was missing an opportunity.

"I will have Athena."

Brenda smiled slowly. "I know."

Symon put the whisky down. He didn't want to dull his senses.

He'd squandered enough days. Sitting in the chair was impossible when there were matters to attend to. He pushed up and out of it, cursing the night and how many hours there were between him and the chance to run Athena to ground.

"Be patient, Symon."

He had his hand on the door when Brenda spoke. It wasn't her warning that made him turn and look at her; it was the resignation in her tone.

She was lonely.

Brenda covered the lapse in composure the moment she realized he'd looked back at her.

"Ye will want to know she chose ye, so let her

come to terms with ye, or she might never admit she desires the union as much as ye do. Women are told so very often how much they should abhor such things as passion. It becomes difficult to think past the lectures."

"Boys are lectured on courage and facing what ye fear and never wavering because of doubt but to go quick and directly toward our goals."

Brenda stiffened.

"It seems we both need to listen a wee bit to the opposite sex, Brenda. I will keep yer words in mind."

"As I should listen to what ye have just said?" Brenda inquired tartly.

He offered her a firm nod before turning toward the door.

"Symon…" Brenda didn't raise her voice. Instead she used the purring tone women had learned to utilize in order to cut through the pride of the men who ruled the world around them.

Symon whirled around so fast his kilt flared up.

"She can't run if you don't chase her," Brenda remarked.

Symon grunted at her.

Brenda raised a slim finger. "I doubt she will break her fast in the hall in the morning."

"I cannae precisely blame her for avoiding the high table," Symon replied, clearly impatient to be gone because he had made a firm decision on what he intended to do.

Brenda turned and sent him a look. "As I said, she can't run if you don't chase her. Now, if ye were to bring her something to eat because ye noticed she'd fled the hall and all the eagerness of yer people to push her into a union she has yet to come to terms with... well...she might find herself grateful...and content to be in yer company."

Symon's face lit with understanding. His lips curved into a very pleased smile. He moved back across the floor and placed a kiss on Brenda's temple. "I do nae tell ye enough how grateful I am for ye, Cousin."

"Talk to her, Symon," Brenda advised him. "Let her discover who ye are beyond the laird of this clan. Me guess is she's had a belly full of men telling her what to do. She'd never have spent months in a wagon if she was content."

"Why do ye think I cannae stomach the idea of letting her go?" Symon said solemnly. "Ye can be very sure I have no heart to be her captor."

"I understand yer reasoning," Brenda answered. "Ye could have sent for one of the girls offered to ye if all ye wanted of a union was obedience."

"We've both had enough of that to last a lifetime," Symon replied gruffly.

"Indeed we have," Brenda said. "So let her learn who ye are."

Symon was gone a second after she spoke.

Leaving Brenda alone with just how envious she was of Athena.

Perhaps she should reply to Bothan Gunn's letter.

Her eyes narrowed. Bothan could listen to the same advice she'd just given Symon. She would not wed a man who had simply decided to claim her.

No, she'd have more or nothing at all.

∼⌘∼

Symon nodded and pulled the door open. For all that he'd done the same thing hundreds of times, tonight, as he crossed into the passageway outside Brenda's chambers, something felt different. There was an odd feeling in the air that made the hair on his body tingle. Symon turned his head, catching something in the dark.

For a moment, all he saw were shadows and the normal things he expected to see in the darkness.

And then there was a wisp of light. Like mist at dawn, it shimmered with the first rays of the rising sun.

Only the moon was covered by clouds tonight.

He blinked and tried to dispel the image. It remained, forming into a woman who turned and lifted her hand in a shy wave.

Tara.

He heard her quiet laugh before she looked up and reached for something above her that he couldn't see.

Many would have made the sign of the cross over themselves. Instead, he could feel his lips curving into a content smile as the passageway returned to darkness and shadows. He'd known she haunted the tower. Had felt her presence and even taken solace in what company there was to be had in a spirit. Guilt assaulted him as he pondered whether he'd kept her from moving on to the next life.

It was likely true, for Tara had come to him as wife, devoted to easing his lot with gentle companionship. Even in death, she'd refused to abandon her duty.

At least not until he'd stopped mourning for her.

It was done now. He felt the sureness of it, as if his heart had suddenly begun beating again.

Aye, he would have Athena, and he suddenly realized he was going to enjoy chasing her.

Enjoy it a very great deal!

✎

*England*

"Mother," Dorothy interrupted the Dowager Countess of North Hampton as she read a newly arrived letter. The maid had just delivered it.

"Why are you dealing with that goldsmith and his daughter?" Dorothy demanded. "Galwell is from finer stock."

The countess held up a slim finger encased in a very finely tailored glove. "I thought so as well. However, Lord Leicester is the Queen's confidant and very old friend."

Dorothy shook her head. "Not since he wed Lettice Knollys in secret last year."

The countess waved her hand through the air, dismissing her daughter's reasoning. "A matter that will be forgotten far sooner than many realize. Leicester was with Her Majesty when they were all banished and labeled bastards and the spawn of traitors. Trust me, Daughter, keeping in his good graces is worth a few letters to discover the truth of the goldsmith's niece. Lord Leicester will want Galwell occupied somewhere other than at court, and it is an excellent opportunity for us to make certain we are due a favor from him. One we shall call in once he is back in the Queen's confidence."

Dorothy fingered the velvet of her skirt. "Niece, is it?"

"Yes," her mother informed her with a smile of victory. "And as it so happens, the girl is the spawn of Henry Lennox."

Dorothy drew in a startled gasp. "I wonder if Galwell knows such."

"I wager not," the countess said as she read through the letter once again. "Even illegitimate, her blood link to the Stewarts is strong. According to my sources, Galwell tried to make the girl his mistress, but she set fire to his house and escaped."

Dorothy's eyes widened as her lips rose into a wicked smile.

"It seems the girl is missing and the uncle has made several trips to see some of his longtime customers. No doubt he is gathering support."

"Galwell Scrope is truly a scoundrel," Dorothy declared softly.

"Many men are, dear, as I have told you often enough. Family is your truest ally. However, we shall make a good one of Lord Leicester with this information."

"Leicester won't be able to force Galwell to wed this girl."

"No," the countess agreed. "However, as it is spring and Her Majesty is now on royal progress, Lord Leicester will be closer to the edge of Scotland where he will be able to share this information with the Dowager Countess Lennox. She will not take kindly to Galwell sullying the Stewart name or the Stewart blood. And as for Galwell himself..." The countess took a moment to smile at her daughter. "Once his father learns of the dowry the girl has, Galwell will be ordered to wed her. I have already sent a letter to Baron Scrope as Lord Leicester requested I do."

"But if he tried to make her his mistress!" Dorothy exclaimed.

The countess raised her delicate eyebrows. "Marriage is about gain, Daughter. Blood or riches, preferably both."

Dorothy nodded. Her own husband preferred the company of young men, which only meant she had to make sure to bring along a few of them when she visited his bedchamber so that they might get on with begetting heirs as well as making very sure none of his lovers ever spoke about the earl's tastes. It wasn't the most horrible thing she might have found herself facing when she wed, and she was a countess. In a few years, once the children were born, she could have all the lovers she desired with her husband's blessing.

Her mother was correct. Queen Elizabeth would forgive Lord Leicester for they were truly in love, and Elizabeth Tudor would be a fool to ever marry. She was Queen in her own right, and all the nations of Europe were holding back their armies as they tried to gain England through the hand of its monarch.

Yes, Elizabeth played the Virgin Queen very well, so she would forgive Robert's need for an heir. He'd be at her side before the summer's end. It would seem Dorothy had a great deal to learn from her mother still. Dorothy leaned closer to her mother.

"How shall we play this?"

❦

*Scotland*

Hidden behind Grant Tower was a lake.

Athena was fascinated by the sparking surface of it.

There was also a mill. The wheel turned in the morning light as she wandered down to explore her surroundings.

There was work aplenty, and she was far from the only one up at first light. Two men were working the mill. They grinned as she came close and tugged on the corners of their bonnets before they went back to their labor.

She walked around the outside of the mill, enjoying the sound of the water.

Another sound intruded, as did a very large dog. It had a thick coat of hair and ran toward her on long legs, not stopping until it had its nose pressed beneath her skirts. The animal sniffed her before sitting back on its haunches and howling long and loudly.

"Good boy," Symon praised the dog as he came around the edge of the mill.

"Did you set a hound to track me?" she asked incredulously.

Symon offered the dog a piece of meat before rubbing its shaggy head for a moment.

"Aye, I did," Symon answered. "But only because ye were more clever than me this morning in escaping the hall. But ye left me there to endure the suggestive looks from everyone."

"Decided to join me?" she inquired.

He shrugged. "Are ye going to make me admit

to me own cowardice, lass? That's right unkind of ye when I've brought ye something to break yer fast with."

Symon set a small bundle on a rock near the river's edge. The ends were tied up around something. He pulled at the knots until they opened, revealing an assortment of food. There was a round of newly baked bread, a hunk of cheese, and half a roasted chicken. He pulled a pair of mugs from beneath the bread and scooped up some of the fresh water.

"You're correct, Lord Grant," she muttered as her belly rumbled. "I am being far too harsh. Even if you do somewhat deserve everything you receive because you brought me here."

He chuckled. "I do nae regret it…well, perhaps I was rethinking the matter as I sat at the high table and realized how many were staring at me."

Symon pulled his dagger and cut the cheese into slices which he offered to her.

She claimed a piece of the cheese. "Why are your people so desperate for you to wed?"

It wasn't a very polite question.

Symon swallowed before fixing her with an honest look. "Me wife died in childbed four winters ago."

"I'm sorry."

"And me father died last season, as did Brenda's husband, only that was more of a blessing, except there was no issue," he continued. "My father lingered, and I was by his side. The years passed. I should have attended to the matter of finding another wife, but it seemed such a cold thing to do when I knew me attention was on me father."

Not many men would have felt the same. She chewed on the chicken leg.

"Ask more questions," he said.

Athena looked at him over the rim of her mug. "You enjoy a woman who chatters?"

He chuckled. "Brenda advised me to allow ye time to come to know me. So ask questions."

She laughed.

And realized it had been a really long time since she'd laughed out loud.

Symon noticed. His gaze rested on her as she looked away because she felt unmasked.

"Thank you for thinking of me this morning."

Symon grunted before pointing the tip of his dagger at her. "Ye've been alone, haven't ye? With that merchant."

"Well, I wasn't going to keep company with Will Tinker and his comrades," Athena exclaimed. "But it was to be expected, that I'd have to keep to myself."

"Ye've got a solid spine, lass. More than one woman would have taken the position of mistress and considered it the best that might be had under the circumstances."

It was a compliment. One of the most honest ones she'd ever received.

"I suppose it was pride that kept me from it," Athena said. "And the knowledge that Uncle Henry had done well by me. Disgracing him hardly seemed a fitting reward. He sheltered me from those who advised him to turn me out. He'd chosen to keep me when my father's family would have seen me die in my swaddling cloth. My uncle is a moral man. I will never disgrace him."

They ate in silence for a long moment.

"I still say ye could grow to like it here," Symon said.

But it was a teasing suggestion now, which made her contemplate it so much more deeply.

"Yes, and you could grow to realize you don't like me at all," she answered. "We really know very little about each other."

She didn't much care for her own words. They felt wrong, as if she was fighting the current, trying to swim upstream when there was nothing better there for her.

"Are ye telling me that ye snore?" he asked.

She laughed again, earning a smile from Symon. "How would I know such a thing?" she asked.

He shrugged. "Fair enough. Perhaps ye should spend the night in me chambers so I can learn the truth of the matter meself."

Athena aimed a smile at him. "Will Brenda be there?"

Symon made a sour face. "That sort of thing does no' happen in our family. Now, I've heard it might be true up on Gordon land…"

"Stop," she admonished him. "You'll end in the stocks with talk such as that."

His eyes flickered with heat. "I assure ye, lass, I'm in far more danger of ending in the stocks for seducing ye."

"So sure I would submit to you?"

Challenging him wasn't the wisest thing she might have chosen to do.

But she enjoyed it more than she'd ever imagined.

Something flashed in his eyes that awakened an answering flicker of heat from her insides.

He suddenly groaned and pushed to his feet. "We'd

best get back before that look on yer face makes me forget my intention to woo ye."

He tied the cloth around what was left of her meal and offered her a hand. She put her hand into his, feeling the connection all the way to her toes.

Yes, she could come to like it here, with him.

In fact, she rather thought she'd already gone and done so.

Not that she was planning on telling him.

No, not just yet.

❧

*England*

Galwell looked at his father in shock. "I had no way of knowing Athena had such a dowry!"

His father, Baron Scrope, sat on his chair with his hand gripping the armrest so his signet ring caught the candlelight.

"It would seem your ability to enchant the Queen has brought us gain, just in a different way," the baron explained. "The girl didn't know of it either. Her father's family are not fools. They have kept the matter secret. If her uncle had investigated, he'd have discovered the inheritance left to the girl."

Galwell smiled with victory. "Elizabeth is becoming enamored of me. She even sent Lord Robert Leicester away tonight in favor of sitting with me."

"Yes, I am well aware of that," the baron said quietly. "Lord Leicester is not a man to be slighted, Galwell. He is the Queen's favorite."

"I am her favorite," Galwell exclaimed.

"You are her current fascination," the baron informed his son. "Someone she is using to remind Leicester of his place, so he remembers that she is the master of her realm."

Galwell's eyes widened with anger.

"Mind your tongue, Son," the baron warned him. "I have known Elizabeth Tudor since her birth and her mother before that. Elizabeth is every bit her father's daughter. She will never share the crown, but she loves Robert Leicester too. His wife is for breeding, and you will wed Athena Trappes for the same purpose."

Galwell paced, his father watching him in his agitation. "Athena won't have me."

"I have already sent for her uncle," the baron replied. "We shall come to an agreement, and I will have him produce the girl. It will be for her kin to make her see the value of obedience. You will answer to me in the same manner."

"She might well be wed to another by now," Galwell answered. "What better way to cover the scandal of her setting fire to my townhome than by arranging a very quick wedding?"

"We shall see," the baron muttered. "However, you will make it known that you are seeking reconciliation with her."

Galwell stomped his foot on the hard floor. "The Queen will be upset with me."

"Yes, she will," the baron agreed. "It is Lord Leicester's favor we are courting now, for that is the favor you can expect to keep. Elizabeth is merely toying with you. Robert Leicester will not forget who clears the path between him and the Queen."

Galwell left his father's house, stewing with anger.

Elizabeth enjoyed his company, and he knew he could make it last if he was just given the time to win her. By the time he'd made it to his townhome, his servants were almost finished packing. He'd depart at first light to accompany the Queen on her progress.

It would give him the time he needed to win her heart. His father might rule the family now, but Galwell was a second son. He'd always known he'd have to secure his own fortune.

The heart of England's Queen was far more important than one tract of land.

༄

*Scotland*

Symon looked into the kitchens at first light, catching his Head of House's attention. Feenet wiped her hands on her apron before she came out to meet him.

Symon looked both ways before speaking.

"See that the mistress is dressed for dinner in something a little less likely to allow her to tend to her own needs."

Feenet took a moment to think through his words before understanding dawned on her. "A dress more suited to the hall, perhaps?"

Symon nodded.

Feenet lowered herself before she turned and went back into the kitchen.

Courting was a matter of strategy, after all. Athena wouldn't wander from the hall if she didn't have a warm enough dress.

"Good morning, Mistress," Feenet declared as the bed-curtains were swept aside to let the morning light in. "We've come to help ye dress."

Athena rubbed her eyes and looked at the window. Dawn had broken, but the hour was still very early.

"You do not need to dress me," Athena said.

Feenet and the two maids with her didn't stop. They came right into Athena's chamber, their arms piled high with clothing. Feenet pulled the bedding down, letting the morning air in.

"It's not right that the laird's guest should be wearing servant's clothing," Feenet informed Athena with a firm look. One of the maids was quick to set her bundle down and gather up the skirt and bodice Athena had worn the day before.

The bodice had laced up the front, making it simple to see to her own needs. Athena looked longingly at it as the maid slipped through the door and disappeared. A moment later, another maid appeared with more clothing.

"Please, this is all too much," Athena tried to argue.

Feenet watched as her staff laid out the dresses. "Ye might be able to say Highlanders are savage on account of how they steal women and all, but..." The Head of House held up a finger. "Ye will no' say we do nae treat our guests well."

One of the maids failed to hold back her mirth. Athena sent a look toward Feenet. "I won't be saying you lack creativity, either."

It would seem the staff had decided on a way to

make certain she and their laird were together. At least during meals.

Feenet grinned and pointed at a green dress. Athena stood while being dressed. It was strange how hard it was to remain in place while the maids brought her layers of clothing and laced everything into position. At least there was no farthingale. The stiffened underskirt that would hold out her skirt like a bell was something she did not miss at all. Walking had taken strict attention so her hips' natural sway didn't make her look like a giant bell being rung.

"And no working in the kitchen," Feenet said as the last sleeve ribbon was secured. "This dress is too fine."

"I was very happy in the other."

Feenet clapped her hands together. "Let's get to table before the laird sends someone up here to investigate why we are late."

There was a flurry of motion as the maids and Head of House swept Athena along in their midst. The hall was full of men. The Grant retainers were enjoying the opportunity to sit and converse before the work of the day began.

"Mistress Athena."

Symon's voice echoed through the hall, full of authority and command. The men grew quiet as they looked toward her. At the end of the aisle, the high ground had a table on it. Symon was standing there, more formal than she had ever seen him. His doublet was buttoned most of the way up his chest, and his bonnet was freshly pressed, a brooch attached to its side with three feathers raised.

The sight of him would have made the knees weak in half the heiresses in Elizabeth Tudor's court.

Athena realized she was no exception.

"Join me." Symon extended his hand to indicate a space beside him. There were no other women at the head table. Tamhas and Lyall were there, their position made clear by how close they sat to the laird.

And another retainer was pulling a chair back for her.

She lowered herself before moving up the center of the hall. For the first time since leaving London, she found herself somewhat thankful to Galwell, for she knew how to carry herself with grace and poise. Which was a very necessary skill because everyone was watching her.

Symon didn't sit until she had.

"You are trying to impress me." She spoke low so her words wouldn't carry.

"Surprised to discover I have polished manners?"

His topaz eyes were full of mischief, and she found it infectious.

"Perhaps I enjoy you as I first encountered you…"

His eyes narrowed. "I seem to have miscalculated and made a target of meself by dressing the part of a laird." His voice dipped low. "Ye are going to tease me unmercifully."

"Shall I remove myself to one of the lower tables… Laird Grant?" she fluttered her eyelashes. "I only wish to please you."

"Truly?" One dark eyebrow arched. "If that's so, I've no' gotten into this doublet for naught. We'll make a fine-looking pair as we take our wedding vows."

Maids were serving the first meal of the day as the

windows brightened with spring sunshine. There was a fresh scent to the air, tempting Athena to simply let the moment carry her along. Symon caught her hand beneath the table.

"Give me hope that yer silence means ye are considering me."

His playfulness had evaporated, leaving her facing a very serious look.

"You don't know me," she muttered, once again losing the battle to keep her thoughts from spilling across her lips. "I might well be a liar."

"Yer thoughts show on yer face. Why do ye think I cannae keep me hands off ye? I see the desire in yer eyes. The way ye undress me with yer gaze. I am no' the only one who needs a blessing from the priest."

Her cheeks heated, earning a chuckle of victory from him. He reached over, pulled a round of bread from a platter, and broke it before placing a generous portion on her plate.

"Eat well, lass." He dropped his voice into a raspy whisper. "Ye will need yer strength today, for I will have ye to wife." His eyes snapped with determination. "Soon."

She wanted to protest.

*You also want to smile.*

The two urges pulled on her, threatening to rip her right in half.

Which made no sense at all.

Well, neither did Symon and his desire to wed her. Not with all the offers he had for his hand.

*Unless…*

Athena looked at the newly churned butter as a thought burst upon her.

He might not have offers at all. She'd heard the tales of the Scottish Highlanders who carried brides off for their dowries. The shipyards in Scotland were notorious—brides often found themselves abducted right off the ships they were on as those ships put in for much-needed provisions.

She'd be wise to question the matter.

*He's proved himself honorable…*

Galwell had played that part well too.

Symon kissed her hand as the meal ended and he went off to begin his day. His departure left her with plenty to think about as Brenda arrived and took her along to work on the account books.

Life flowed around them. The bread rose, and the scent of dinner filled the passageways. Beyond the towers was a lovely view of newly turned fields.

Athena was tempted to join the melody. Cast her cares and questions to the winds to see where they would land.

But marriage was different for a woman. The wife was chattel and the husband free to treat her as he might. More than one bride had discovered her true worth was her dowry and maidenhead.

There were chambers in the towers that were far too silent, places Symon might place her once he had the gain he thought to get.

It hurt to think of him in such a way, and yet she forced herself to ponder the matter. No matter what, she would never be trustingly naive again.

Not even when it came to Symon Grant.

❧

Supper in Grant Hall was a time of merriment.

Feenet beamed with pride as platters of meat and new vegetables were carried in. The Grant retainers pounded on the tabletops to show their appreciation.

Once the fare had been passed around, cider came from the kitchens along with cheese and fruit.

"Forgive me, I am so very tired."

Athena didn't make eye contact with Symon. She didn't know if it was true that he could see her thoughts; however, she had precious little experience with lying, so it was best to keep her gaze lowered. One of the retainers who seemed assigned to stand behind them while they ate pulled her chair back.

"The Grant accounts are in such good order, the books wore ye out!" Tamhas declared from the other side of Symon.

"Brenda was likely relieved to see ye had some skill with accounts," Symon added. "She has no liking for the chore."

"I am happy to be of service." Athena lowered herself before hurrying from the hall.

She chided herself when she realized how fast she was moving, forcing herself to slow down and appear ready for bed.

She peeked back at the head table when she was almost around the edge of the passageway. Tamhas was taking full advantage of Symon's undivided attention, speaking intently with one finger sticking out at his laird.

The moment was perfect.

Everyone was enjoying the cider, and the sound of music and laughter spilled into the hallway. Athena hurried along, recalling the way far more easily now that she had spent more time inside the tower. What had once appeared to be indistinguishable passageways were now something she might navigate successfully.

She made her way to the doors of Symon's study and opened them in spite of the guilt trying to strangle her.

She couldn't afford to be timid.

And besides, he'd shown them to her first, so she was not looking at anything he hadn't been willing to share.

*You are making excuses to cover your snooping…*

She didn't shy away from the thought. If Symon was good to his word, she might just give in. Discover happiness wasn't something she had to forgo in life.

But she felt exposed thinking in that manner. As though she'd forgotten the cost of being whimsical instead of keeping herself firmly focused on logic. For certain it sounded like a simple enough way to conduct herself when she heard lectures on the topic.

Yet the practical application wasn't proving so easy.

Nearly impossible, actually…

No one had lit the candles, but enough light came through the windows for her to see. Even in the murky light, she made out the letters. They were no longer open on the tabletop. Instead they were folded. Laid neatly on top of some of them was a newly penned and wax-sealed letter addressed to the sender of the letters. She reached for one of the original letters and unfolded it, holding it close to her face so she might read it.

He'd spoken the truth.

"I spent a good amount of time today answering those letters."

She jumped, whirling around to find Symon perched on the edge of his desk. He enjoyed her shock, his lips parting in a grin.

"As I told ye before, lass." His eyes flashed with determination. "Ye are no' so meek, and I know it well. Ye seem to have forgotten how we met."

"I haven't…forgotten." Yet she did attempt to keep her mind from returning to the way he'd been there, in the shadows of the night while she danced. "Although I suppose I deserve to be considered brazen when I—"

"When ye danced around the fire in a shirt," he finished for her. "I am making sure the rest of the Highlands knows I have settled on me choice of bride."

"Yet…" She was caught in a moment of utter bewilderment. "You know little of me. There is dowry to be had, but it will not be any great fortune."

He straightened away from the desk, working at the buttons on his doublet. It had only been closed halfway at his midsection, and he made quick work of it before tossing the garment aside.

"I know," he informed her firmly as he came toward her, "that I've spent an embarrassing amount of time today thinking about how much I enjoyed having yer hands on me last night and wishing Feenet had no' come along to interrupt us, even though I'll admit me cousin was right to ensure ye had a chaperone."

He chuckled, the sound full of promise.

Dark promise.

Or at least the sort of promise best fulfilled under the cover of darkness.

He pulled the laces at the collar of his shirt free so it fell open, baring his skin. "Come here, Athena, and do what ye wanted to last evening."

She wanted to.

No, the word was *crave*. For the hunger she felt for him was far too deep to be merely want.

She was suddenly full of impulses and half aware that part of her had hoped he'd follow her and confront her.

She felt bound too tightly in the corset and gown.

"Did Brenda advise you to tempt me with things that should not be spoken of? Is this the wooing you think will win me?" She didn't care for how peevish she sounded. Simple conversation escaped her grasp as her blood hummed through her veins like she'd indulged in too much wine.

Symon only tossed his head back and laughed.

"You cannot be amused by my prickly distemper."

He looked back at her. "I am, because I see ye're flustered by me presence. Ye're trying to be a shrew to convince me to leave."

He'd edged closer. In the semidarkness, she caught the way his gaze moved over her face, lingering on the burning spot that betrayed how she blushed for him.

She'd been lulled into a sense of safety by his low tone. Symon reached out and gripped a handful of her skirt, pulling her forward a moment later.

So easily she was in his embrace, bound against him as she tried to flatten her hands on his chest to push free.

Instead she heard a little sound of delight cross her lips as she felt his hardness.

"As for Brenda"—Symon tipped her chin up so

their gazes locked—"me cousin made sure to inform me that women like to be pleasured as much as men, and I *cannae* wait to pleasure ye, lass."

And he didn't wait to kiss her but claimed her mouth in a kiss that was fierce and strong. She shifted beneath its power, not really trying to escape, merely uncertain how to endure all the need flickering inside her.

She felt like her very body caged her. Freedom was what she craved, freedom from all the things binding her and holding her in line.

His shirt was one of those things, for it was between them. She pushed at it, another sound of contentment escaping her when she succeeded in cupping his bare shoulders.

He was hard, built to endure his environment, and in that moment, she was completely enamored of his strength. Her core contracted, making her aware of how empty she was.

She strained closer to him, desperation making her pull at the fabric of his shirt. He suddenly released her, reaching up and behind his neck to pull at the garment. He bared his chest, tossing the shirt aside and facing her.

"Is that what ye wanted, lass?" he asked.

She nodded.

Oh, she shouldn't have, and yet it seemed the worst sort of lie to deny the way his kiss made her seek his flesh.

"I like the sound of the idea meself…" He cupped her shoulder and turned her around and pulled the top of her lace free.

"Symon…"

Was it a warning? Or encouragement? Perhaps it

was relief because the gown bodice loosened as she felt her nipples contracting. Unlike the first time he'd unlaced her, tonight he pulled at the loops with impatient fingers.

Her dress slumped to the floor in a puddle around her ankles, and her hip roll fell when he opened it.

She shivered, uncertainty breaking through the moment. She crossed her arms over her breasts, the thin fabric of her smock feeling like a whisper between them.

"The firelight showed me yer breasts…" He came up behind her, wrapping his arms around her as he flattened his hands on her belly. She shuddered, aching for more and yet caught in the harsh grip of uncertainty.

"I want to fill me hands with them…" His voice was full of dark intention. Anticipation spiked up from where it had been twisting through her core. Now it touched off a craving in her breasts, one she'd never thought possible.

But she wanted him to make good on his promise.

Symon didn't disappoint her. He smoothed his hands up her torso until he was holding both of her breasts.

"Perfect," he growled, taking their weight before teasing her hard nipples with his thumbs.

She let out a sigh, leaning back against him, arching to offer her body to him.

Surrender?

No, it was more of a demand.

Or a challenge, and he seemed worthy of it, sending delight through her. Introducing her to a level of pleasure she'd never realized her body could feel. He pressed a kiss against her neck, adding to the craving growing in her core. She would have done anything in that moment to keep his hands on her. Nothing mattered except finding out what else she might experience.

He kissed the side of her neck, and she arched so that he might place another kiss farther down. Her eyes slid shut as she let the current take her.

It wasn't submission.

He was her companion.

She turned and reached up to lay her hands against his neck, needing to participate more completely. His expression tightened as his eyes closed.

"That's the way, lass…" He offered encouragement in a husky tone. When he opened his eyes, desire flickered in them, and she knew without a doubt he was seeing the same thing in her gaze.

Someone pounded on the door.

It wasn't a knock but a solid thumping.

Symon cursed. Low and darkly. "I am going to murder whoever that is."

"Ye won't," Brenda informed him as she came in without invitation. "Ye will thank me for coming down here and bringing the lady a dressing robe."

Athena likely burned to a cinder in that moment.

"Ye are no' wed yet, and there will be gossip aplenty if she is seen returning to her chambers looking thoroughly disheveled."

Symon growled but released Athena. "She came in here of her own will, Brenda."

Brenda's poise was noteworthy, because where Athena felt like she was going to burn to a crisp right there from shame, the other woman merely came forward and helped cover her smock with the dressing robe.

"Consider it a step in courting, Cousin," Brenda advised him. "If she loathed ye, she'd no' be curious about yer private affairs."

"Brenda, Symon was not misbehaving," Athena said.

Brenda made a soft sound beneath her breath. "He knows more than ye do about...well, about matters, and being laird means that there are expectations to be maintained." Brenda sent her a look that made it clear Symon was not the only once receiving a lesson from her. "We'll have to go to the bathhouse to make things seem correct."

Brenda might have been discussing what herbs to use when seasoning a chicken. Her voice was smooth and even, but she suddenly flashed Athena a smile.

"Me cousin and I," Brenda began, "both had matches arranged for us. It's the truth that we spent a few evenings discussing how dreadful it was no' to be allowed our choice." She looked past Athena to where Symon was pulling his shirt on. "I do hope ye enjoy the opportunity to woo the woman of yer choice!"

Symon answered in Gaelic. Whatever he said, Brenda pressed her lips tightly together to stifle her amusement before guiding Athena down the passageway toward the bathhouse.

Athena discovered herself thinking something profane as well. Clearly there was a reason matches were arranged.

Courting was frustrating beyond belief!

～❦～

He could ride to London and contract with Athena's uncle.

Symon paced across the length of his study and realized he was seriously contemplating undertaking the journey.

But shame was quick to take a jab at him.

Was he not up to courting? He'd seen more than one man treat his wife poorly because he had never had to win her affection. Elizabeth Tudor had half the crown princes in Europe dancing attendance on her because the Virgin Queen of England would be a fine prize to win and her father had never contracted her.

Besides, he knew something earned was better than anything given. That was the difference between him and Galwell. Symon understood the value of winning Athena's heart.

But Christ, her uncle had done his duty tenfold in keeping her chaste.

He poured himself a measure of whisky and downed it before chuckling at his own expense.

Aye, she was a maiden in every way, and yet she had danced on May Night. She was not wanton. Passion was something she held secret against her heart.

He'd have to entice her to share it with him.

For a moment, he indulged in the memory of her turning to put her hands on him. So very comfortable with letting him hold her breasts.

It had been a victory, earning that trust from her.

All of the battles he'd won paled in comparison. When it came to claiming victory in a man's world, his confidence was firm.

Now, as he contemplated coaxing Athena into his bed, well, it was the truth that he felt like an untried lad.

Not bed... He wanted to coax her to wed.

He could seduce her. She craved him as much as he wanted her. Left to the moment, he'd have claimed her there on his desk, and knowing it was the solid truth shamed him a bit. While taking her might be a quick remedy to the situation, he wondered if it was the wisest.

He'd always known she hadn't come to her own decision to make him her choice.

He wanted that too.

Perhaps just as much as he craved her body.

And he was going to have it.

But first, there was Brenda.

Symon slowly grinned. Victory went to those who were wise enough to make a grab for it when the situation was right.

He was going to have to make certain his sweet cousin was distracted so he could finish courting Athena. His cousin was correct—he was more experienced.

And Athena wasn't the only one who had a passionate spirit. Brenda did as well, and she held it back just as much.

It was time to make certain Brenda was faced with a challenge to her determination to remain alone for the rest of her life.

❧

"Good morning, Mistress."

"Mistress."

"Fine morning to ye, ma'am."

Brenda's efforts had not been as effective as Athena had hoped.

The morning light brought the Grants offering her

nods and greetings. The retainers, who looked worthy
of any fireside story that she'd heard in her childhood
concerning savage Highlanders, reached up to tug on
the corners of their bonnets when they crossed her
path and did their best to smile at her.

The maids lowered themselves.

The older women, the ones who carried the respect
of their fellow clan members, offered her greetings and
called her "mistress."

"A fine morning to ye," Feenet called out when she
spied Athena using a ladle to fill a bowl with porridge
instead of going into the hall to eat. "Look what I've
pulled from the storerooms…"

A maid brought a stool for Athena to sit on while
she ate. The Head of House held up a chunk of sugar.
She sniffed it long and deeply.

"So sweet," Feenet exclaimed. "It will make a fine
tart for yer wedding celebration."

"We are not—"

Feenet's eyes narrowed in the manner that only
a parent's could do. She put the sugar down and
propped a hand on her hip. "I've never seen a pair
more in need of a blessing from the Church. Better to
take yer vows now before ye find yerself shuffling yer
feet in shame as ye seek forgiveness for falling from
grace. This castle is too large for Brenda to keep finding where ye and the laird have snuck off to."

The maids giggled.

Athena slipped off the stool, leaving her half-
eaten porridge behind. The Head of House merely
shook her head at her before shooing her from the
kitchen. "Mark my words, Mistress, unless ye leave

for England this very hour, ye'll no' escape what fate has decided upon."

Fate... Athena knew its hand all too well.

And yet there was something about Symon that made it all seem worth the blows.

She'd have never met him if it hadn't been for Galwell's treachery.

She looked at Feenet. "I will think upon the matter."

The Head of House bestowed an approving smile on her before she turned and began issuing instructions to the kitchen staff in Gaelic. Bright smiles appeared on the faces of the maids as the younger ones blushed and giggled.

Feenet clearly didn't have any doubt about what conclusion Athena would come to.

Well, the Head of House was correct about one thing.

It was time to make a final choice.

~

"What are we really going to do with her?"

Will Tinker turned and found that his men had elected Craig to be the one among them to question him.

"Well now," Will began as he looked past the stall he was hiding behind. Out in the distance, the old man made steady progress toward the towers. "We might discover who she is, see if we could truly ransom her for more than the merchant is willing to pay."

There were a couple of nods in response.

"If the family won't pay enough," Will continued, "we'll take her down to the Lowlands. A madam will pay better for a virgin there. In the ports where some captain will want to make sure he does nae get the pox."

"Give me that letter!"

Will ducked out of sight as Brenda came around the corner. She was trailing a young retainer who was nearly running to escape her.

"I cannae, Mistress Brenda. The laird charged me with the duty of seeing it delivered."

The woman growled and reached for the man, hooking her hands into his doublet as she tried to take the letter by force.

"Brenda."

Symon Grant was the one who called out to his cousin. She released the retainer and turned slowly to look at him. Will shoved his fist into his mouth to keep from laughing, for the way the red-haired woman glared at Laird Grant promised a fine show of temper.

"How dare ye stoop so low as to write to Bothan Gunn because I kept ye from deflowering Athena last night?" Brenda demanded.

"I do nae need permission to send a letter to a fellow chief, Brenda," Symon informed her in a gruff voice.

Brenda propped her hands on her hips. "Ye are avoiding the issue, trying to distract me. Athena has been here less than a week! There is no reason for ye to take such offense over her no' wedding ye just yet."

"I am no' the only one who needs to wed again, and we agreed—"

"I did no' give ye me word to accept Bothan Gunn," Brenda interrupted him. The retainer backed away, his eyes wide at the way Brenda was going after the laird.

"You are intent on ignoring the man," Symon replied. "Ye should have replied to his letter. The

Grants do nae need trouble with the Gunns because ye are negligent in responding to his offer. He is a chief, Brenda."

"I won't have him, and ye swore…" She slapped him in the middle of his chest. "Ye swore I would be me own woman."

"A letter"—Symon cut through her tirade—"is no' a contract. But I thanked the man for his inquiry and made it clear he must deal with ye on the matter."

Brenda was silent for a long moment. Will watched the way she pursed her lips before coming to some conclusion.

"And ye just thought to reply to Chief Gunn's letter today? I have had it all winter. Ye are trying to distract me."

Symon crossed his arms over his chest. "I will no' hurt Athena, and I will no' dishonor her either. Ye need to let us be so we can come to an agreement."

"Exactly why I do nae leave the pair of ye alone," Brenda defended herself. "The pair of ye cannae keep yer hands off each other. Once ye have her, she'll wed ye because she'll think herself soiled. Is that what ye want, Cousin? I thought ye said ye wanted something different than ye had with an arranged match."

Will tugged on the sleeve of his companion. The old man was coming back, Athena's blue gown easy to see against a newly turned field. Behind them, Symon and Brenda were still arguing. Will jerked his head toward the riverbed. It was roaring with spring runoff and would make the perfect place to claim their prize.

No one would hear her scream.

☙

Perhaps she was being foolish in not taking Symon's offer.

Athena had walked a fair ways from the towers when she stopped and looked about. The fields were being plowed. All around her, the Grants were working to plant and produce a harvest. The air was fresh, far sweeter than in London. In the distance, snow still capped the mountains, and the air was crisp.

Were the Highlands less civilized than London?

Indeed, and she decided she adored the difference.

*You mean you adore Symon Grant…*

Yes, no matter how illogical it might be.

Smitten.

Aye, that was the word for it.

And yet she realized something else. She was happy. At some point, she'd plucked a flower and was walking with it between her fingertips as she hummed, not a care in the world as she thought of Symon and the way he'd sent ripples of anticipation through her the night before.

It had rained throughout the night, but the sky was clear now except for fluffy white clouds.

A fine day for a wedding.

*For your wedding…*

She felt something shift inside her, filling her with a confidence she'd never felt before. Everything was completely right; her lips lifted into a smile as she turned and faced the tower.

She was going to marry Symon Grant before the sun set.

"Mistress…"

Athena turned. The older man was breathless, panting with how fast he was moving.

"Ye…must help…me. My little grandson…he's fallen…needs a woman's touch…"

The flower dropped from her fingers as she grabbed the front of her skirt.

"Up there…where me son is…"

The older man pointed with his walking stick.

Athena didn't hesitate. She caught sight of someone waving from the riverbank.

"Hurry!" The old man urged her forward without him.

She lifted her feet and ran. The river roared with spring runoff. The children had been warned to stay away from it, but the younger ones often needed more minding. Her heart was in her throat as she contemplated what she might find.

⁓

"I do want her to choose me of her own free will," Symon insisted, but he suddenly looked past Brenda toward the open door of the stable.

"Then ye shall have to give her time to accept ye," Brenda insisted.

Symon snarled before lunging past her. Brenda turned in time to see Athena running across the field. She made it to the riverbank without realizing Symon was heading toward her. A moment later she was out of sight.

"Come with me," Brenda instructed the retainer. "There's trouble."

⁓

The men were down in the gully carved out by the water's strength. They had on Grant colors and were leaning down near the water's edge.

"Let me see him…"

She was beside them before one of the men turned his face up to where she might see it. Her eyes rounded in horror as she recognized Will Tinker. A moment later, someone hit her with something hard across the temple. She reeled, stumbling back. In some part of her brain, she realized the river was dangerous, yet she preferred it to the gleam in Will Tinker's eyes.

"Athena!"

She looked up as Symon shouted her name. He crested the edge of the gully as the water caught her skirts. She pitched back, falling into the water. Symon's face blurred as she was dragged under.

She should have wed him the day before.

For now she'd never know him.

But he followed her. Diving into the water, plunging deep so he could clamp his hands around her. She felt his strength, but the current was far more powerful. Just as nature had always done, she proved her ability to bend them into submission by refusing to allow Symon to pull her from the grip of the current.

The water caught at her skirts, pulling so hard it felt as if her limbs would be yanked from their sockets. Her lungs burned, and the current tumbled her, bringing her up for one quick breath before dragging her down to linger in a long, drawn-out death.

It wasn't the pain in her body that horrified her. No, it was the way Symon strained and struggled to save her. She fought with all her strength, but the river was too powerful, and he would not abandon her.

He would join her in death, and for that she knew there would never be any peace for her.

꧁

"Get after them!" Brenda shouted.

The three retainers didn't obey her.

She turned a hard look toward them and discovered them grinning at her.

The young retainer from the stable jumped down next to her. He began to unbuckle his belt in preparation for dropping his kilt so he could enter the river.

But he jerked as one of the men ran him through. Brenda stared in horror as his body contorted and he looked down to see the tip of a sword protruding from his midsection, covered in his own blood. His lips moved in silent shock before the man who held the sword turned and dropped him into the river.

She needed to run.

But the other two men were on her too quickly. One of them swung a limb at her head. It connected with a hard thump that sent pain through her skull and down her spine. She fought against it, but the darkness claimed her, leaving her at their mercy.

꧁

Will pulled Brenda off the ground and slung her over his shoulder.

"She's the laird's cousin," one of his men warned.

"In England, she's just a wild savage Scot," Will answered. "And a beauty at that. We'll dress her in some furs and fit her with a collar and sell her. I know a madam who needs fresh entertainment for the nobles of the Virgin Queen's court."

"She'll not agree to such entertainments."

"Madam La Merci has proven methods of dealing with stubborn merchandise," Will informed them cheerfully. "In fact, she has some clients who prefer wild stock. Gives them a change from their obedient wives."

His men accepted his explanation, following him as he made his way upstream to where their horses were. Will tossed Brenda across the back of a horse and covered her with a pair of hides, making sure to tuck them up and around her feet. On the road, no one questioned them, their stolen Grant kilts doing a fine job of beguiling all those they passed.

Not the one they'd come for, and yet he had always been a man to accept what fate offered. Will whistled happily as he headed south toward England, where he would at last earn the fortune he'd broken trust to earn.

Oh yes, he'd earned it and planned to enjoy the fruits of his labors just as surely as any man out sowing seed. Had he killed? Aye. But how else did the lairds gain and keep their titles? Old Laird McGregor was a fine example of a man hiding behind a mantle of lies and demanding devotion from his clan all the time.

Was he disgraced?

No. Will had spoken the truth and been stripped of his colors for it. Well, he'd learned that day that the only thing in life that mattered was going after what he wanted.

Mercy was for the broken.

# Five

DEATH REJECTED THEM.

Or at least it felt like the very river spat them back into life after it was finished tormenting them.

One moment she was caught in the grip of the water, and the next she was reeling from a hard landing on a granite rock outcropping.

Symon cursed but yanked her up by the back of her corset. "Climb, lass."

She didn't need to be told twice. The harsh surface abraded her fingertips, but Athena grabbed at it and pulled herself up and away from the water. It roared behind them, a harsh reminder of how deadly its strength was.

Symon gained his feet first. He braced his feet wide and looked around. In the last of the light, all Athena saw when she joined him was a deep gully carved out of the land by the raging spring runoff. Trees teetered on the edge, their roots exposed as the ground had been eaten away.

Somewhere behind them, a boulder shifted, banging into another with a crash.

"We need to climb." Symon grasped her by the upper arm, propelling her farther from the water. "The current could shift back this way at any time."

As if fate wasn't quite content with allowing them relief from almost dying, a crack of thunder jolted them. A moment later, rain pelted them as a stiff wind chilled them to the bone.

Athena climbed. Her muscles ached, but the pain was a sweet confirmation of life. Symon made the crest of the gully first, surveying what was on the other side before turning to offer her a hand.

"We're in luck. There's a croft of some sort." He pulled her out of the riverbed.

In the dying light, she didn't see what he meant right away.

"There, lass."

He pointed to a circle of stones that had been built up. Upon closer consideration, she realized there was a roof covered in peat moss.

"No fire, so it's abandoned," he muttered. "Let's get out of this rain before we freeze."

"It would be a shame to die of cold after we managed to escape the river," she offered as a means of lightening her mood.

Symon didn't reply. He found the door of the dwelling and pushed it in. He peered inside for a long moment before nodding approval.

"No one's here."

He moved in and found a stone hearth. Someone had already stacked wood inside it for a fire. Symon struck a flint stone that was also nearby as Athena stared in wonder at the flames that burst to life.

"It's too good to be true," she whispered in awe, stretching out her hands to warm them.

"The herders keep these ready for when they are out in the spring with the flocks," he explained.

Steam rose off his kilt as he stood near the fire.

"I am properly grateful."

Symon grunted at her.

It was a sound of disapproval and no mistake. Athena turned wide eyes toward him.

"Do nae pretend to no' understand it's yer doing that we're here." He faced off with her. "It's a damned fine thing that I am no' yer husband, for ye need to be taken in hand. Yer foolishness could have seen us both dead this day."

"My foolishness?" she questioned.

"Aye, foolishness, and it's the truth that part of me wants to send ye back to yer uncle with all haste! Ye've already seen what Will Tinker would do to ye if he found ye helpless. I cannae understand why ye would try to leave alone simply because I told ye I'd wed ye if ye'd have me!"

He was furious. Symon ran a hand through his hair as he stopped to draw in breath.

"I did not…try to escape," she insisted, the fire forgotten as she faced off with him.

Symon grunted, clearly not believing her.

"That old man came up, saying his grandson had been hurt. I went with him…he was wearing your colors, and then I realized it was truly Will Tinker waiting for me, and someone swung a tree branch at my head." She shoved her hand into her hair and pushed it away from her throbbing temple.

She'd thought him furious.

Athena realized she hadn't truly seen raw rage on Symon's face until he focused on her head. He reached out and turned her so the light from the fire illuminated her face.

"What…" He bit back a word of profanity. "What was his name? The old man?"

"I don't know," she exclaimed. "He was using a walking stick, and I never thought he meant me any harm or would lie about such a thing as a child needing help."

She pulled away from him but only made it a couple of steps before he reached out and caught her wrist. Pulling her back towards the flames and turning her loose as though he had no taste for touching her.

"Stay by the fire, or ye'll catch yer death in those wet clothes."

"You're wet too," she murmured, hurt edging her words. "And you haven't apologized either. I am not so afraid of you, Symon Grant, that I'd do something so foolish."

"Ye're afraid of the way I raise yer passion, Athena." He reached out and caught a handful of her tattered skirt when she recoiled from him, pulling her close so there was no missing the way the shiver from the chill was being replaced with a quiver caused by his proximity. "For ye are a maiden, and it's an unfair fact that women are expected to remain chaste until they wed."

"Men are too," she argued, the brazen impulse too great to control. "I've read the Scriptures. Men simply don't obey because they are not the ones shamed when the wedding sheets aren't bloodied."

He hovered over her, his mouth just close enough

for her to rise up and press hers against it. But he didn't kiss her. Instead he held himself steady, watching as she felt passion catching hold of her just as easily as the wood caught fire.

"Aye, it's true," he agreed before releasing her with a soft sound of frustration. "And it's also true that I'd rip the head off any man who taught ye the way of being a woman."

She snorted at him. "And yet someone taught you how to be a man."

They shouldn't be having the debate. No, it was scarlet and unholy, but there was no way she could have held her tongue.

"I am not...*afraid* of you." She refused to be frightened. Athena turned on him and stabbed him in the middle of his chest with her finger. "I will not be bent by fear. Galwell thought to make me submit, but I will not, do you understand me?"

He captured her wrist, closing his fingers around it and turning her around before stepping up behind her and binding her in place. She felt his breath against her ear and his heart beating behind her.

"I understand ye, lass," he rasped out next to her ear. "I ken things ye do nae about what makes ye snap and hiss at me..."

She strained, but there was something in his tone, a dark promise that weakened her resolve as anticipation began to throb inside her. It was more than her insides too—the feeling was centered in her core, between the folds of her sex.

"I'll keep me word, but I am going to introduce ye to passion..."

She didn't understand.

She should have voiced an argument.

The words got sucked back into her mouth as he reached down and pulled a handful of her wet skirt up. His grip was so powerful that he bared her to her knees and then to her waist with a second pull.

"Symon…" Her voice was husky and shocked. She heard him chuckle in response.

He cupped her sex next. She let out a sound that was neither protest nor encouragement. She was losing the ability to decipher anything except the way it felt to have him touch her.

He was so hard against her back. The binding hold should have enraged her, and yet she felt a surge of need rising up, almost as if she enjoyed knowing how strong he was.

Like a confirmation of his worthiness.

"Yer pearl is here," he whispered, rubbing her mound gently.

With nothing between his fingers and her skin, one of his fingers slipped between the folds guarding her sex. He touched something there, the place that was throbbing, and she listened to her own cry filling the little hut.

"It's the center of yer passion, lass…the place where a man can move ye to ecstasy if he's wise enough to play the part of yer lover."

Ecstasy…lover…they were forbidden words, and yet she discovered herself eager to understand them beyond the boundaries of the word *sin*.

It couldn't be wrong to feel so good.

His finger rubbed her, slowly sending a warm flood of pleasure into her core.

"I am going to be yer lover, Athena…"

Husky and deep, his tone was a whisper next to her ear. Between her thighs, he was building a blaze of need, stoking the throbbing his kiss always started into a roaring flame.

She reached back, needing to hold him tight. She arched toward his hand, seeking more pressure and release from the need consuming her. Her heart pounded, the cold forgotten as he sent intense pleasure through her core. There was no thinking, only response, and her body seemed to know exactly what to do.

Strain toward her lover…

Her hips arched as she dug her fingers into his thighs, and suddenly everything was twisting and bursting in a pleasure that sent a cry across her lips while she writhed with the extremes of it.

Symon held her through it, stroking her pearl a few final times while she struggled to pull enough breath into her lungs to stay awake. Warm and satisfied, she thought slipping into slumber seemed a perfect ending to the moment.

∽✦∾

*Gordon land*

"Ye look almost civilized," Diocail Gordon muttered.

Bothan Gunn offered his host lowered brows. But he'd arrived in a doublet buttoned all the way to his collar and with his sleeves on as well. His hair was clean and brushed back, and even his boots looked free of dirt.

"Do not frighten my son," Jane warned Bothan as he continued to glower at her husband Diocail.

Bothan wasn't about to tell Diocail's new bride that he was the one more scared of their newborn babe because he was expected to carry the infant to its baptism as the godfather.

He had never held such a delicate creature.

But Jane offered up the swaddled bundle, the baby looking at him with blue eyes. Tradition dictated that the parents could not attend. Jane wouldn't be allowed back into the sanctuary until she had been "churched." Old ways no one was willing to defy in case there was truth to them.

The baby was a soft bundle. Bothan gathered him close before turning and moving off toward the door of the laird's chamber. It was his luck to arrive on Gordon land when Diocail's son arrived. He'd have been long gone if Diocail hadn't asked him to stand godfather to the babe.

It was an honor.

Yet he was preoccupied with thoughts of Brenda Grant.

At least it was still winter on his land. The Gunns lived much farther north than the Gordons. It would give him time to seek out the woman who had lived in his thoughts for the last year.

He grinned as he thought of her reaction.

It would be fiery, just like her hair.

Which only strengthened his determination to claim her.

The baby squirmed, alarming him. Ailis Robertson stretched her neck out to peer around his shoulder to check his hold on the infant. She didn't make any comment, which allowed him a measure of confidence.

It was good, in a way, that he was there to participate in the ceremony surrounding the birth of a child.

For he had every intention of ensuring Brenda Grant gave him a son.

～

"Ye're passionate, Athena, just like the goddess ye are named for," Symon whispered as he nuzzled her neck. "Ye need to get out of this wet dress."

He didn't wait for her to grant him permission. Instead he popped the lace free and pulled it loose.

"You are always undressing me." Her thoughts were still muddled, allowing the words to spill over her lips.

"It's the truth I enjoy it," Symon informed her smugly. But he leaned in, letting her feel his breath against her nape. "So do ye."

She did.

Her dress slumped to the floor. She stepped out of it, feeling her cheeks heat as her wits sharpened, allowing her to think about what he'd just done.

*What you thoroughly enjoyed...*

"In this case, we'll need to spread yer dress out by the fire if there is any hope of it drying. Stay in it, and yer underclothing will never dry while it's raining."

He had unbuckled his belt and had his kilt over his arm. He tossed it up over one of the exposed beams that supported the roof so it hung down in two long lengths of fabric.

"Give that to me." Symon held his hand out for her dress.

Still in her corset, she felt less exposed than she really should have. But hugging a wet dress to her wasn't the way to make it through the night. Outside the little stone house, the night was split open by lightning. Thunder boomed so loudly it threatened to shake the stones sheltering them from the fury of the storm.

"Thank God we got out of the riverbed," she said as Symon tossed her dress over another rafter and added a log to the fire.

He offered her a grunt.

"You are still angry with me." She knew it, could tell by the sound he'd made. "I told you I wasn't trying to escape."

"Aye, I understand well enough wanting to help someone who appears to be in need," he interrupted her. "Why were ye so far from the towers? And if ye intended to leave, why did ye no' take some of me men along? Do ye venture out onto the streets of London Town alone? Does yer uncle allow such?"

She'd been correct. Symon was angry with her. He stood facing off with her, his shirt starting to dry with the aid of the fire.

Which allowed her to see straight through it, since he was standing between her and the flames.

His cock was sticking straight up. Closeted she might be, but she was no fool when it came to the basic facts of anatomy.

Or how they fit together.

"Ye are a beauty, and I cannae see how ye would have been allowed to disregard the dangers of going wherever ye please without chaperone or escort. Me own father took a strap to me arse when I was a lad for running off because I thought it a fine jest." He grunted again. "Any number of things might have befallen ye. If I had no' seen ye—"

"I needed to think, for the last time I agreed to marry, I misjudged things so very horribly. I simply was absorbed with the idea of wedding you, and by the time I realized I should wed you, I was so far from the castle, and then the man cried out...oh... Henry taught me better...he did. You mustn't think him a fool."

Symon's jaw was tight. She drew in a deep breath and let it out, resigning herself to his distemper. He meant well. So she truly should accept his gruffness as a kindness, for he thought to protect her from the evil of the world.

Her temper didn't care to listen, and her eyes narrowed. "Just because I agree to wed you, Symon Grant, do not think I will become meek and obedient. It's the truth I am finished with being told where my place is continuously."

He reached out and caught her by the part of her smock that was covering her thighs, pulling her close and locking her against him with a solid arm around her back.

"Ye can be sure I will enjoy telling ye that yer place is in me bed, Athena," he muttered. "Over and over and over again."

There was so little between them.

Athena shivered, yet it was not with cold but awareness.

"I give ye me word I will wed ye the moment a priest is near to perform the ceremony." He cupped her chin and raised her face so their gazes were fused. "Do ye accept me word, lass?"

There seemed some great significance in his question. She searched his face, trying to comprehend.

"It's called a handfast. A time-honored tradition here in the Highlands. I offer ye me word, and ye accept. Any issue from our union will be considered legitimate by the clan. But do nae worry, we'll have the Church's blessing as well once I get ye back home."

Yet he planned to have her here.

Anticipation went tearing through her, making her realize she was not nearly as satisfied by their first encounter.

No, she craved something much deeper.

And so did he. His cock was hard against her; even her corset didn't hide it.

Yet he waited for her agreement.

"Athena?" he questioned her. "Did I hear ye wrong?"

"You didn't," she answered in a whisper because of how nervous she was. "I just never thought…to make such a decision on my own."

He snorted. "Ye just said ye had decided to wed me."

Galwell had been frustrated with her as well. Yet there was a vast difference in the way Symon looked at her.

He was waiting and would hold himself to his word. Honor.

He embodied it, and it attracted her to him in a manner she'd never expected to find in a man. Something shifted inside her, a certainty of some sort that made his embrace feel like the most natural thing.

As though she were exactly where she belonged for the first time in her life. Somehow, childhood was losing its hold on her, cracking like the shell of an egg to allow her to stretch her limbs and begin life.

"I did say I will wed you, Symon Grant, and I accept your word." She spoke clearly and firmly.

His eyes narrowed, and his lips curled in a very pleased expression. It was very male, and she drank it in until he lowered his head and kissed her.

Gone were the hard, insisting kisses he'd used before. Now, there was an unbridled feel to the way he claimed her mouth.

And she felt different as she kissed him back.

As though it wasn't forbidden.

She flattened her hands on his chest, indulging in the freedom to touch him. Never had she experienced such a connection between herself and another soul. It breathed life into the word *intimacy*, unlocking an understanding that felt like it was soul-deep.

He trailed kisses along her jawline and down the side of her neck. She let out a soft sound of delight as ripples of enjoyment raised gooseflesh across her skin.

"Do ye want me to shave the beard off?"

His question startled her. Athena opened her eyes and tried to force her mind to work.

Which wasn't what she wanted at that moment at all.

"I want you to stop talking," she insisted, tugging at his shirt. "And take this off."

He groaned and turned her around so he could get at the back of her corset. "I see merit in allowing a woman to tell me what to do."

"When we're alone, you can be sure I will not be submissive," she said, realizing it was more of a promise, for Symon's eyes lit with anticipation.

She liked knowing she could affect him in such a

way. Excite him as much as he did to her. Something shifted inside her, and she realized it was confidence.

But she was nervous.

Her belly did a little flip as she felt her breasts sagging with the opening of her corset. It was a relief in some ways, for she had felt bound in the thing.

Boldness.

Yes, and she embraced it with full consciousness of her actions, but that didn't mean she wasn't a bit uncertain.

Symon wrapped his arms around her, still behind her, giving her a strong embrace that steadied her nerves. The position afforded her a look toward the small bed the croft had.

"There is no sheet," she said as she realized the bed was little more than a wooden frame with rope strung through it to support a rough-looking mattress that was likely stuffed with chaff from the last season's harvest.

"Every man wearing me colors knows ye're a maiden, Athena. There is an innocence in ye that is plain to any man with a set of eyes in his head." He stroked her. Cupped her shoulders and rubbed her arms with slow and steady strokes.

She heard herself sigh.

"Brenda will no doubt enjoy setting straight anyone who dares to question the matter," he remarked.

Athena laughed softly. "Your cousin is a true force of nature."

"So our priest is often warning me."

Athena shivered when his hands reached her thighs. No one had ever stroked her thighs.

Symon did, flattening his hands on her skin and drawing them up her legs beneath her chemise.

"And you?" she asked.

He gripped her hips, sending a jolt of need through her core. Playfulness evaporated as hard passion began to rule her again. She could feel it in him as well, some understanding that was new and yet very keen.

"For although it is rough, I am enjoying knowing ye are mine and mine alone at this moment, Athena."

He scooped her off her feet, stealing her breath with the demonstration of how strong he was. There were times her trust of him blinded her to the fact that he was so very much larger than she was.

"I do nae want to share ye with anyone."

He laid her down, covering her as he kissed her.

Breathless and needy, she reached up and threaded her hands through his hair. Conversation wasn't what she longed for. No, her body craved an end to ignorance and an introduction to womanhood. He parted her thighs with his weight, and she let out a breathless little sound as she cradled him. Far from the awkward experience she'd imagined, there was a symmetry to the way they fit together. The way she knew how to move.

He brushed the hair back from her face, but she could see the way he clenched his jaw.

"Be done with it," she whispered, reaching down so she could get her hands beneath the edge of his shirt. "Enough waiting."

He liked her demand.

In a very male sort of way, his eyes narrowed, his lips thinning. He shifted, proving he'd been holding back.

Now, he swept his fingers through her spread slit,

teasing her pearl with the tips before slipping down to the entrance of her body.

She was wet.

But not from the water.

His fingertip dipped into a well of fluid that had seeped from her passage.

"Perfect," he muttered before he shifted again, easing his cock into position.

The first touch sent a jolt of awareness through her. It was so intense she couldn't remain still, and yet she had no idea what to do.

He did though, pressing his hips forward so that her passage stretched around the girth of his cock. She arched to receive him, her fingers curling into talons on his hips when pain arrived with a sudden intensity.

She gasped, but he thrust forward, lodging himself completely in her sheath.

"Christ," he gasped, his body shuddering.

Her fingernails had drawn his blood. "I didn't... mean to hurt you..."

He chuckled at her. "Scratch me, lass. Show me yer claws."

His tone was raspy, his body hard, and it was exactly what she craved.

Strength.

Boldness.

She lifted her hips, taking his thrusts as the motion kindled a renewed need inside her. The pain was only a dull ache, the motion of their bodies far more pleasing than anything she'd ever experienced. Her heart raced, everything but her lover forgotten.

She strained toward him, only to have him grip her

wrists and pin them to the bed by her head. He reared back, pressing his entire length deep inside her.

The look on his face captivated her.

It was full of lust, and yet it was tempered by enjoyment.

"Ye're mine now, Athena," he informed her. "Ye'll be me wife."

She wanted to watch his face but couldn't keep her eyes open. Nothing seemed to matter except lifting up to take his cock. Pleasure boiled up, nearing an explosive level. She felt her body drawing tight, and then she cried out as it all burst. It snapped through her, twisting and wringing through her core. The walls of her passage clenched around his length as she clamped him between her thighs.

He gasped and then growled as he hammered into her a few final times. His seed flooded her, completing the moment as she felt him quivering just as surely as she was.

❧

"Get yer cock too close to me, and I'll tear it off," Brenda promised Will Tinker.

He chuckled, but she saw the worry in his eyes. He was soft around his belly from too much excess and not enough work.

"What did I tell ye, lads?" Will boasted to his friends. "She'll be the wild Highlander lass; men will pay a great deal to try their hand at riding her. Perhaps we'll even get a nobleman to pay for the exclusive right to own her."

He snickered. But fighting against her bonds only

tore more of her skin. She felt the slide of blood behind her where her wrists were securely tied together. There was even a thick coil of rope around her body, which kept her arms tight against her sides. When Will went to shove a gag back between her lips, there was little she could do.

Once she was silenced again, he grunted with satisfaction and yanked the thick sheepskin down over the back of the cart she'd woken up in. It was small and cramped, the cart bed narrow to make it usable in the rough terrain. Will Tinker had bound her wrists to her ankles to fit her inside it. When the cart moved, she was jostled around with no way to protect herself.

But she would not despair.

It wasn't the first time she'd face a dire fate and prevailed.

∾

Bothan Gunn wasn't one to sleep when he had something that needed completing.

Or, in this case, something he'd decided to set his mind to accomplishing. First light illuminated him and his men as they rode out of Diocail Gordon's stables. Their mounts were well suited to the harsh Highlands. Moving south, he headed toward Grant land, enjoying the warming weather.

"Looks like they are riding out to meet us," Maddox said near evening.

In the distance, a group of Grant retainers rode hard. Bothan held his fist up, commanding his men to stop so the Grants wouldn't take their arrival as a threat.

"Ye've good timing, Chief Gunn," Lyall Grant

declared as he pulled his horse up. The animal had been ridden hard, making Bothan's eyes narrow. Lyall moved in close so his words wouldn't carry.

"What is wrong?" Bothan demanded.

"The laird is missing, and his cousin too. The stable boy saw them running down to the river, and then they were all gone, but there was blood on the rocks," Lyall explained. "A lot of blood. I'm riding up to warn Diocail Gordon."

"Symon's cousin Brenda?" Bothan asked.

"Aye," Lyall confirmed. "Tamhas has taken more men and gone down the river in search of them."

"I will join the hunt," Bothan declared.

"There is no time to waste," Lyall said. "They are the last of the line. There will be a bloodbath if we do nae recover at least one of them. I know there are those who would delight in such. I am no' one of them."

"That is to yer credit." Bothan kneed his horse forward. There wasn't time for conversation. He felt his muscles tightening as the fact that Brenda was missing pounded through his brain.

The woman had the worst luck of any female he'd ever encountered.

That fact only strengthened his determination to find her and take her home, where he could ensure she spent the rest of her days sheltered.

And in his bed.

He admitted to thinking about that part of the arrangement overly much.

And he couldn't wait to tell her so.

Athena sighed.

She stretched and let out a little contented sound. Someone stroked her face, easing her from slumber into the morning light.

"I would just as soon linger here with ye, lass," Symon said as he sat up and took her along with him since she had slept with her head pillowed on his chest. "Yet I must get ye back to the towers where I do nae worry about who might happen upon us."

She rubbed her eyes and used her fingers to brush her tangled hair back from her face. Light came from beneath the door, allowing her to see more of the little house. The outer walls were all formed with stones. Mortar had been used to glue them together, and the roof was higher at the center where tree trunks met to support the moss.

There was a musty smell lingering in the air. Symon reached up and touched the fabric of his kilt where it was still draped over one of the rafters. He nodded and tugged it down. It didn't pile in a wet mess, proving it had dried during the night. Symon was quick to start pleating it before laying it down and using his belt to secure it around his waist.

Athena felt far less accomplished as she tried to find her garments.

"Come here, lass," Symon teased her as he cupped her shoulder and turned her about so he could lace her corset closed.

"Your cousin enjoyed putting me in a dress I couldn't get into and out of on my own," Athena groused.

"Brenda was giving you time to come to terms with wedding me." Symon tied off the corset and reached up to pull her gown down. "Making it a wee bit harder for me to get me hands on ye."

Athena turned and gave him a raised eyebrow. "You think I haven't heard of tossing skirts before?"

Symon met her look with a smug one of his own. "Ye've no' tried it," he said wickedly. "The stain on yer smock tells me that right enough."

She humphed at him. "You don't have a right to insist on purity."

"I was wed before," Symon defended himself as he shrugged into his doublet.

Athena crossed her arms and sent him a hard look.

"Aye…well…as I said, I'd likely take off the head of the man who taught ye how to be a woman before me. So 'tis better to know I was the first."

She should have remained cross with him, but a bubble of joy stuck in her chest. No frustration seemed sharp enough to puncture it.

"Come…" He pulled her close for a kiss. "Let us find our way back to where we can bar the door of our chamber and debate any issue ye desire."

She kissed him back before following him out the door. He had to duck beneath the roofline. He turned and offered her his hand, tugging her into the morning light.

"Ye look like a pair of rabbits emerging from yer burrow."

Symon snarled, pushing Athena behind him. In the new light of day, the men on horses were easy to see.

"Who are ye?" the one in the center demanded.

"Grant," Symon answered.

The man tilted his head to one side. "I gathered that

from yer colors, man, just as ye can see I'm a Stewart. Ye're off yer land, Grant."

"The lass fell into the river," Symon explained.

"Did she, now?" the man asked. "Was that after ye ran her husband through?"

He looked over to the side. Athena let out a gasp, but Symon growled as he moved over to where one of his men was laid out on the ground. The river had removed most of the blood, leaving the young man pale as snow and just as lifeless.

"Christ," Symon muttered as he searched his man's face and then looked at the wound that had ended his life. "Sweet mother of God, I swear Will Tinker will pay for this." Symon pushed to his feet. "I am Symon Grant."

"Laird Symon Grant?"

Symon nodded. "Will Tinker is a disgraced McGregor and responsible for this work. I plan to see him answer for it."

"I am Domnall Stewart, in service to the King." He dismounted and patted his stallion on the neck. "We pulled yer retainer up here to bury him properly."

"I am in yer debt," Symon murmured.

"As to that," Domnall said as his men dismounted and began the process of selecting a spot to dig in, "I am charged with making certain the Highland lairds arrive in Edinburgh to pledge themselves to King James."

"I will attend to it once me wife is back on me land," Symon informed Domnall.

"Best she comes along as well. Young James likes to know his nobles. It's a fine trait in a king, to be certain."

Athena watched the way Symon stiffened. He

didn't answer, though; instead he added his effort to making sure his retainer was laid to rest.

He likely blamed her for the young man's death.

Guilt crashed down on her, and she didn't even try to avoid the weight.

If she'd taken time to consider that wandering off by herself wasn't wise, the young man being wrapped in his kilt wouldn't have been put into an early grave.

She knew better.

And even if Henry had failed to teach her of the perils of the world, she had certainly tasted the harsh edges of reality in the last few weeks for herself.

Symon had every reason to reproach her now.

Athena closed her eyes and focused on a prayer for the young man. At least it allowed those taking curious looks at her to think her eyes were red for grief.

They didn't need to know the true reason for her heartbreak.

And it was truly that, for now she understood what folly love was. The pain ripping through her was far worse than she might ever have expected.

She loved him, and he could not have a wife who took such risks with his men. The Grant clansmen would hardly welcome her back.

*Be careful what you wish for...*

How many times had she heard the saying? So very many, and now the meaning was clear as she faced the prospect of Domnall Stewart and his men. They were a force to be reckoned with. All of them armed and with horses. Due to her inattention, Symon didn't even have a bonnet on his head.

And the worst part of it all was she knew he'd stand

and protect her with his life if necessary because honor dictated he do so.

She wasn't worthy of it.

Of him.

The prayers finished, Symon turned on Domnall. "I give ye me word I will attend the King once me wife is home."

"Ye Highland lairds are doing a fine job of ignoring the summons ye have received from Edinburgh. The Earl of Morton sent them as does the King now. I've me orders, man. Ye'll be riding with us, no' going to take shelter behind yer tower."

Symon stiffened. "What is the point of having me give the King me pledge of honor if ye are calling me a liar right here?"

Domnall slowly grinned. "Fair enough. However, I will no' allow ye to ride down to Edinburgh with yer men."

"So ye would have me riding without protection for me wife?" Symon demanded.

"Now ye're insulting me, Laird Grant," Domnall insisted. "Me men will provide the escort and protection. Now ye can mount up, or I'll have ye tossed across a saddle."

The Stewart retainers circled them. Symon towered over them, but their sheer numbers would defeat him. He shielded her with his large frame again, noble in every action no matter the rage he must be feeling toward her.

"Symon," she muttered. "See reason."

He turned a furious look on her. Athena was certain she felt it burning through to her very heart. Domnall stepped slightly aside, exposing a man who held out a set of reins for Symon. He grunted and reached back to clamp his fingers around her wrist.

The hold was painful.

*Of course. You have proven yourself unworthy.*

Symon pulled up next to the horse and cupped his hands together so she might use them as a mounting aid.

She couldn't meet his eyes.

Those topaz orbs that fascinated her so.

No, she would not weep and make him feel guilty with her tears.

She was the one who was ashamed. The least she might do was bear up with the same amount of dignity he was. They would both prove their upbringing proud by presenting a composed demeanor to the world.

A noble front.

Like a dignified walk to the scaffold before laying your head on the block and stretching out your arms to let the executioner know you were ready for the ax to descend.

She would not shame Uncle Henry.

But in her heart, what truly fueled her determination was the way Symon held his chin high as the Stewart retainers closed in around him.

It was her doing.

He was a magnificent Highland laird, a creature who had earned his position, and now she'd landed him in the hands of his enemies.

Indeed, she deserved the guilt assaulting her.

And the heartache too.

For Symon Grant could never have a woman who had disgraced him so very completely.

Never.

# Six

JAMES THE SIXTH OF SCOTLAND WAS ENAMORED OF everything French.

The court was full of men and women attempting to gain the favor of the young King by playing to his current fascination.

Athena was having none of it.

"I said no, and I mean it."

The four maids facing her down weren't impressed. In fact, one of them giggled in a very arrogant manner.

"Your husband will like it...very...very much," the oldest of them insisted.

Fresh from a bath, Athena stood in a dressing robe. Beyond the closed doors of the rooms she'd been shown to were burly guards. Domnall had made it plain she would be staying in the chambers until she was summoned.

It had seemed a perfectly acceptable arrangement when a bath had arrived. Three days of hard riding had her ready to beg for the opportunity to be clean.

"You silly girl," the maid declared. She suddenly grabbed a handful of her own skirt and yanked it high to expose her own mons. "This is the way to be truly ready to receive a lover like your husband. Stop protesting like a virgin, and lie down. It does not take very long at all. A bit of wax, and the hair will be gone!"

"Yes, yes," one of the other girls insisted. "He will be able to lick your little pearl, and it is...*bliss!*"

If only Symon didn't hate her...

"You likely have fleas from all the riding on the horse," another of the girls added. "Your dress was filthy, as though you slept with the pigs."

That much was true. Between the river and the excessive riding, she had been bedraggled beyond comprehension.

*Fleas?*

It was too horrible an idea to contemplate. The maids read her indecision on her face, rushing her while she pondered the idea. They pulled her back to a couch, opening her robe before setting to work grooming her in the French fashion.

Thank Christ she had never wed Galwell.

Court customs were horrible.

❧

James the Sixth of Scotland was a boy of fifteen.

He'd taken control of his country only two years before, although Symon wasn't all too sure about who was truly ruling. Royal guards opened the double doors, allowing Symon into the King's private receiving room. There was a dais on one end where the King sat on a throne with a canopy embroidered with the royal Stewart coat of arms raised over his head. Two royal guards stood at attention behind the boy, their gazes fixed straight ahead while the young King gripped a staff in his right hand.

Symon lowered himself.

"Could you have not gone to see the tailor?" a man asked from where he sat on the far side of the room. He was elegant and old enough to be James's father. There was a faint curl of disgust on his lips as he raked Symon from head to toe. "You have come before your monarch in rags."

Symon straightened and looked at the King. "Yer men denied me the opportunity to return home and prepare for this audience. When they found me, I'd just managed to pull me wife out of a river."

There was a slap of palm against the armrest of the chair the man sat in. "You could have asked for a tailor to be summoned."

"I am a Highlander. The clothing a tailor here might provide is no' suited to me home." Symon tempered his tone with all of the patience his mother had warned him he'd need someday. There were times in life when you could be happy or right but not both. He might tell the popinjay mocking him he thought the man a fool, but the man wouldn't be there with the King if he didn't hold influence over the boy. So, Symon wouldn't find himself very happy at the end of the meeting if he offended them with a truth they didn't care to hear.

"Esmé, Laird Grant is clearly a frugal man. It is a virtue," James said quietly.

For such a young man, he was well-spoken. Symon expected no less of the King, for he had been crowned since before his first birthday and reared to sit on the throne he now occupied.

"As you like, James," the man acquiesced.

"Esmé Stewart is my confidant," James informed Symon. "He is very knowledgeable when it comes to the French court."

Symon held his tongue. Mindless chatter wasn't his strong point.

"All of the Highland lairds were summoned to court," the King said, "yet you did not answer the summons."

Symon felt his grip on his temper slipping. "Me cousin Brenda returned to me land after having been abused by the Earl of Morton in a most grievous fashion at this court. The truth is I do nae have much good to say about what happened to me blood here, so I thought it best to stay well away. Or do ye no' have enough men gathered out in the hall waiting to air their arguments with ye?"

James looked toward Esmé. The man lifted one hand into the air in a gesture of unimportance.

"Do nae dismiss the fact that I will no' hold with abuse done to the women in me family." Symon lost the battle to hold his tongue.

"Brenda Grant has red hair," James stated. "Many claim she is an enchantress."

Symon felt his blood chill. There had been rumors of the King's fascination with witch-hunting. It would seem there was truth to the tales.

"More than a few Highlanders have red hair," Symon answered. "And Brenda fought to escape from here. If she were immoral, she'd have stayed and tried her hand at enticing a lord into marriage. No' returned to the Highlands and her father's house where she is naught but a widow. She has only a modest life and is content. Those are no' the actions of an enchantress."

James nodded slowly. "You have sound reasoning."

Symon reached up and tugged on the corner of his cap. "Will ye accept me pledge of loyalty?"

"Your captains are not here to witness such," James said.

"As I explained, Yer Majesty, yer men denied me the chance to return home."

James nodded once again. There was something almost unnatural about the way the boy held himself. No lad of fifteen was so controlled. Someone had instilled composure in him, and Symon didn't care very much for the fact that he knew there was really only one way to force a child to grow up too quickly. Someone had applied the rod to him.

Often.

"You shall be given safe passage out of the gate. I will hear your pledge of loyalty when you return with your captains," the King announced.

Symon reached up and tugged on the corner of his bonnet again.

"Your wife shall stay here."

Symon froze. The King watched the effect his words had on the laird.

"No honorable man leaves his wife," Symon informed him.

"Of course not, but this is not an unsafe place," James continued. "The Earl of Morton was a rough man. However, this is Scotland, and the men here will not be governed by a light hand. He is gone, and you will make certain to tell your fellow lairds in the Highlands to mind my summons. You will not see her until you have done as I command."

James pounded his staff against the floor.

The doors opened, and the royal guards behind the throne aimed their attention toward him.

The audience was over.

James had spoken.

Symon fought the urge to argue. He'd stood against raiders and enemies without flinching; today, it took all his strength to back away from James.

He turned around once he'd made it out of the receiving room, turning and leaving the men attempting to escort him far behind because of how much longer his strides were.

The Earl of Morton might be gone, but there was still someone pulling the King's strings.

Someone Symon wanted to kill very much at that moment.

❧

"Ye do nae have to trail me, man," Symon growled at Domnall. "I heard the King."

Domnall stood in the stable doorway, his hands clasping his wide belt. "It seems so."

Symon checked the saddle on the horse he'd been given to ride and gave the animal a firm pat before leading it out.

"Me men will look after yer wife," Domnall said.

Symon turned and sent him a deadly look. "I find she's been treated like me cousin Brenda was inside these walls, and ye can be certain I will be looking to ye to answer for it."

Domnall didn't falter under the glare. "Ye have me word on the matter."

Symon wasn't content. But the King's word was final, and in a fashion, he understood it was better for Scotland if there was a strong ruler on the throne. It meant there would be peace, and he found that far preferable to having a war take him away from Athena once he settled her in his home.

He mounted and headed toward the main gate.

❧

"Oh *non*," one of the maids exclaimed. "Our effort is…wasted."

Athena escaped from the couch, rising to look out of the window where the maid was looking.

Symon was riding out of the gates.

"So sweet," one of the other maids said as she noted the tears slipping down Athena's cheeks. She used a fine linen cloth to wipe them away. "You are still enamored of your husband."

They fussed about her as she stared after Symon until he disappeared.

He was gone, and so was her reason for drawing breath.

Yet her chest expanded, and her heart was still beating.

Death was too great a kindness, it would seem.

She turned and looked toward the maids.

"I would like to dress in something simple."

They pouted at her, not approving of her choices at all. They frowned when she selected wool skirts over silk ones, pursing their lips when she declined shoes in favor of boots.

Practical and sensible. The two things she had departed London determined to embrace.

It seemed she was going to get her wish after all. How very foolish she had been.

❧

Athena still had the money Uncle Henry had given her.

Secured in her boot, it had survived her trip down the river.

She tucked one of the smaller coins into her bodice before heading toward the door of her chambers. The palace was an old castle, the passageways formed of dark stone. There were servants moving through the passages, their arms full of everything from letters to food.

Her plain clothing allowed her to blend rather well with them. Outside, the day was fair enough. She kept walking, joining the large number of people leaving the castle through the main gates. Beyond them lay the city. She'd come through it with Myles, stopping to do business before the merchant had decided to venture into the Highlands.

She finally had something to thank Will Tinker for. His numerous slaps and thumps on the head had kept her attention sharp during the journey, so now her memory offered up a good recollection of where to head. She recalled the inn where Myles had inquired about what roads to take, and she knew the men there had been for hire.

With a bit of luck, she'd find someone on their way to England who would be interested in increasing their profit by having a paying traveler along.

Truly, it was time for her to have a change of fortune. Fate couldn't be so unkind as to leave without a morsel of good fortune after so many harsh collisions with unfairness.

*Meeting Symon was worth it all…*

She didn't bother to argue with herself. After all, what was the point? She could hardly lie to herself. In her heart, she wasn't repentant. Even if she was quite certain she would see him riding away from her for the rest of her life.

"Well now…"

Startled, Athena realized she'd drifted into her thoughts so deeply, she hadn't taken note of where she was. The inn Myles had stopped at was a full two blocks behind her. She'd crossed into the section of town where women leaned out of upper-floor windows with their bodices open, displaying their wares for the men drinking themselves stupid.

"This is fine luck…fine luck, me boys!"

Athena blinked, but Will Tinker's face was still there, his eyes glowing with happiness as he yanked her toward him.

"One little word, and I'll gut ye as clean as a fish."

He jabbed the tip of his knife through her clothing so she felt it drawing blood. He held her beside him, taking her along with him as she looked around.

*For what? You're in Scotland…*

And all around her were rough-looking men with clubs hanging from their belts. They stood guard over the doorways of the brothels, while the madams attempted to entice costumers inside.

She would only be merchandise to them.

"How much?" A huge man wiped the ale from his

whiskers on his sleeve as he stepped into Will's path. "How much for that lovely?"

"She is no doxy…but a courtesan." A woman came through a doorway, her burly man following with his club in hand. "Come inside, I have lasses for you to enjoy."

The man grunted. He raked Athena from head to toe before he grinned and turned to follow the madam inside.

Will forced her though the door and up a narrow flight of stairs. One of his men lifted a bar off a door and yanked it open. The room beyond it was naught but an attic space. It was dark, and she dug her heels in, but he shoved her inside.

Athena stumbled over something, hitting her head because there wasn't enough height to stand up fully in the space.

What she tripped over groaned.

"It would seem I've found ye at last," Brenda Grant muttered, disgruntled. "However, I'll have ye know, my intention was to rescue ye, no' the other way around."

Symon's cousin was bound tight, a coil of rope wound around her body.

"Still," Brenda said, "seeing ye alive is the first bit of good news I've had in days, so I am no' complaining, even if ye did walk over me."

❧

Symon didn't go far.

He pulled his horse to a stop, indulging in a grin.

Domnall had his duty, but so did Symon, and there

was no way he would leave Athena in the place where
Brenda had faced so much abuse.

He started to turn his horse toward the woods
when a whistle caught his attention. A group of men
was coming down the road toward him, the pace they
were riding at kicking up dirt.

"Laird!"

Symon slowly grinned, recognizing Tamhas.

"Ye're a sight for sore eyes, man," Symon said as
the group pulled to a stop around him.

"As are ye," Tamhas replied. "We found a puddle
of blood on the riverbank, and more than one feared
it might be yers."

"Young Kory," Symon muttered with bitterness
rising up from his stomach. "Will Tinker used an old
man to lure me wife away with a tale of his injured
grandson."

"Wife?" It was Bothan Gunn who asked the question.

The chief rode near the back of his men. Symon
reached up and tugged on the corner of his bonnet.
"Aye, handfasted for the moment. The King's men
found us and forced us here to give me pledge, but
he'll no' accept it without me captains present, and
he's kept me wife."

"It would seem the rumors are true. James still thinks
to make the Highlands kneel," Bothan Gunn replied.

"I have no quarrel with pledging me loyalty, for it's
the truth I'm happy to see a king on the throne at last
after so many years of regents," Symon replied. "And
I'm grateful ye had the sense to follow me, Tamhas,
for now I can reclaim me wife. I was going to ride
back and steal her away in spite of the King's order,

for there is no way I'd leave her here where Brenda was treated so harshly."

"Where is Brenda?" Bothan asked.

Symon went still. "I have no' seen her, but she was with Kory when I went after Athena."

It was a grim thought, one he'd avoided because there was little point in worrying about something he could do nothing about.

Bothan's expression hardened. "Let's retrieve yer wife and deal with the King so we can find yer cousin."

Symon nodded.

He turned, feeling his confidence surge. It seemed luck was finally coming back to give him a chance at claiming the happiness he'd sought for so long. He refused to think about how much of a blow it would be if they never found Brenda.

His cousin had proven her tenacity before, and he wouldn't insult her by giving up on her now.

Brenda was a survivor.

She was a Grant, after all.

⁓

Athena tried to stifle her moan. But the knots holding the rope around Brenda were too tight to work loose.

"Damn Will Tinker," she muttered as she rubbed her fingers. Blood oozed out from two fingernails she'd broken in her attempts to untie Brenda.

"I'd sooner see him castrated," Brenda retorted, "and left alive to know it."

Athena looked around the attic space they were in. The window had its shutters nailed shut. She gripped the upper edge and tried to open them.

True iron nails had been used. They'd been driven deep into the wood, so all she glimpsed were the ends of them. There were bits of wood missing where other unfortunate souls who had found themselves imprisoned in the space had tried to used their fingernails to pry them free.

Someone was coming up the narrow stairs. Athena heard the bar on the other side of the door being lifted before light flooded in from outside.

"Move one foot toward me, and ye both can go hungry."

It was the one called Craig. He eyed Athena for a moment before he grunted and dropped two bowls and a jug onto the floor just inside the space. He shut the door and barred it, leaving them with only the faint light that managed to come through the crack where the window shutters met in the center of the window.

"Supper…how grand," Brenda muttered.

Athena picked up one of the bowls. "There isn't a spoon."

Of course not. Will Tinker had brought her to a place where they knew their trade well. A spoon might be used to pry the nails free. Edinburgh was where all the roads met. There were all manner of merchants in the town, honest and dishonest alike.

Instead there was a piece of stale bread stuck into the rough stew. It was stone cold, fat congealed on the top of it. She contemplated refusing it but forced herself to eat every bite of her serving.

Brenda needed the nourishment as well. There was a pinched look on the other woman's face that spoke of a very hard journey down from the Highlands.

"Here," Athena murmured as she used the bread to scoop up some of the stew. "You need your strength."

Brenda opened her mouth, making a face when she chewed the first mouthful.

"What happened to me cousin?" Brenda asked the question quietly. "I saw him go into the river after ye—"

"He survived," Athena was quick to say. "But… there was a young man…"

Brenda let out a sigh and closed her eyes for a moment. Despair was etched into her face. "He followed me…I saw them run him through, may Christ forgive me."

"I am the one who needs forgiveness," Athena confessed, "but I do not deserve it. So do not feel you need to temper your anger."

Brenda opened her eyes. "What do you mean?"

Athena toyed with the bowl. "If I hadn't walked so far from the tower, neither you nor Symon would have come after me. I know better—my uncle taught me to have a care. The man wouldn't be dead if it weren't for me."

Brenda's eyes narrowed. It was the reaction Athena expected, and still, it rent her already tattered heart once more.

"The same might be said of me," Brenda muttered. "I was so set on keeping me cousin's letter from going to Bothan Gunn…" She shook her head. "Ye do nae know the Highlands as I do—raids are common. I should have rung the bell in the stable, no' gone after ye. If I'd rung it, Will Tinker would be dead. Things would no' have been different for Kory though."

*Kory.*

Athena looked down at her hands, turning the bowl as she absorbed the retainer's name.

The bowl was brown-glazed pottery. She fingered the rim of it, noting the rough edges where a chip was missing.

Athena looked back at the window as an idea formed with the help of the meal in her belly. Reaching for the jug, she offered it to Brenda. Once it was empty, Athena used it to smash the bowl. They both broke into several pieces. Selecting one that was curved, she tested the edge to see how sharp it was and looked at Brenda.

"Well now," Brenda said. "There's something ye cannae do with a spoon, sure enough."

The rope didn't give easily. There was more blood on Athena's fingers by the time she sawed through it.

"Sweet Mary," Brenda muttered as she lifted her arms for the first time. Tears left streaks down her cheeks as she rotated her shoulders.

Athena looked toward the window. The curved pottery was sharp. She suddenly grinned as she moved toward the shutters and started to dig around the nails. The wood was old and splintered as she persisted.

"Ye're clever," Brenda said as she selected one of the other broken pieces and started in on a different nail. "Will Tinker won't be making pets of us just yet."

"Not while I draw breath," Athena remarked.

❧

Esmé Stewart contemplated the letter from his cousin. The Dowager Countess of North Hampton had discovered a very interesting secret. She was quite good at such things, playing the part of a devoted grandmother while listening so very intently to everything and everyone around her.

Land was the true currency of wealth.

And it would seem Athena Trappes was heiress to a rather nice bit of it, courtesy of a grandmother who had willed it to her female descendants. Since Athena's noble father had never sired any other children, the inheritance was hers to claim.

Esmé enjoyed the humor of the situation. Athena's noble kin had neglected to tell her guardian of the inheritance.

However, it was Stewart land, and Esmé was a Stewart.

And then there was the matter of Galwell Scrope and Lord Robert Leicester. The confidant of the English Queen was a man Esmé needed as a friend. Making certain Elizabeth returned to Leicester's side was worth the effort of intervening in the matter of Athena Trappes.

It was only business, however.

The sort that needed attention so his family would remain strong and he might continue to be James's best confidant.

She'd have to wed Galwell after all.

❧

"At last." Athena felt tears easing down her cheeks and realized she was crying with joy.

It had been a hard-won happiness, though. Light from the late-afternoon sun flooded the small attic space as Brenda pulled one of the shutters open. The last nail lay in Athena's palm. Her skin was marked with blood from where the pottery shard had cut into her fingers as she forced herself to grasp it.

But the shutters were open.

"Now we'll put that rope to some good use," Brenda declared in a hushed tone as she moved to where her bonds lay in a heap.

Athena looked up, spotting a rafter. Brenda tossed the rope over it and knotted it firmly. Will had likely not wanted to waste rope by cutting it, so he'd used the entire length to bind Brenda.

Now, it would serve them in reaching nearly to the ground. Brenda tied knots in it a foot apart before she looked to Athena. "Ready?"

"Yes." Athena looked out the window, searching the street for signs of Will or his men.

"The moment ye reach the ground, run," Brenda advised. "Do nae wait for me."

The other buildings along the street all had upper attic spaces with closed window shutters. It was a good bet there were other madams accustomed to breaking their new girls in with a little imprisonment.

But in the afternoon light, it was quiet as those who plied their trade at night slept before their customers came to seek them out. Below them, the house was quiet too.

"Tuck yer skirts up," Athena advised.

Brenda nodded before complying.

They locked gazes, determination settling into them both as they took deep breaths and Brenda picked up the rope. She tossed it out the window as Athena lifted her leg and went outside.

She wasn't sure she had the strength to grip the rope. Not that it mattered. Her need to escape was far greater. Athena grabbed at the rope with both hands while her body weight dragged her down toward the street below. The rope slid through her hands, burning them while she felt herself falling.

She landed in a bone-jarring heap, pain jolting through her body. She stumbled as she attempted to stay on her feet and Brenda came down nearly on top of her.

"Hey now…"

A man stood up from where he'd been sitting near the front entrance.

"Run!" Brenda shouted.

Athena reached back for Brenda instead, grabbing her hand as they took off down the street.

"I'll crack yer skulls!" the man declared.

He was close. Athena knew it but didn't dare risk a glance behind them. Another burly man guarding a tavern door in front of them rose up as they dashed past. The end of the block came, bringing hope, but she heard the swish of the club, pushing Brenda away as it sailed through the air between them.

"I am Brenda Grant!" Brenda shouted. "Touch me, and ye will answer to all the Grants!"

She aimed her voice at the men coming out to block their path. They were stuck, the man smacking the club against his palm as he closed the distance between them.

"Don't much care who ye be," he sneered. "I've been paid to keep ye in hand, and I am no' going hungry—"

Two hands suddenly appeared on the side of his head. Huge hands. They wrenched his head about, causing a cracking sound before the man slumped to the ground in a dead heap.

"Ye should have cared," Symon Grant remarked as he stood over the body. He looked past them to the others. "No one wrongs a Grant and lives."

Symon.

Athena blinked, certain her mind had broken, leaving her insane and imagining him there.

But he looked at her, locking his topaz eyes with hers, and she felt the connection all the way down to her toes.

He was real.

"Thank Christ," Brenda muttered, grabbing Athena and moving toward her cousin.

There were still men on the street, silently watching them as they decided whether to take Symon's challenge. Symon pushed the women behind him as the crowd began to realize they were dealing with more than just Symon. The feathers raised on the side of his cap made it clear he was a laird. They disappeared back into the shadowy doorways where the last of the evening light reflected off their eyes like rats in the dark.

Not that it mattered.

Symon reached down and clasped her wrist in his hand, his fingers wrapping all the way around her wrist.

All that mattered was that she'd freed Brenda. There was a victory in the action. Perhaps not redemption, but atonement at the least.

Symon pulled her toward his horse and mounted.

Tamhas offered her his interlaced fingers to use in mounting.

She savored the feeling of his arms around her, not caring about the tears that eased from her eyes. Pride mattered not at all. Only the stolen moment of being held close by the man she loved.

Because, of course, it would be for the very last time.

❧

"Where is Will Tinker? Ye'll tell me which house he took ye to."

Bothan Gunn asked the question of Brenda, although it was clearly more of a demand. Stained with blood and dirt, Brenda lifted her bruised and scraped chin and faced off with him.

"We managed quite well," Brenda replied.

The Earl of Sutherland kept a house in Edinburgh for when he came to court. The staff opened the doors wide when Symon informed them who he was.

"Athena." Symon turned to her. "Tell me which house he took ye to."

"So you can return and do murder?" she asked.

"Justice," Symon insisted. "Or have ye forgotten Kory so soon?"

She felt the blood drain from her face. "I have not. I would never forget that he died because of my foolishness."

Bothan had been facing off with Brenda. The Gunn chief turned to look at her with a question in his eyes.

"As much my doing as yers, Athena. Tamhas has warned me more than once about leaving on me own," Symon said.

There was a grunt from Tamhas. The captain was enjoying the attention of the servants who were eager to have something to do other than clean an empty house. A manservant had appeared with a gleaming tray holding mugs of cider.

Symon and Bothan ignored the refreshment, intent on only one thing.

"Ye go back down there, and Will Tinker won't be the only man ye kill—his friends will come out of the gutter to defend him," Brenda insisted. "I for one would just as soon go north where we can get back to living. This town has naught but filth and pain in it."

She looked down at her hands and started trying to wipe the blood off her fingers. Then she let out a frustrated sound before she pushed past Bothan and escaped through a doorway.

Bothan started after her. Symon reached out and caught his arm. "Give her some time, Gunn. Me cousin looks as though she's had a rough time of it."

Bothan wasn't content. His complexion darkened, and his attention shifted to Athena.

"I won't tell you either," Athena informed them both. "Brenda is correct. You will both end up in a fight. Better to return to your home free men."

"That bastard came onto me land and put his hands on ye. It cannae go unchallenged," Symon insisted, with Bothan nodding his agreement.

"It can, for Will Tinker is the sort of man who cares nothing for his name or word. Those who do business with him know him for the scum he is," Athena replied.

"Ye are me wife," Symon insisted.

She stepped back, uncertain as to what to make of his declaration. She saw the determination flickering in his topaz eyes, but her mind couldn't seem to grasp the idea. Not when she knew he had to detest her.

"Excuse me, Bothan." Symon spoke quietly to his fellow chief without taking his eyes off her. "It seems I need to have a bit of time with me *wife*…she's confused."

Symon scooped her up a moment later, stealing her breath with just how easily he took her weight.

She seemed to forget how large a man he really was. *Because you trust him…*

It was true and something she didn't lament, for he'd proven himself to her. Which was a good thing because he took her through a doorway and up a flight of stairs and into a chamber. Symon turned her loose before bracing himself in front of the closed chamber door with a look that sent a shiver down her spine.

"Ye…" he began softly. "Ye are me wife, Athena."

"Your people will hate me for the way I caused Kory's death," she began, dragging a deep breath into her lungs to steady herself and say what she knew was logical and just. "So…I do not expect you to honor the arrangement we had. I understand you must be concerned with your people's opinion of your wife."

He cocked his head to one side, his eyes narrowing. "What ye need to understand, lass…is that I have had ye, with yer agreement on the matter."

"Kory would not be dead if I had not walked away without an escort."

Symon offered her a nod. "He'd also no' be dead if I had no' decided to distract Brenda from acting as chaperone to ye with a letter to Bothan Gunn."

"You what?" Athena asked incredulously.

Symon's lips twitched into a rather smug grin. "Enjoying me confession? Good. It's the truth that I was trying to find a way to keep me cousin from interfering in me courtship of ye."

"I believe the word is *seduction*."

Symon's grin grew. "I was certainly hoping it would come to that."

And it had indeed come to pass.

Her cheeks heated. His attention shifted to where she knew her skin was turning crimson. His lips thinned, and she recognized the look of hunger flashing in his eyes.

It triggered something inside of her. Like a spark falling from a flint stone to a pile of tinder. The entire purpose was to allow a flame to ignite.

And she felt it flicker to life deep inside her belly.

Symon read her feelings right on her face. He nodded slowly before he began to come toward her.

"Wait…" It wasn't what she wanted to say. No, her flesh was heating for him, her nipples drawing into tight points behind her bodice.

"I'm going to toss yer skirts, sweet Athena," he promised her with a wicked gleam in his eyes. "And once I satisfy ye, I am going to strip ye bare and love ye until ye have no more strength to argue with me."

"You cannot—"

He was looming over her now. Something flashed in his eyes, a warning that curled her toes with anticipation. "I can," he rasped out, stroking the side of her face as he slid his hand back to clasp her nape. "And it will be me pleasure to convince ye to join me in passion."

He sealed her reply beneath his kiss. Symon didn't tease her with soft kisses. He took her mouth with a demand that froze her breath in her chest. It was searing hot and carnal in every motion. He pressed her lips open with his, holding her nape with a grip that kept her his captive.

Even if she was a very willing one.

There was no way to deny it. Need and hunger were living forces inside her; the wanton side of her nature seemed in tune with him, responding to his kiss just as surely as she would have flowed into a dance she'd rehearsed.

Instinct told her how to kiss him back, and her memory of their night together fanned the flames licking at her insides. Her clitoris throbbed, eager for attention from his hand.

Symon didn't plan to let her linger very long with need clawing at her insides. He pressed her back, placing her against a wall as he grabbed a handful of her skirts and pulled them high.

"Christ, ye drive me to madness," he whispered next to her ear. "Tell me ye cannae wait any more than I can…"

His tone was edged with the same frustration she felt. She'd just never expected to hear Symon Grant brought to the same level of craving as he reduced her to.

His hand was on her thigh, sliding up and down it for a moment. She arched back, sensation driving her nearly mad as it went racing along the surface of her skin.

"I crave you, Symon. God knows I should not."

He lifted his head, locking gazes with her. "Why does it distress ye so, Athena?"

"Because..." He gripped her hip, sending a jolt of excitement through her core.

"Because...why?" he demanded in a raspy tone.

He slipped his hand down and over the curve of her bottom and then along the underside of her thigh as he lifted it up so his hips nestled between hers.

"Why, Athena?" he demanded, his eyes flashing with determination to pry the answer from her.

"Because I cannot think when you touch me..."

A confession...

Her weakness...

His lips twitched in response, the glint in his topaz eyes hardening with purpose. His cock was hard behind the layer of wool that made up the front of his kilt. He'd locked her knee around his waist. Nothing mattered but the certain knowledge that he was pulling up the barrier between them, making her gasp as she lifted her hips up toward him.

The first brush of his cock against her slit made her moan. Her passage clenched, eager and needy to be stretched.

"What have ye done to yerself?" he asked in a hoarse whisper.

Her eyes had slid shut as the need to see became irrelevant to the way she wanted to just sink down into the moment of being taken.

"Athena?" He was suddenly moving back, reaching for the tie that kept her bodice closed. It popped open, and he plunged his fingers into the lacing, pulling the lace free so the garment opened wide.

She'd forgotten about the French maids...

"Oh...well..."

Athena found herself stammering. Her clothing was falling away. Symon tugged and pulled at her laces, determined to bare her. The light of evening still lit the room, making her shift away as her skirts fell down to puddle at her ankles.

"The maids at the palace were French, so they..." It seemed impossible to actually say. She stepped out of her clothing, slipping away from Symon while he paused to give her time to explain. Her chemise fluttered just above her knees.

"Show me." There was a wicked gleam in his eyes.

Something about the way he watched her filled her with confidence.

Or perhaps it was more precise to call it boldness.

She wanted to captivate him. He was huge and impossibly strong. Dark and dangerous even if her trust of him made her forget from time to time.

And his gaze was on her, his jaw tight as he waited for her to grant his request. She fingered the edge of her chemise, tugging it up to bare her thighs. His eyes narrowed, his lips thinning with hunger.

Vanity wasn't a good trait, but she admitted she enjoyed knowing he was captivated by her.

"Sweet Christ," he murmured as her sex came into sight.

"They insisted," she offered as she hesitated to draw her last garment completely off.

He moved toward her, cupping her chin and pressing a kiss against her lips. "Get into bed and stay there, lass. I'll be back in just a wee bit. Need to shave this beard off before I come near ye, or I'll scratch yer tender skin."

He turned and left, moving so fast the back pleats of his kilt swayed.

*"He will be able to lick your little pearl, and it is…bliss!"*

The maid's prediction rose from her memory.

Her cheeks flushed again, and so did the rest of her body.

She'd heard rumors. London was a town full of all manner of entertainments, holy and not so holy. Her uncle's housekeeper had taken to whispering a few things to her once Galwell had begun to court her.

Things a woman should know, she'd explained.

Athena paced around in a circle and found herself facing the bed once more. Lying down and waiting for Symon held no appeal, even if she'd have been put to bed after her wedding in just such a way.

No…Symon was not like Galwell.

She circled around again, taking the time to look at the chamber. There was a dressing table. Athena went toward it, searching through the drawers until she found a comb. She dug the pins from her hair until it fell down. Using the comb, she brushed it all out until it was a fluffy cloud.

The sun had set, the shadows growing darker. Using a flint stone, she struck it into the tinder pile and held a candle in the flame. A golden pool of light grew from the candle. Athena carried it to another candle on the mantel and lit it.

"That's how I first saw ye…" Symon's voice came from the darkness. "Lit by the light of fire and wearing almost naught."

He emerged from the shadows by the door, wearing only a shirt. His face was clean and the rest of him too. Water still glistened in his dark hair. It was a strange thing to think, but she realized she'd never seen his feet.

He chuckled softly and drew his shirt up and over his head. There was a confidence in him she envied. For he stood there, firm and unwavering in nothing but skin.

Well, she wasn't going to be a mouse…

Setting the candle down, Athena pulled her chemise over her head. Her hair floated down to rest against her back as she watched Symon take her in.

He didn't rush. No, he took his time, sweeping his gaze over every inch of her. His expression captivated her, filling her with confidence because she saw the approval on his face.

"I wanted to ravish ye, there in the light of the May fire," he rasped as he moved closer. "Ye enchanted me, and by Christ, I was happy to fall under yer spell."

He'd reached her, stopping one pace from her. She would have sworn she felt his body heat. Her skin was so sensitive that she sucked in her breath when he settled his hand on her hip.

"Ye wanted me to steal that kiss…"

Athena felt her lips curving into a smile. "Looking for absolution?"

His eyes flashed at her. "I'm looking for an accomplice…one to join me in mayhem—"

"You mean debauchery."

He flashed his teeth at her. "I most assuredly do, lass."

"Well then," she muttered, hardly recognizing her voice for how husky it sounded. "I must do my part…"

She reached forward and touched his cock.

He sucked in his breath, spurring her on.

She teased his length with her fingertips. She was surprised by how soft his skin was, but beneath that, his cock was hard and rigid. Hunger returned to gnaw at her insides, but she realized she craved the anticipation as much as the actual moment.

Perhaps he did too…

She closed her hand around his length, pulling and milking him as she watched the way his face drew taut. The grip on her hip tightened, his chest rising and falling faster.

He captured her nape and kissed her, his lips demanding, and she met them with a hunger of her own. They twisted toward one another, touching, turning, moving in a tangle of limbs and unbound hair.

Symon gathered up a handful and growled softly as he buried his face in the strands. She heard him inhale and realized she liked the way his skin smelled as well.

So carnal…

And yet so very enjoyable.

"Now, I am going to enjoy what I shaved for." He scooped her off her feet, cradling her against his chest as he took her toward the bed. With only the two candles lit, the bed was shrouded in darkness.

It suited the moment, for she craved the unknown things rumored to be lurking in the night shadows.

Symon didn't disappoint her. He pressed her thighs wide, slipping down her body so she felt the touch of his breath against the wet folds of her sex.

The first touch of his lips against her clit sent her arching away from him, not from the desire to evade him but from the sheer volume of sensation the connection yielded.

Her body was truly a mystery, one she had never guessed might be lurking for her to discover.

Symon chuckled, stroking her folds as he looked up her body. "The French do know a thing or two about being good lovers…"

"I don't want to know where you learned…those things."

His eyes narrowed. "I promise to make certain ye know where I am every night for the rest of our lives, Athena. For I'll be right here…"

He stroked her open sex and lowered his head to her exposed clitoris. She writhed, twisting and gripping at the sheet beneath her while he tormented her with his tongue. He started with long laps along the entire length of her slit, and then he closed his mouth over her pearl, sucking on it while she lost the ability to keep her cries to herself.

There was simply too much pleasure.

She cried out with it, straining up toward his mouth as she felt the moment of release growing closer. Symon took her to the edge of madness before granting her release. It broke in a mind-numbing burst of pleasure. She was trapped in the moment, arching up.

It released her, dropping her back down onto the bed where Symon was waiting to take her back up the peak she'd just fallen from. He stroked her first, using his large hands to rub her limbs and then cup her breasts.

"I wanted to handle these…that night by the May fire as well…" He leaned down, sucking one of her nipples into his mouth and sending a jolt of pleasure down her spine. "Truth is I feared ye might blacken me eye if I tried it—"

"You are twice my size, Symon." She threaded her hands through his hair. "I could never hurt you."

He settled on top of her, smoothing his hand along her cheek. "Ye can, lass. Never doubt ye have the ability to cut me to the bone with yer rejection. I'd no' survive that."

She went still. "I almost died…when I saw you riding away…"

His jaw tightened. "The King forced me. But it's the truth I turned around and came back for ye. I will never leave ye, even if it puts me life at risk."

She slapped his shoulder. "Do not ever risk your life. I cannot live without you. If there are times we must be apart, then I will suffer them."

"Tell me ye're me wife."

His voice was still low, but she heard the demand edging his tone.

"We haven't taken vows," she answered.

His hand tightened in her hair as he shifted so that his cock nudged the wet folds guarding her entrance.

"I'm no' interested in fucking ye for the release it grants me. I want more, and I'll no' have ye unless ye swear ye are me wife because ye consider yerself bound to me as surely as I know I am bound to the very bottom of me soul to ye."

"I love you, Symon Grant." She wasn't sure when she decided to say the words, only that they felt like they flowed from her, more honest than anything else she had ever allowed to cross her lips.

He pushed into her. She lifted her hips, welcoming him as her eyes slid shut. She didn't want to talk, she wanted to feel.

Needed to, really…

It was an obsession, one she knew she had to have, even if it meant her death once it was finished. He was hard and everything she yearned for. All of the heartache made her more aware of how very real he was, how much she needed to savor having him there.

She couldn't stay still. Athena wanted to stroke him, rise up to meet him, lock him against her so there wasn't any space left between them.

So they became one…

Was that whimsy?

Perhaps.

She didn't know and wasn't going to ponder it. He was what she craved, and by some stroke of luck, he was there where she might indulge in him.

Their passion crested too fast. The passion rushed them toward the final moment of ecstasy. But she didn't lament it because it dropped them both into a contented pile of spent flesh. True to his word, he wanted more than the release. Symon lay on his back for only a few moments as he labored to catch his breath, and then he pulled her close, gathering her up against his body so her head was pillowed on his chest and the sound of his heart lulled her into sleep.

❧

Will Tinker only survived because he never overlooked an opportunity to put coin in his hand. His men looked to him as they made their way out of the brothel while the doorman slapped his club against his grubby hand in warning, just in case they had a mind to argue with the madam over her putting them out.

"What now?"

Will contemplated the question as they blended into the men walking along the street. He suddenly stopped.

"What was he doing here?" Will asked.

"Who?"

"Laird Grant," Will answered. "And the English lass. I never thought to ask why she was walking this way. Where did she come from?"

His men didn't know.

"There might be coin to be earned yet tonight," Will said. "The Earl of Sutherland keeps himself a fancy house on the other side of town. Think we should go see if there is something to be learned from the staff. Something we might be able to sell."

It gave them a direction to go. Will did so with a happy grin on his lips. His fortune was bright because he was always looking for a way to shine it. Today was no different.

⤞⤝

Symon's belly rumbled.

He shifted away from Athena, tucking the bedding around her.

The sight of her sleeping so contentedly warmed his heart.

But his belly growled long and deeply once again, reminding him that he'd not eaten much. He doubted Athena had either, but she was too exhausted to stir.

He put on only his shirt before moving out into the hallway. Bothan was sitting at the table on the main floor. The Gunn chief looked up and waved him down to join him.

"The servants are clearly bored," Bothan muttered as Symon reached him. "They are trying to burst me at the seams with all this food."

The table was nearly full. There were plates of cheese and fruits. Fresh bread and honey. Symon lifted a top off a tureen to find the stew inside it still warm. He grinned as he filled a plate and began to eat.

"Ye appear to be more content with yer situation than earlier today," Bothan remarked.

Symon flashed him a grin. "To tell the truth, I did no' have enough sympathy for yer plight, my friend. This courting business is more frustrating than I ever thought it might be. Well worth the effort, though."

"I'm forced to take yer word on the matter," Bothan grumbled. "Yer cousin has no' emerged from abovestairs. With how eager the staff is for something to do, I do nae think to see her before we depart."

"Ye can wager it will be early," Symon replied. "Brenda will want to be away from this town as quickly as she might."

"And ye?" Bothan inquired with a raised eyebrow. "Is yer business finished here?"

Symon drew in a deep breath. "The King demanded I give him me pledge but only with me captains to witness it. He'll be wanting yers as well if he discovers ye are here."

Bothan slowly grinned. "I suppose it's a fine thing the King does nae know we're here. I've heard enough about forced weddings and other mayhem to set me mind against seeing this King until he's grown enough to have the sense of a man."

"If that's so, ye might not want to linger," Symon warned him. "This town is full of spies, and the men surrounding the King are happy to provide the coin for bits of information. I gave me word that I'd return, so I must."

"Yer cousin will need an escort home," Bothan declared firmly.

Symon sent him a hard look. "So if Brenda wishes to be away at first light, she'll have to accept yer offer?"

Bothan nodded, unashamed of how calculated his situation was. Bothan lifted his mug in a toast.

"Admit it, Symon, ye admire me for thinking that one through."

"More like I pity ye." Symon joined him in drinking. "For Brenda will make ye pay for it."

Bothan smiled slowly. "I am looking forward to it."

❧

Athena didn't want to wake up.

Symon had no mercy, though. He threw the bed-curtains open without a care for how she pulled a pillow over her face.

"Ye're coming out of that bed, lass," he warned. The bed rocked as he placed a knee on it and plucked the pillow from her.

"It's barely first light," she groused.

"Aye," he agreed as he shrugged into his shirt. "And high time ye made an honest man of me. Get dressed, or I promise ye I will bring a priest in here to get the deed accomplished."

She wanted to be cross with him, but his enthusiasm warmed her heart. Even if the floor chilled her toes when she stood. The morning light had little warmth to it as she went searching for her chemise.

"On second thought," Symon muttered, hooking her around her waist and pulling her back against him, "perhaps I am rushing things a bit."

His cock was hard against her bottom as he nuzzled her neck.

"Of course you aren't," she teased him, trying to pry his hand loose. "I couldn't live with myself if I knew you suffered a guilty conscious over my actions."

He nipped the side of her neck before releasing her. "Ye did enchant me."

Athena put her chemise on, pulling it down so she could shoot him a hard look. "You stole a kiss."

"I am a Highlander. It's expected." He knelt down and began pleating his kilt. "Me father told me over and over of the expectation of me position since I was a wee little laddie."

"I highly doubt he offered instructions on stealing kisses."

Symon looked up and winked at her. "Clearly ye did nae know me sire."

Athena tied one of her garters around the top of her sock to keep it secure above her knee. "Not when you were a *wee laddie*…"

Symon shrugged and lay down. He'd threaded a belt beneath the pleated wool, leaving a few feet of it on either side that he flattened over his front. He buckled the belt before rolling over and gaining his feet.

She doubted she'd ever tire of watching the way he moved. Galwell had always had his servants there to dress him and fuss over his appearance.

"Ye're thinking about him." Symon's voice had hardened.

Athena had been tying her boot closed. He cupped her chin and lifted it so their eyes locked.

"I do nae much care to know it, Athena." He'd gone somber, his expression tight.

She stood and stared him straight in the eye. "You should, for the only reason I think of Galwell at all is because I notice how very unlike him you are. And that I am grateful I have the opportunity to learn just how wrong I was to think him a good man."

Symon smiled slowly. She watched the approval flicker in his eyes. "Leave yer hair down, lass. Ye were pure when we handfasted."

He threaded his fingers through her hair as she tugged on the lace threaded through the eyelets in the front of her gown and knotted it.

Someone laid their fist on the door.

"Trouble," Bothan shouted through the door.

Symon was turning before the word sank into her head. He pulled the door open, letting in the sound of boots hitting the wood floor.

Symon was already at the bottom of the stairs when she made it to the top.

"Open in the name of the King!"

The servants who had so eagerly welcomed them the night before cowered in the corner, two of the maids hiding behind their aprons as if the fabric would shield them.

Brenda appeared beside Athena, a pinched look on her face. "Appears there is no end to the pain the palace will rain on our lives." She walked up behind Athena and began to braid her hair as Symon opened the door.

❧

"Domnall Stewart," Symon addressed the man standing on the step. "Delighted to see ye again."

Domnall offered him a smirk before coming through the door as though he was welcome. Symon couldn't really refuse to admit him, and it rubbed his temper to know the man knew it well.

"Ye are supposed to be riding to yer lands, Laird Grant," Domnall said as three of his men took up position in the room. "Yet ye are here."

"Me captains are as well," Symon replied. "So everything is in good order."

Symon pointed toward Tamhas and Craig.

Domnall considered the men, his gaze stopping on Bothan.

"Chief Bothan Gunn," Bothan supplied. "Laird Grant tells me the King is eager to meet all of his lairds."

Domnall looked up the stairs to where Athena and Brenda stood. "Ye were told no' to see yer wife until ye returned and gave yer pledge to the King."

Symon stepped between Domnall and Athena. "And ye gave me yer word that me wife would be safe. Yet I found her escaping from a brothel where the madam was set to auction her off."

Domnall bristled. "She'd slipped away by the time me men arrived at her door. Not that I expect ye to accept such an excuse."

Symon stared at the man for a long moment before he let out a hard grunt. "Athena has a talent for slipping away unnoticed."

Tamhas scoffed while Athena felt her cheeks heat.

"I'll take ye all to the King," Domnall said.

"We do nae need escort," Symon said. "I gave me word, man, and I will honor it."

"Yet yer fellow chief did not," Domnall snapped back. "And the last Gunn chief murdered one of the King's regents."

"I had naught to do with that," Bothan declared, his captain shifting up closer behind him.

"The only duty I am charged with is making certain both of ye appear before the King," Domnall stated firmly. "I am saddled with duty as well, but I see the wisdom in Scotland being united behind one king. The Highland clans need to be represented well."

It was a sound way of thinking. Even Athena recognized the sense in what Domnall said. England might have a queen, but under Elizabeth's rule, the country had enjoyed more years of peace than anyone remembered. Her rule had allowed men such as Athena's uncle Henry the opportunity to become artists and merchants. Even Myles Basset came to mind, for he'd never have been trading in Scotland if there was war.

She headed down the stairs, but Brenda lingered. Domnall looked up to where she stood.

"I must take all of ye," he said softly.

Athena turned, still close enough to notice how

white Brenda's knuckles were. She was stiff and frozen. She blinked when Athena turned to look at her, shaking her head as she seemed to break out of whatever had hold of her. She started down the stairs.

Symon hadn't moved—he was looking at Brenda, concern in his eyes.

"Are we going to stand here, then?" she inquired as she looked at Domnall. "I thought I heard ye say the King was expecting us."

Domnall reached up and tugged on the corner of his cap before one of his men pulled the door open.

"Aye," Symon muttered. "Let's finish this business so we can go home."

Athena liked the sound of his words.

She just wished she didn't feel the tension bleeding off all of them.

Clearly nothing was certain.

❧

Athena found herself staring at the boy sitting on the throne, so very still and sedate.

"Yer Majesty." Symon lowered himself and gestured toward Tamhas and Craig. "Me captains."

"You have not been gone long enough to reach your lands, Lord Grant."

Symon inclined his head. "If ye recall the circumstance of how I came to be before ye in the first place, I'd gone into the river after me wife. Me men were searching for me. We met on the road."

James shifted his attention to Athena. "Are you a Catholic?"

Athena felt a shiver race down her spine. The

tension between Catholic and Protestant churches was just as high in Scotland as it was in England. Blood was spilt often over the rift in faith.

"No, I am not." She spoke quietly as she lowered herself.

"Then how is it," Esmé Stewart asked from where he sat off to one side, "how is it that you claim to be wed?"

"We're handfasted," Symon declared firmly, looking straight at the King. "A time-honored tradition in Scotland. She is me wife, the union consummated."

"And I stand witness to the union," Bothan Gunn added. "In the Highlands, couples often have to wait for a member of the clergy to be available. A man is bound by his word before other men."

"Me pledge of loyalty would be worth naught to ye, Yer Majesty, if me pledge to Athena is considered nothing."

"There is no contract," Esmé declared. "And she is a Stewart."

Everyone looked at her. Athena held her chin steady and stared straight back at the King. "My sire was a Stewart who abandoned me when I was born a female. My mother died in childbed, and my father's family left me to the mercy of my uncle. Never once has my sire's blood given so much as a silver penny for my care."

"You are legitimate," the King stated.

"What matters is the land left to you by your grandmother," Esmé insisted, "and the contract you have with Galwell Scrope."

Athena felt the breath freeze in her lungs.

"A contract he never finished," Athena declared. "He claimed his father was making him a grander match."

"He did not know about the land dowry," Esmé informed her.

"I have never heard of it either," Athena admitted.

"You must return to England and wed Galwell," Esmé insisted.

"Did ye no' hear me?" Symon growled. "Our union is consummated."

"Yet not blessed by the Church," Esmé answered "And she would have to convert before you can be married. Better to send her back to England where she can wed within her own faith and you can find a wife within your faith."

"Me pledge is worth nothing to ye," Symon informed the King, "if me word to Athena is no' respected. Ye are me king. Do nae take me wife from me."

Esmé started to speak. The King held up his hand. He was thinking the matter through, and Esmé didn't appear pleased by the fact that James wasn't doing exactly what he wanted.

"I will confer with my counselors," James said at last. "Domnall Stewart, you shall make certain Athena does not wander from her chambers this time. I expect her to be there when I send for her."

He lifted his staff and stamped it against the floor.

Symon didn't want to leave. His body was tight, and the guards behind the dais James sat on moved forward.

Bothan pulled him away at last. Outside the doors, Domnall and his men were ready, giving them no time to escape.

*Be careful what you wish for…*

Athena felt sick as she realized she might just get to wed Galwell as she'd thought she wanted.

❧

"Bleeding Christ," Symon swore the moment they were behind closed doors.

"Agreed," Bothan responded.

They both paced around the chambers they'd been shown to. Their captains looked around the stone walls with critical eyes.

Maddox whistled as he pointed at a window.

Bothan grunted. "I cannae leave while Brenda is here."

"Domnall is no fool," Symon growled. "He'll take Brenda and Athena deeper into the palace." He moved closer to the window. "Even still, I will no' sit here and wait for that cursed French man to take me wife."

"I never intended ye to."

Symon whipped around. Domnall was standing inside the chamber.

"Ye are clearly a fool," Symon declared softly, "to face me behind closed doors. I've no' a kind thought in me head for ye. Me wife would no' be here if ye had no' insisted on bringing us here."

Bothan grabbed Symon before he lunged at the Stewart retainer.

"I am loyal to the King," Domnall declared, "but Esmé Stewart, well, he's another matter."

Symon went still. "Explain."

"That Frenchman is unnatural," Domnall declared

with a sneer of disgust. "And too friendly with the King for my liking."

"Just what we need," Bothan growled. "A king who buggers boys."

"James is too young to understand what he wants," Domnall said, clearly trying to dredge up hope for the future. "Trust me, there are men working to separate him from the influence of Esmé Stewart."

"Are they planning to take action today?" Symon demanded. "Because if they aren't, ye're wasting me time, man, for the King is thinking to send me wife back to a man who tried to force her to become his mistress."

"The King ordered me to keep yer wife in her chambers." Domnall declared. "But he did no' tell me she could no' have visitors."

Symon shared a hard look with the man.

"Me men are instructed to keep her in those chambers," Domnall explained. "But if a priest were to come to offer her solace, he'd be allowed in. Me men will no' allow ye in—there is no way to know who is in the pay of Esmé Stewart, but I will no' stand by while he plays his games. I brought ye here because I was bound by duty, no' so that Frenchman can find ways to become richer." He sent Symon a hard look. "Do nae get caught. So long as I do nae know ye are missing, I have no reason to look for ye. So leave a few of yer men here for when yer supper arrives. The kitchen staff is full of those willing to sell information."

"Ye might have to let the man live," Bothan said once the door was closed.

Symon sent him a deadly look. "Brenda is here as well."

Bothan's expression darkened. "These walls are pressing in on me."

Symon nodded. But the thought of escaping the room didn't do much to improve his demeanor. His freedom meant little when Athena was a captive. He'd free her.

Even if it cost him his life.

⁓

The day crept by.

Oh, the chambers Athena and Brenda had been shown to were spacious and well stocked with amusements for them.

There was no possible way she might settle in to read a book, though.

"Symon won't allow them to send you back," Brenda said.

"I don't think the King will take disobedience very well," Athena responded. "I'd rather go than see Symon facing consequences." She locked gazes with Brenda. "I couldn't bear it."

"Ye truly did nae know of the land?" Brenda asked.

Athena shook her head. "I wager Galwell would never have tried to force me to be his mistress if he'd known. In truth, it's a blessing, for I would have wed him willingly. I never suspected how foul his character truly was."

Brenda smiled ruefully. "Many a man hides a black heart. And then there are plenty who wear their sordid ways proudly."

"I will no' leave ye here, Brenda."

Athena jumped. She would have shrieked, but Symon clamped a hand over her mouth, pulling her back against his hard body.

"Easy lass," he cooed against her ear.

Brenda had frozen, but she'd flattened a hand over her own mouth to remain silent.

"Where…did you come from?" Athena demanded.

Symon flashed her a smug grin. "Have ye no' learned yet that I will find ye, lass?"

Bothan Gunn watched them with a grin on his lips. But he melted back against a wall when someone pounded on the door.

Symon hid behind the arched opening that led to the bedchambers beyond the receiving chamber.

"Ye've a visitor," one of the men guarding her door said as he pushed it open. He looked at whoever was waiting to enter. "Just the priest," he said. "The rest of ye can stay out here."

Tamhas and Maddox tugged on the corners of their caps as they caught her eye. The two captains clasped their wide belts as the priest came through the doors and the guards closed them firmly.

"They allowed you in," Athena said.

"Domnall's orders are to keep ye in," Symon explained, "so we'll have to get married right here."

The expression on the priest's face told her he knew what he was there for.

It was what she longed for…

"We shouldn't."

Symon tilted his head to one side, looking at her incredulously.

"Your king might be angry if we wed without his

permission," Athena explained in a rush. "Elizabeth Tudor banished her favorite Robert Leicester—"

"Banishment would be a fine gift," Bothan declared, earning a snort from Brenda.

"He could have you hanged for treason," Athena declared. "I couldn't bear it."

"Wedding you isn't treason," Symon argued.

"This is about land," Athena shot back. "Blood is spilled over land, and you know it. Don't be a fool."

"I became a fool the moment I laid eyes on ye, Athena." Symon caught her hand, pulling her to a stop. "Ye're right about Esmé Stewart. The man is motivated by greed. But I have faith in me king."

And she couldn't bear to ask him to abandon that faith. No, it was part of him. She nodded, and he pulled her next to him as he turned them to face the priest.

For better or worse, they were getting married.

❧

"Why are you hesitating?" Esmé asked James. "It is a matter of noble land remaining in noble hands."

"The Highland lords are noble," the Earl of Gowrie insisted as he pointed at the Frenchman. "Do nae advise the King to offend half his country."

Esmé glowered. "She must be returned. It is Stewart land."

"Land changes hands in marriage," Gowrie insisted.

"But they are not truly wed." Esmé was unwilling to yield on the matter.

The Earl of Angus slapped his hand down on the table. "A handfast is a wedding in the Highlands. This is Scotland. Mary tried to force it to become France, and she lost her crown for it. England has tried to destroy us a few times as well."

"Esmé has a good point," James spoke up. "Since they have not been wed yet, and the girl did have a contract with Galwell, perhaps she should be returned to honor her word."

"Ye'll insult Laird Grant if ye do," Gowrie insisted. "He's declared her his wife and done it in front of Chief Gunn."

"So the King should cower anytime one of these Highland lords declares something?" Esmé asked with a smirk. "Those lords need to unite under your rule, James. They still cling to the Catholic faith and their clans. You must make it clear you rule Scotland."

"It sounds to me as though ye are making certain we all understand that whatever ye advise the King to do, he will," Gowrie declared. "We've had enough regents, man."

"My Lord Gowrie," James admonished the earl, "Esmé Stewart is a valued adviser."

"He is no' a Scotsman," Gowrie spoke gravely. "For all that ye do nae care to hear me say it so plainly, understand I am no' a coward. I'm speaking plainly to ye, saying the things others are whispering behind yer back. I watched yer mother lose her crown because she could nae see the necessity of maintaining unity. Send that girl back to England for the sake of his family fortune, and there will be resentment over the matter."

"A great deal of it," Angus added. "Symon Grant is laird and the last of his line. It sounds to me as though this Galwell Scrope did nae even want to wed the girl until he learned of the land."

"She did say he tried to make her his mistress," James said. "I believe we need to hear more of the matter." He lifted his hand, and one of the men behind him came forward. "Bring Mistress Athena Trappes to me here."

The man inclined his head before he left.

❧

"Ye're me wife now," Symon declared as the priest finished. "No one can argue the matter."

Bothan slowly grinned. "There is the matter of the consummation."

Athena sent him a look intended to shame him. Brenda beat her to it though. "Trust a man to think that is the most important part of a wedding."

Bothan folded his arms over his chest. "Ye cannae beget children without it, lass."

The priest frowned at Bothan. The Gunn chief cleared his throat and tugged on the corner of his bonnet. "My apologies."

The priest made the sign of the cross over him.

Someone knocked and pushed the door in without waiting.

Four royal guards stood in the open doorway, staring at Symon and Bothan, the men at the door sputtering.

"The King will know of this," one of them growled.

"I hope so," Symon answered. "Sincerely I do."

❧

"Annul it," Esmé insisted. "On the grounds of prior contract."

"Galwell Scrope broke the contract," Athena spoke

up. She was taking a risk, for there were plenty of men in the room who believed a woman should be silent until spoken to.

The look the King sent her said he was one of them.

She held her hands up to him, adopting a more submissive posture. "Should I not take him at his word, Your Majesty? Should I not seek a union that is in accordance with God's law? Galwell Scrope demanded I become his mistress."

There was a soft clearing of a throat. James looked toward the minister sitting at the table with his counselors. "Virtue is to be respected and encouraged."

James nodded before looking toward Symon. "Why did you disobey me, Lord Grant?"

Symon tilted his head and sent the King a steady glance. "I explained it to ye, Sire. We handfasted, which means I was honor bound to wed the lass as soon as a priest was available. That moment was today. I do nae shirk from me duty."

The King drew back in his chair for a moment. "I see."

"This is nonsense," Esmé spat out.

"Keeping me word is something I consider far more important than worrying about how ye are going to respond," Symon informed Esmé.

"You simply want the land now that you know about it." Esmé sniffed.

"That is possible," James said.

Athena felt the muscles in her neck tighten. He was so young, and yet everyone in the room would do whatever he said.

Their fate truly was in his young hands.

The evening service bells began to toll. The minister stood and inclined his head before striding off to disappear into the passageway, obedient to the call to prayer.

"This matter will be decided in the morning," James informed them all solemnly.

The royal guards pushed them back in response, moving them beyond the King's receiving chamber. Two huge doors were pushed closed the moment they were past them.

But as those doors closed, Esmé Stewart sent her a look that chilled her blood.

❧

"Where did ye get that?" Brenda asked.

Athena looked up and let her skirt flutter back down. "My uncle Henry made sure to give me some coin before he sent me on the road with Myles. In case I had need of it."

She held up the gold angel.

Brenda smiled slowly before she lifted her foot and braced it on a bench. She pulled her skirt aside and dug beneath her own garter to retrieve a coin. "It's wise advice." She flipped the coin toward Athena. "Use that one and keep the gold. We might need that gold later."

"You didn't ask me what I planned to do."

Brenda sent her a knowing look. "Ye love Symon, I see it in yer eyes. It's certain he can't come to ye, so ye are going to him. He'd advise me to talk ye out of it, mind ye."

Athena sent Brenda a hard look. It earned her a chuckle from Brenda.

"I am going," Athena informed her firmly. "If your king sends me back to Galwell tomorrow, I won't go having wasted my last night with the man I love."

Brenda took a length of linen from where it lay on the tabletop after they'd removed the bread that had been delivered for their supper. "Best cover that hair of yers. It's quite unique in color. The guards will spot ye if ye don't."

Brenda tied and tucked the linen around Athena's hair. She stood back and contemplated her work.

"Try yer luck," Brenda said.

Athena turned toward the door. Determination so hot flashed through her that she almost felt her will would be enough to make the man standing outside their door agree to her wishes.

She opened the door and found herself facing a very large man. He tilted his head down and sent her a glare.

"I want to see my husband," she said as she held up the coin. "It may well be our last chance to be together."

Something flickered in the guard's eyes, and he looked at his companion, who looked both ways before shrugging. "Esmé Stewart needs to go back to France if ye ask me, no' increase his holdings here. Take her to see her husband."

❦

Brenda smiled as the door closed and Athena remained on the other side of it. So strange to discover something good happening inside the castle.

She had never known anything but pain within these walls.

She lifted her foot and placed it on the bench once

more. This time, she pulled a dagger from where it was strapped to her thigh. Too many things had happened inside the stone walls for her to sleep.

Instead she moved to a chair in the corner and sat down. The dagger was a good companion as the candle burned low.

❧

"The King might decide in yer favor," Bothan said softly.

"I do nae care for the odds," Symon grumbled.

Bothan grunted. "The odds against us making it past those guards now are far worse." He reached to the center of the table and picked up part of a round of bread that was sitting there. "Do yerself a favor, lad. Eat while ye can, for who knows what fate will give ye tomorrow."

The door suddenly opened without any warning. The benches went skidding back as both Symon and Bothan stood. The guard shoved someone through and pulled the door shut.

"Christ, Athena," Symon growled. "What are ye doing?"

Athena blinked, enjoying the moment of victory. Her husband was glaring at her though. "I'm spending the night with you. And don't pretend you wouldn't be so bold as to bribe a guard so you could join me. The King will find it harder to annul a consummated union."

"Ye cannae trust the guards here. He might have taken yer bribe and raped ye in some storeroom where there were no witnesses and no one close enough to hear ye cry," Symon reprimanded her.

She lifted her chin and shot him a hard look.

Bothan Gunn started laughing. It started as a chuckle and turned into full belly-shaking amusement that had him sitting back down on the bench.

"Ye are no' helping," Symon informed his friend.

Bothan's mouth settled into a smirk that he aimed at Symon without a shred of remorse. "She's worth keeping. If ye do nae see the fire in her as something to treasure, perhaps I should try me hand at stealing her from ye."

Athena took a step back.

But Symon snorted at his friend. "Well spoken." A moment later he turned and looked at her. She caught her breath because in his eyes was a hard glint of need.

It was lust.

And she adored the sight of it.

Boldness snaked through her, destroying any last bits of reservation she might have had over being so very blunt in exactly why she was there. Let Bothan Gunn know they were going to bed.

They were married, after all.

Yet there was nothing submissive about her feelings about her position as wife. Symon captured her hand, enclosing it in his larger one before tugging her toward the doors at the back of the room.

The doors opened into a private dressing chamber. Symon kept going until he'd reached the set of doors in the back of that room, which opened into a bedchamber.

"Do ye have any idea how much I enjoy knowing ye came to me when others knew yer intentions?" He was standing in front of the closed doors, working the buttons of his doublet and then shrugging out of the garment. "Or how much I want to scold ye for taking the risk?" he continued.

"Do you understand how important it is for me not to waste what might be our last night together?" she countered, reaching up to pull the linen off her head.

"If the King sends ye to England, I will come for ye." His tone hardened with resolve.

"You will not." Athena forced the words past her lips. Symon tossed his kilt aside, his expression darkening. "You will not put your life at risk."

"The King will no' send troops into the Highlands, and I would no' be the first Highlander to suffer the displeasure of the King."

"The Duke of Norfolk thought the same way, thought himself beyond the Queen's reach in the North," Athena answered as she pulled the lace from the eyelets on the front of her bodice. "Elizabeth had him beheaded and his title tainted. Do you wish that on our children?"

"I wish there to be children that are ours, Athena!" He caught her up against him, pressing a kiss against her mouth to silence her.

She wouldn't lie—it was exactly what she craved. Him.

He lifted her out of the puddle of her clothing, using all of the strength she adored to carry her to the bed.

She pulled him down with her, unwilling to allow him to pull his shirt off. Instead, she pushed at it, kissing him back and rolling him onto his back as she came up on top of him.

"You will not put your life at risk, Symon Grant!"

She lifted up and came down on his cock. It was hard and blunt, and she sucked in a deep breath as he cupped her hips, guiding her.

Her heart pounded with the need to move faster, to ride him just as hard and fast as he'd taken her. She wanted him to know she would demand him and take him too.

"Look at me!" he growled.

She opened her eyes and gasped. Pleasure blazed in his eyes.

A moment later, he was rolling her beneath him, earning a snarl of defiance from her.

He chuckled at her. "Ye are mine, and I am going to claim ye now."

He thrust hard into her spread body, pushing her closer to climax as she lifted up to take every last bit of his length. Climax rushed toward her, but she kept her eyes open, watching as his narrowed and his jaw clenched.

His seed released a moment before her own pleasure crested. She felt her body clenching around him, witnessed the way his face contorted with release. It all combined into a moment of sheer intensity that wrung a cry from her lips as pleasure tore through her.

White-hot and so intense she lost track of anything except the man she was clinging to.

Symon didn't let her fall. He collapsed onto the bed beside her, curling around her as the night sheltered them from everything except each other.

⤐

"You know I am correct."

Symon had been watching her from the bed. In

the gray light of dawn, Athena pulled a comb through her hair, beginning to prepare for the day that would not spare them its arrival. The two doors between the bedchamber and the outer room were open now, proving that the world was not going to allow them to forget about it.

She heard Symon coming closer, his feet bare against the floor.

Such an intimate sound, and she took a moment to savor it as he reached out and fingered her unbound hair.

"Promise me, Symon. I cannot live with the idea of you being executed for disobeying your king."

She turned and looked at him.

"Ye would have me cower?" Symon shook his head with frustration. "It is no' in me nature."

"It was in your nature to take me with you to your home." She stood up and faced off with him. "I love you. Admit you are pleased to hear me say it."

"I am," he growled. "For I love ye too, Athena. Why do you think I will no' allow ye to be given to another man?"

"If you lose your head, you will have nothing to say about it," she answered with tears glistening in her eyes. "And I will have to watch it, your death. And live with the memory for the rest of my days. Better to know you are alive…"

He grunted, and she hit him.

"You are so stubborn," she hissed. "What of your people? You and Brenda are the last of your line. If you die here, there will be fighting and blood spilled. You told me so yourself."

"The lass is correct, Laird."

Symon turned and shot Lyall a hard look, but the captain only tugged on the corner of his bonnet where he stood just beyond the doorway to the outer chamber.

"Whatever the King decides must be obeyed," Lyall finished. "For all that I will wish a pox on him if he does nae see the sense in no' sending her back to England."

Symon was silent. Athena saw the understanding in his eyes. She laid her hand over his heart before sitting back down and beginning to braid her hair.

Symon would do what he had to.

Just as she would.

Duty wasn't nearly as satisfying as she had always been told it would be.

However, it was every bit as demanding.

❧

The King received them in his throne room again.

The raised dais with its canopy was regal, as were the two guards standing behind the throne the young monarch sat on. He was perfect in manner and bearing, and Esmé Stewart was in the corner looking far too confident.

Athena felt her insides clench.

"You spent the night with your wife, Lord Grant?" the King asked. "Knowing I might send her to England today?"

"Someday, I hope you understand how dear a wife can be, if ye are fortunate enough to be wed to a woman who touches yer heart."

James contemplated Symon for a long moment. "Did your father arrange your first marriage?"

Symon nodded. "However, he allowed me to voice me opinion in the matter."

"You selected your first wife from women of correct social standing?" James asked.

Symon nodded.

"Yet now you would bring home to your clan a woman you found at a market fair."

Symon surprised the King by grinning. "By the sound of ye, Sire, someone has tried to make ye think Athena is no' worthy of being lady of the Grants."

The young King lost his composure for a moment as his gaze slipped to Esmé.

"If she were no' worthy, why then would another man want her so badly he'd go to so much trouble to convince ye to take her from me?" Symon finished softly. "For I am a loyal man, and I'll bend me knee to ye and no' ever break me word, but I will no' ever forget the slight of ye taking the woman I have pledged meself to."

"How dare you threaten the King," Esmé growled.

Athena felt her heart stop. The guards behind the King shifted their attention to Symon, waiting on the word to take action.

"I spoke the truth, and if ye are a wise king, ye'll understand the worth of knowing where I stand without trying to wonder if I am play-acting the part of a loyal subject."

James held his hand up. His young face had settled into a firm expression.

"The solution shall be this," James said. "Lord Grant, you will give me your pledge, in front of these lords, and I will be pleased."

Athena felt time was tormenting her, creeping along as she waited for the young monarch to continue. He looked at her.

"Athena Trappes is Lord Grant's wife."

Esmé Stewart let out a little snort of disapproval.

"I cannot break the bonds of matrimony," James continued, "for it is a state in which a woman is best settled and kept from mischief."

Athena reverenced deeply.

Symon lowered himself to his knee and kissed the King's signet ring. Esmé sat back in his chair, letting out a huff.

But the royal guards returned to looking straight ahead.

Perhaps it was over.

Air moved in and out of Athena's lungs easily for the first time that day. Symon and his men started to back up, but the King lifted his hand.

"The Stewart property passes to Lord Grant through his wife and shall be settled upon Brenda Grant, who will have it as her dowry when she weds Galwell Scrope."

Athena gasped.

"Your Majesty, I gave me word to me father on his deathbed that I would never force Brenda to wed," Symon protested.

"And you are keeping your pledge, Lord Grant," James informed Symon. "I am her king, and I demand this wedding as a means of keeping peace."

Symon shook his head.

"You have given me your pledge, Lord Grant. Obey me or face the consequences," James insisted. "I assure you, they will be grave."

"I will obey, Yer Majesty," Brenda spoke up. Symon turned to her, his body rigid with fury. "And ye will no' argue with me, Cousin. Now leave before I am forced to watch ye hang for yer stubborn pride."

"Brenda…no…I cannae allow it…"

"Ye have kept yer word, Cousin, and ye have a wife," Brenda declared. "Do nae make her a widow so soon."

James lifted his staff and stamped it against the floor. Behind them the doors opened as the guards behind James looked at them to ensure they left in accordance with the King's wishes.

Esmé strode forward, taking Brenda by the arm. She jerked away from him as a group of guards formed around them and took Brenda down the hall.

But Esmé sent a smirk toward Symon before he left.

"I am going to have to kill that man," Bothan Gunn muttered under his breath.

"Some of us will thank ye for the service."

Symon turned his head to discover the Earl of Angus standing nearby. "There is always someone listening at court. Remember that."

The earl jerked his head toward the passageway. He kept going until they were outside where the earl's men had horses waiting. "Elizabeth Tudor is on her summer progress in the north of England. Esmé Stewart is going to take yer cousin down there to see this business finished quickly." He nodded toward his men. "Fresh horses, everything ye need."

Symon nodded and offered the earl his hand. They clasped wrists.

"Ye must allow the marriage to take place."

Symon growled.

The earl kept Symon close with the hold on his wrist. "Retrieve yer cousin now, and Esmé Stewart—curse and rot him—will only run back to the King and have ye branded a traitor. Don't mistake how powerful he is with the young King. He'll have me marching me men up to yer land. Find another way."

Symon didn't care for the earl's words.

But there was a flash of red hair as Brenda emerged from the passageway. There were a dozen burly retainers trailing her.

"I will have words with me cousin," she informed them.

The captain looked down at her. "He can join ye over here."

Symon moved toward Brenda as the retainers fell back.

Brenda hugged him tightly. "Go home," she whispered against his ear. "I know ye plan to ride after me. Do not. I am going to marry him."

Symon growled at her. "I can no' allow ye to do it, Brenda."

She locked gazes with him. "We shall both do what must be done for the Grants. If ye ride after me, ye shall be branded a traitor. Perhaps if ye did no' have a new wife, ye might do as ye please, but I forbid it, Symon." Brenda released him. "It is hardly the first time I have been wed for the benefit of the family. Nor am I the only woman facing it. Promise me ye will never force such a fate on any daughters ye have." She looked past Symon toward Bothan. "And ye shall not do murder."

He nodded reluctantly. Brenda offered him a smile

before she turned and returned to the inside of the palace, the retainers closing around her.

Symon waited until they were far enough away before he locked gazes with Bothan.

The Gunn chief slowly grinned.

∽

Someone rang the bells as they approached Grant Tower.

By the time they rode through the gates, the yard was full. Symon swung out of the saddle and came around to lift Athena off the back of her mare before he turned and looked at the expectant faces of his people.

"Yer mistress is home."

A cheer went up. Symon sent her a wink before Tamhas offered him something.

"Feenet, hang this in the hall."

Athena's eyes widened as she recognized her smock. The blood had dried dark brown but the Grants hooted with appreciation as the Head of House held it up proudly.

Symon scooped her off her feet and carried her inside. He didn't stop until he'd climbed three flights of stairs and taken her through the doors that led to his chamber.

"I wanted to put ye right…here," he muttered as he placed her on the huge bed, "from the moment I saw ye."

"I'm sorry about Brenda."

Symon grunted. "Do ye truly believe I'd have come home if I did nae trust Bothan would see her delivered from harm's way?"

The tension that had kept her shoulders tight for the entire ride home suddenly eased.

"It would seem I have misjudged you," she offered softly.

He stood and unbuckled his belt, allowing his kilt to slither down his legs to the floor. "I see I am going to have to take ye in hand, Athena."

She watched him unbutton the cuffs of his shirt before he pulled the garment over his head and dropped it.

"Would your bed be my proper place?" she asked in a husky tone.

"Let's give it a try and see how things go. It's the truth I think we'll have to have a fair number of discussions on the matter of just what position I prefer ye in."

❧

"You aren't as content in the matter as you try to tell me you are."

Symon grunted as Athena lifted her head off his chest. The window shutters were still open, allowing the moonlight in, because they hadn't left the bed long enough for anyone to attend to the chore of closing them.

"It's me duty to put yer fears to rest," he answered her.

"And is it not mine to share your burdens?" she asked.

Symon pressed her head back down onto his chest. "Ye ease me load by being here, where I was always alone for the past few years."

Athena rubbed her hand across his belly. "Perhaps Uncle Henry could help Brenda."

Symon's body stiffened. "How so?"

"He was going to gather support against Galwell,"

Athena answered as she lifted her head and looked at him. "Elizabeth Tudor will not take it kindly if she discovers one of her lords is playing women falsely."

Symon slowly grinned. He shifted from beneath her, rolling out of the bed as he rustled around in their discarded clothing to find his shirt. It was the only thing he put on before he strode toward the door.

He stopped at the last moment and reversed course, coming back to sit beside her.

"I love ye, Athena. For yer wit and yer flesh." He kissed her soundly before rising. "I'm going to write him a letter."

"I love you, Symon Grant."

He froze at the door, turning around to look at her with his hand on the door. The look on his face brought tears into her eyes. She didn't fight them though. They were born of happiness, and happiness was too rare a thing in the world.

So she'd embrace every moment of it.

Every moment she had to share with Symon.

A lifetime wouldn't be long enough.

Of that she was certain.

∽

It wasn't the first time she'd been sent to marry a man because of the gain it would deliver to her family fortune.

Brenda looked at the border of England and stiffened her spine.

She wasn't even very upset about the whole business. After all, she was much stronger than when her father had wed her to a Campbell at the tender age of seventeen.

*Ye are upset…*

No, she was not. Brenda forbade her inner voice to argue with her. But a face rose from her memory in defiance of her determination to focus on the path in front of her.

Bothan Gunn.

Anyone who didn't understand how dangerous he might be was indeed a fool.

She'd rejected him.

He wasn't the first man to meet that fate, but he was the only face that refused to be banished from her mind.

She would have to tighten her discipline.

For the road in front of her was toward England, and Bothan was a chief from the Highlands. He belonged there, among the snowcapped mountains, not below her in the stench of overcrowded English cities.

She would not think of him again.

And that was final.

⌒∾

*Grant Tower*

Symon was watching her sleep.

Athena woke with a soft gasp to find him with his head resting in his hand as he lay on his side with his elbow propped up beside her.

"Ye must stop worrying," she murmured as she reached up to stroke his face. Her belly wasn't even rounding yet, but her waistline was thicker as their babe began to grow.

Symon's concern grew every day too.

"Or is it…that I do, in fact, snore?" she asked softly.

He chuckled, placing his hand on her belly. "Ye don't snore, *wife*…"

She enjoyed the way he stressed the word *wife*. "You realize that when you worry…you doubt God?"

Symon's brow furrowed.

Athena nodded. "Yes, after all, we were brought together…under the most extreme circumstances. And I am here…and our child is growing—"

"So I must trust in this will of God?" Symon asked her.

Athena covered his hand where it was on her belly. "Yes, just as you will tell me to trust that Brenda will be with us when we baptize our child."

Symon nodded and lay down beside her, gathering her close. "For all that it frustrates me almost beyond me endurance, I admit there is no man I would put me faith in quite so much as Bothan Gunn. He'll bring Brenda home."

Or die trying.

Athena knew her husband didn't say the last part, but he was thinking it.

She was too.

Brenda's fate was hanging over them like a storm cloud. Of course, no life was perfect, and Athena had received so much more than she'd ever thought possible. Happiness was like a living force inside her, something she was grateful for every moment of the day.

And night, she thought wickedly.

Symon had kept his word and become her lover just as she'd done her part by learning to be an equal partner in their union.

Athena sighed, letting his scent and warmth lull her back into slumber.

God wouldn't let them down.

Fate would deliver Brenda.

For although Athena didn't know Bothan Gunn well, she trusted Symon's judgment on the matter.

Bothan pulled his horse to a halt.

Maddox, his captain, came up beside him.

"I never thought to lay eyes on that," Maddox declared.

Bothan turned to look at him. "Or cross it."

Before them were the borderlands. England lay on the other side of them. He didn't belong there, but Bothan set his stallion into motion. Because Brenda Grant didn't belong in England any more than he did.

She was wild.

And he was going to ensure she could stay unbridled by those who didn't understand the value of a woman with the spark of life burning in her. Let the English keep their wives in submissive obedience. He craved a wife who would singe him with her heat and give him children with the strength to rise up to the challenge of living in the Highlands.

Brenda was that woman.

She'd spit in his eye, though.

He slowly grinned as he contemplated the battle ahead.

It was a fact he was going to enjoy it.

And so would Brenda.

He'd see to that…personally.

KEEP READING FOR A LOOK AT THE NEXT BOOK
IN THE HIGHLAND WEDDINGS SERIES

# Wicked Highland Ways

1579

FROM THE BACK OF HER HORSE, BRENDA GRANT contemplated the road in front of her and felt nothing.

That was the saddest thing about what was going to be her second marriage. She felt nothing much about it at all. She wouldn't expect to feel happy about being ordered by a king who was only fifteen years old to leave Scotland and wed a man she'd never met.

But feeling naught? She would have expected at least to feel a sense of injustice. For it was vastly unfair for her to have to wed at James the Sixth's command. Of course, she would hardly be the first person to suffer from a royal intent to smooth the ruffled feathers of a friend. Nor would it be the first marriage contracted for the gain it would bring to the groom's family.

Her temper stirred at last as she thought about the Frenchman who had fought so hard to ensure the land that was now Brenda's dowry was returned to his English cousin. However, the flare of anger didn't last very long; it sputtered out before her mare had crossed even half a mile. At this point, Brenda didn't expect any better from life than to be used by men for their personal gain.

*Jaded.*

It was bound to happen. Her first marriage had smashed her illusions to little bits, her tears drying when she realized her husband only viewed her as an amusement to bring him notice from his friends. His father had eagerly collected her dowry as the wedding was celebrated in fine style at the Scottish court.

And she'd been bedded in full view of over a dozen of her husband's friends. Drunken sots who had leered at her and enjoyed her horror, all the while calling themselves noble lords.

Now, it seemed impossible that she had ever been so tender. Had been naive enough to think her future might include love or something as simple as a marriage where husband and wife treated one another with kindness.

*Yet there had been a time…*

Brenda stiffened, banishing the memory, because she had decided long ago never again to allow her first husband to hurt her. She'd wed at her father's command for the alliance it would bring her clan. Her first marriage had prevented bloodshed. It had been her duty.

Truthfully, her anger should be directed at her Campbell relations, who had enjoyed seeing her tender illusions shredded on her wedding night and throughout her first year of marriage, when her husband had seated his mistresses at the head table alongside her and the laird of the clan Campbell.

*Well, her husband was dead now…*

She was her own woman again.

Her lips rose into a sarcastic twist as she looked around at her mounted escort. At least she had been her own woman until her cousin had found Athena Trappes. The English girl had been escaping from the very man Brenda was now on her way to wed. He'd made a large fuss over a piece of Athena's dowry, enough to have the Scottish King willing to placate him by making it part of Brenda's dowry instead.

Galwell Scrope would soon see that nobles and royals tended to arrange matters to suit themselves. Galwell wouldn't be expecting Brenda. If Galwell expected the delicate Athena to return, Brenda imagined a fiery Highlander woman would be quite a shock to the English nobleman.

However amusing it was to contemplate how unhappy Galwell might be, Brenda knew for certain that she would be the one to suffer for his disgruntlement.

There it was—the way life had always treated her. There was no kindness, only a very determined decree that she never be happy for too long. As soon as she believed she was safe, fate would reach out and slice her open with its talon.

At least there was the comfort of knowing she was ensuring her cousin Symon was happy and her clan in good standing with the King. She took pleasure in knowing that Athena was happy too, and Galwell wouldn't find her substitute so easy to intimidate. Brenda had learned how to live as chattel and Athena would never have to know how the position chafed. And Symon wouldn't face the displeasure of his king.

Brenda smiled again. Symon had wanted to protect her.

He was a good man. Which was why she'd spoken up and declared she'd obey the King when Symon had wanted to protest. He would have gotten himself thrown into chains for defying the young king. Brenda didn't fault her cousin—no, James had neatly twisted the situation so Symon might keep his new bride, but at the expense of having Brenda promised to the English nobleman instead. The man only wanted the land. It was common enough. So there was no reason for Symon to anger his king. No reason for Brenda not to step up and do as the King demanded. No reason to think about how much she didn't want to wed again.

Yes, it was her duty to wed Galwell Scrope. She'd face whatever came her way, as she always had. As the Highlander she was.

She would do her duty.

❧

Chief Bothan Gunn pulled his horse to a halt. He reached forward to rub its neck as he contemplated the view before him.

Maddox, his captain, came up beside him, tilting his head to one side as he waited to see why Bothan had stopped.

"I never thought to lay eyes on *that*," Maddox declared when Bothan remained silent. His voice drew out the last word, making it clear Maddox cared little for the place they were heading.

Bothan turned to look at him. "Or cross into it."

Before them were the borderlands. England lay

beyond. He didn't belong there—but Bothan set his
stallion into motion, because Brenda Grant wasn't
suited to England any more than he was.

She was wild.

And he was going to ensure she could remain
unbridled by those who didn't understand the value
of a woman with the spark of life burning in her. Let
the English keep their wives in submissive obedience.
He craved a wife who would singe him with her heat
and give him children with the strength to live in the
Highlands. Brenda was that woman.

She'd spit in his eye, though. At least a few times,
until he proved his worth to her.

He slowly grinned as he contemplated the battle
ahead. It was a fact; he was going to enjoy it. And so
would Brenda.

He'd see to that…personally.

Of course, first he had to rescue her. At least there
was *something* pleasing about his journey into England.
Snatching a prize from the hands of the English—well,
that he would enjoy. They told tales in England of
wild savages such as himself.

*Highlanders.*

He did not plan to change the way the English
thought about him. No, he was riding into their land
to retrieve the woman he craved. Any who stepped
between them was going to discover he was tenfold
worse than any story they had ever heard.

❧

The English captain escorting her was happy to be on
homeland at last. His face bore the marks of his worry,

and Brenda watched the way he ran a hand over his face before sitting down at a long table in the common room of the tavern where they'd stopped for the night.

He caught her looking down at him from the top of the stairs.

"You will find your supper above stairs, Mistress," he called out. The man was well suited to his position. His tone was full of authority, with no hint of insecurity.

But she knew he was just a bit shaken by her appearance. She allowed her eyes to narrow, and enjoyed the way his lips thinned in a hard line. He was wise enough to know she might be a great deal of trouble if she decided to be a thorn in his side.

"I would like some water," Brenda said as she came smoothly down the steps. A few of his men cast her harassed looks. They were drunk on their own arrogance, thinking her nothing more than a nuisance.

Oh my, if only they knew just how difficult she might be if she hadn't given her word to see the wedding through. They misjudged her simply because she'd been riding without any comment for so long. They mistook her compliance for docility.

"Drink the ale in your room, woman," one of them groused at her. "Water will poison you. Ye'll get the fever from it."

The captain didn't take his eyes off her. She watched as he gauged her reaction to his man's order, a flicker of surprise in his eyes as she merely keep moving at the same pace. His jaw was set but he didn't stop her, so Brenda turned and moved towards the back of the common room, heading towards the door to the kitchen.

"Addams, go with her," the captain ordered from behind her. Brenda heard a bench skid against the wooden floor of the tavern as Addams stood with a grumble and reluctantly fell into step behind her.

The kitchen was smoky. At the end of the day the fire was allowed to burn down to conserve wood. Peat was often laid on top of the coals to keep them alive until the morning. It made for a slow, smoldering fire that smelled of a barn floor. The back door was open wide to let the smoke escape, but now that they were in the city, the air beyond the doors smelled even less pleasant.

Another marriage wasn't the only reason Brenda loathed her return to what so many considered civilization. She'd take the Highlands over the congested city any day.

The cook was yawning and sitting by the fire as he nursed a mug of cider. His apron was stained and grubby. He looked up as Brenda came through the doorway, clearly not interested in another request from his patrons.

"She insists on water," Addams spoke up.

The cook started to rise, resigned to his duty. "I will fetch it, sir," Brenda said sweetly. The cook settled back down and pointed toward a barrel sitting near the open back door. As Brenda picked up a pitcher and took it towards the barrel, Addams grunted and crossed his arms over his chest.

"No one drinks water," he goaded.

"We drink it often in Scotland," Brenda answered.

"Best get used to the way we live in England," Addams informed her as he came up to snatch the pitcher from her fingers. He dipped it into the water without a care for what might be on the outside of the vessel.

Brenda offered him a disapproving glare. He shot her a smug grin that froze on his lips as he looked over her shoulder and dropped the pitcher into the barrel.

Someone pulled her back, encircling her waist with a hard arm and lifting her off her feet. In the next instant, Addams was knocked in the jaw with a hard fist as a man grabbed a handful of his doublet front to keep him from flying into the wall. Addams's head jerked back, and his eyes rolled back in his head before the man lowered him to the floor to sit in an unconscious heap.

"He needs a wee nap to think about the tone he was using with ye," Bothan Gunn informed her firmly.

Brenda didn't care for the way her heart accelerated. Perhaps if she could have attributed it to fear, it might not have mattered, but she knew that wasn't the cause.

"Chief Bothan Gunn," she murmured as she caught sight of his captain offering a coin to the cook. The man took it in a blink of an eye before settling down and casting his attention back to the hearth. "Ye should no' have followed me."

Bothan Gunn was a very tall man. He had to stay away from the edges of the kitchen because the roof sloped, preventing him from standing upright. They were still close enough to the border that his kilt wouldn't have caused too great a disturbance among the men he'd walked past in the yard. But she knew him for what he was—a Highlander. The English around them might make the mistake of believing all

Scots were the same. Brenda knew better, and anyone who took the time to look at Bothan Gunn would see he was far harder than any lowlander was.

Bolder too, because he was standing there. Somehow, she wasn't really surprised. Bothan Gunn had always been bold.

"Did ye think I would no' come for ye, Brenda?" he asked softly, his lips twitching up into a grin.

*She'd hoped…*

Brenda stiffened, chastising herself for the stray thought. She couldn't afford such ideas. Especially with regards to Chief Bothan Gunn. It wasn't *his* clan the king of Scotland would hold accountable if she didn't go through with her wedding.

Duty. So very sharp edged. She felt like the very word left open wounds in her soul. She drew in a deep breath, looking at Bothan and the freedom he represented and knowing she had to deny herself.

"I didn't realize ye were one to waste yer time," she muttered as she reached into the barrel and retrieved the pitcher. Her tone wasn't as composed as she would have liked. And the way his eyes narrowed suggested he saw through her attempt at poise.

"Keeping ye from being forced to wed a black-hearted bastard is no' what I'd call a waste of me time," Bothan informed her

He eased closer to her. She caught a glimpse of his blue eyes in the dim light and realized she was savoring the moment, putting off answering him because he was correct—she had no liking for her circumstances.

Still, duty was duty. And Bothan was not just a man. He was Chief of the Gunn. It was somewhat more than laird because he'd been elected by his fellow clansmen. He didn't just have their loyalty, he'd earned it beside them. She drew in a deep breath and stood her ground.

"Me cousin will be branded a traitor if I do no' wed Galwell Scrope." Brenda forced the words past her lips. "I will not shirk from my duty to me family and laird. And ye would not have me if I did. Yer clansmen would vote against ye if ye brought home a woman who turned her back on her kin. Ye should go now, for there is no reason for ye to stay."

Her words seemed to give Bothan pause. That in itself was remarkable. There was something about him, a sense she gained by being so close to him, which made her shudder as she recognized his strength on some deep level. It was a strange idea, something she'd never encountered before in a man. She was no maid and not even a young woman, and yet Bothan affected her so very differently than any man she'd known.

If only she might indulge herself and discover just why she was drawn to him.

*Do nae!*

She had no idea why her inner voice warned her away from him so intensely, only that it raised goose-flesh along her arms. His lips thinned, which made her think he knew precisely what she was feeling.

"This wedding is an unjust thing, demanded of ye by a boy who is no' yet man enough to understand he is being manipulated by his friend Esmé Stewart. James may be a king of Scotland but he is still a lad," Bothan insisted. "Come away with me, Brenda. I will no' leave ye here."

She was so very tempted, and still she felt herself stuck in place, bound by the repercussions that would land on her cousin Symon Grant.

"Ye must leave me, for I will not shrink from this wedding. My kin will suffer if I do." She wished she didn't sound so despondent. Just because she had no fondness for her predicament didn't mean she should allow her feelings to bleed into her tone. Dignity would be poor comfort when she was alone with her plight, but it was the only thing she seemed to have any control over.

Bothan cocked his head to one side. He had dark hair, black as ink, as though he'd been carved out of the darkest hours of night sky. He was reaching for her, stretching out to capture her hand with his large one.

Part of her liked the idea of being drawn into the dark hours of the night where she might at last be free…

She drew in a startled breath, recoiling as their flesh met.

"I will perform my duty," she said firmly. "Just as ye would, as me cousin Symon has always done. Do no' insult me by telling me it is acceptable for me to run away like a coward because I am a woman."

She jerked her hand free, but all he did was release her fingers in favor of catching a handful of her skirt. His grip kept her in place as he moved so close that she had to tip her head back to maintain eye contact.

"There are a fair number of things I've contemplated telling ye to do because ye are a woman," he muttered softly.

She caught the flicker of a promise in his eyes. It should have raised her temper, for she'd told him more than once she would not have him. Instead, her insides twisted with anticipation.

"And it's the truth I've thought ye frightened of me more than once," Bothan continued.

She let out a hiss, flattening her hands on his chest to push him back. "I am no' afraid of ye, Chief Gunn."

Bothan didn't budge. He stood steady, while her breath became raspy and she felt like her insides were warming, melting the wall she was trying to maintain between them.

"Perhaps it is more correct to say ye are overwhelmed, as I am with you." He shifted so he was whispering next to her ear. "I understand that, lass. It's the truth, I contemplated staying in the north Highlands, far away from ye so I'd no' have to admit how much ye enchant me. Find meself a bride who did no' stir me the way ye do."

A shiver went down her spine. Her flesh responded to him so immediately, there seemed no way to prevent it.

"I will not allow me cousin to be branded a traitor." Brenda shifted her head so she could lock gazes with him. "I cannae believe ye'd have a woman so lacking in loyalty to her family. Ye may be very certain yer men will no' thank ye for bringing home a mistress with scandal staining her name."

His expression tightened. For a moment, she was staring at Chief Gunn. A man who would do what needed doing for the sake of the men who had pledged their loyalty to him. An understanding passed between them, one which left her with a sense of achievement. She knew she had earned his respect.

"It's the truth, I would have overlooked it because of the injustice of asking this duty of ye," he offered. "But ye're right, there would be others who would always consider it a flaw in yer character."

His agreement left a bitterness on her tongue. Bothan was a man of his word. He'd leave her to her fate now, and she would miss him, no matter how much she forbade herself to. At least there was a measure of satisfaction now, which stemmed from knowing he approved of her.

"Goodbye, Chief Gunn," Brenda stated firmly. Her tone was more for herself than him.

His lips twitched. "Ye'd send me off without a kiss? Unkind of ye, lass."

She should do exactly that. Not that she didn't want to discover what his kiss tasted like.

No, she should refuse because she knew without a doubt that she would never forget what it felt like to be kissed by him. The memory would be a torment.

"It would be unwise," she muttered, pushing at him.

His teeth flashed at her as he grinned. "Aye, on that point we agree."

She watched his fingers release her skirt, and disappointment stabbed through her, a lament for the thing she was going to be denied.

"No' that I'm ever the one to take the wisest course of action." He slid his hand up and around her hip, locking his arm around her waist and pulling her completely against him. "The truth is I prefer to play with fire. Which is why I've come looking for ye, Brenda. The offers for obedient brides in me study leave me cold."

She gasped, looking up at him as Bothan caught the back of her head in his opposite hand.

"I'll have a kiss from ye, Brenda, for ye've denied me it for over a year now," he accused her softly.

Bothan wasn't planning on taking the kiss quickly. He took his time, pressing his mouth to hers. Lingering over the first brush of their lips as he turned his head and fitted their lips together.

She shuddered.

He shifted with her, holding her as her body responded almost brutally to the contact. There was an eruption of sensation, one she was helpless to control.

And she wasn't alone. She felt him quake as well, the tremor running through his limbs as he pressed her mouth open for a deeper kiss.

Reason vanished as they tasted one another. Passion ignited between them, roaring to life in the space of a heartbeat. Brenda reached for him, certain she couldn't survive without the feel of him beneath her palms. Need was a living force inside her, beating against the hold she'd maintained against it for so long.

"Now that you've had your kiss, it's time to leave the lady in my keeping."

Bothan released her in a flash. He'd turned and pushed her behind him before she realized it was the captain speaking from the doorway of the kitchen. Her senses were still swimming with intoxication, leaving her blinking in shock as the English captain eyed them.

The captain was wise enough to stand back out of Bothan's reach.

"It's my duty to deliver her to the Queen, and the

lady has explained her intentions quite clearly," the captain continued. "So do not lay my men low again, Chief Gunn."

The two men faced off, taking measure of each other for a long moment. Brenda let out a huff before coming around Bothan.

"He will listen to you, Captain," she said. "Because I have made it clear I intend to honor my word to my king. Chief Gunn is a man of honor."

# About the Author

Mary Wine is a multi-published author in romantic suspense, fantasy, and Western romance. Her interest in historical reenactment and costuming also inspired her to turn her pen to historical romance with her popular Highlander series. She lives with her husband and sons in Southern California, where the whole family enjoys participating in historical reenactment.